You Were Always Magic

Erica L Molinaro

For those who took a little longer to bloom.
It's never too late.

Rock Island
Washington Island
Plum Island Lighthouse
Green Bay
Northport
Gills Rock
Ellison Bay
Pilot Island Lighthouse
Newport State Park
Rowleys Bay
Eagle Bluff Lighthouse
Sister Bay
Chambers Island
Ephraim
North Bay
Fish Creek
Cana Island Lighthouse
Baileys Harbor
Juddville
Old Baileys Harbor Bird Cage Lighthouse
Egg Harbor
Jacksonport
Lake Michigan
Carlsville
Whitefish Dunes State Park
Valmy
Whitefish Bay
Institute
Sturgeon Bay

Chapter One

The high season was well and truly over once Wilson's Restaurant and Ice Cream Parlor closed to everyone but the blow-up Halloween decorations on the restaurant's porch. The novelty ghouls and ghosts would eventually give way to turkeys with pilgrim hats and then Santa Claus as the weather cooled. The Pumpkin Patch Festival's leftovers were seeding the ground for next year's sprouts. Door County was preparing for a long winter's nap, happily basking in the quiet until the tourists descended once more come spring.

In a bakery just outside of the sleepy town of Egg Harbor, Josephine Phines was not thinking of Carie Waverland.

Jo stood in her bakery, hands clasped in front of her mouth and her brow furrowed, staring at the space she had cleared for her new countertop oven. She was resolutely not thinking of Carie. Instead, she wondered was the oven close enough to the prep table? To an electrical outlet? Where would Carie stay this winter if she didn't take the apartment upstairs?

She shook her head. She was very concerned with the placement of her newest acquisition for her bakery.

She sighed, rubbing her hands over her face. "Nothing can ever just be easy, can it?"

Jo closed her eyes and took a deep breath in through her nose. She wasn't thinking about empty spaces in her kitchen that may never be adequately filled again. She focused on how her morning baking routine would be impacted by the extra oven space. She thought about the breakfast sandwiches she could put on her menu. Recipe testing would keep her occupied. She wouldn't have to think of her guest room being empty.

Jo's phone buzzed on the counter. She frowned at the unfamiliar number and nearly dismissed the call.

Had Carie gotten a new number?

She stared at the phone as it buzzed again. She looked at her ceiling, praying for strength or grace or a familiar voice at the other end of the line.

"Hello?"

"Auntie Josephine?"

Jo frowned at the unexpected voice, tamping down a twist of disappointment. "Lisa?"

A sniff. "Yeah."

Jo rarely heard from her family. Their adherence to tradition and rigid definition of values forced a schism between them years ago. After simmering resentments, hurt feelings and expectations came to a head, Jo had fled north to Wisconsin. Her mother ignored her, while her sister with her perfect family and Sunday church picnics had kept her distance. Jo had only met her niece a few times. She had last seen Lisa hiding behind her mother at their great aunt's birthday party. Something dire must have happened to warrant a phone call.

Jo shoved down her questions. She asked the most obvious one. "What's wrong, hon?"

Lisa sniffed again. "Um...I...I know this is weird because we don't really talk. I mean, I don't think I've ever just talked to you, but I don't know who else to call."

"It's okay."

Lisa inhaled sharply, clearly fighting back tears. "I really fucked up. Mom and dad kicked me out."

Jo's breath caught in her throat. "Calm down, hon. Can you start from the beginning?"

"Yeah...yes...um...we fought a lot about school when I first started applying to college. Dad wanted me to get some kind of business degree, which makes sense, I know that it does, but it just isn't my thing. I wanted more of a liberal arts thing, but he and mom said that would be a waste of money."

Jo winced in sympathy. It was a familiar refrain. She had heard the same thing when she first applied to college. The arts just weren't an option in their family.

"I promise that I tried. I really did, but it didn't matter. I just don't get that stuff. It's been three semesters, and it just isn't clicking. They just sent home grades, and mine were terrible. I got this letter a few days later than said I was being dismissed for poor performance."

Celeste and Todd would have gone nuclear over that. Jo had never been close with her sister or her husband, but anything short of perfection in school was unacceptable. They had met in the pre-law program at the University of Chicago, bonding over their shared pursuit of the summa cum laude distinction. Even an A minus would be looked down upon in their house.

"We had a huge fight about it. Like, I've never seen them so mad before. They said I wasn't trying hard enough, but I promise you I was. It got so heated that they told me to leave."

"I'm so sorry that happened," Jo said, trying to inject as much of her empathy into her voice as she could. She was pretty sure that Lisa didn't hear any of it. The girl had dissolved into heaving sobs as she tried to finish her story.

"They let me pack before I left," she said, "I grabbed a few old notebooks because I was just throwing things into a bag to get the hell out of there. When I started looking through what I grabbed, I found your number."

She trailed off. Jo could only hear her sniffles over the phone line. She remembered years ago being in Lisa's exact position, but with no one to call and nowhere to go. She took a breath and decided the best distraction for the winter would be a house guest.

"Do you have a car?"

"Yeah."

"You're still in Wheaton?"

"Uh huh."

Jo recited her address. "Just plug that in your phone and head up this way. I have a spare room you can stay in while you figure everything out."

"Oh."

Jo told herself not to be offended at the surprise in Lisa's tone. Who knew what the family had told her? Knowing them, they probably hadn't said anything. Ignore and suppress could have been the Phines family motto. Maybe it was surprising for a stranger to offer a port in the storm, but Jo didn't think she could bear this winter alone.

"You don't have to--"

"I know I don't. I want to. A change of scenery and some distance will help."

"Okay...um...I need to stop for a few things, but I'll be up later tonight."

"Drive safe."

Jo set her phone back on the counter, staring at it for a moment after. The room would be filled with a relative stranger. The lingering traces of Carie would be papered over with a new guest.

But Jo wasn't thinking about her, so it was fine.

～ℓℓ～

Lisa was walking back to her car with a variety of meats and cheeses and a random bottle of fruit wine that cost less than ten dollars. She paused just outside the doors of the Mars Cheese Castle, realizing that she knew nothing of her aunt's preferences. If Josephine was vegan, Lisa's haul would be a bit insensitive. Lisa could play it off as snacks for herself and maybe offer to pay for a dinner out with money that she definitely had. Her parents must not have cut off her emergency credit card yet because Lisa was able to spitefully fill up her gas tank and buy a whole mess of nibbles for her aunt with it.

With a deep breath, Lisa continued to her car, loaded up her purchases and continued her push north. It was just about five thirty and getting a bit dark. They hadn't set a time for Lisa to arrive, but the idea of arriving late made her guts gurgle.

If she was remembering correctly, her aunt had lived on the Door Peninsula of Wisconsin for at least fifteen years. A quiet collection of lakeside towns, Door County was a summer resort destination, not a place to set down permanent roots. At least, that was how it was framed the few times Lisa heard it discussed. Maybe her aunt had moved there because she was sure the family wouldn't follow.

Lisa had no idea what had happened to cause her aunt to be written out of their family history, and she hadn't been in a rush to ask. Her parents never spoke of her aunt. There were no pictures of her in either their house or her grandmother's. Lisa had only seen Josephine in old photo albums with a tight strained smile. She was a secret no one was willing to discuss.

Lisa pulled out of the parking lot, flipped on a true crime podcast for background noise and merged back onto the interstate. She had about three hours to go, and it wouldn't be getting any lighter out.

For as close as it was, Lisa had only been up to Wisconsin twice. First had been on a trip to the Wisconsin Dells, where her mother had retreated to a day spa and her father refused to take her to the water parks because keeping an eye on her on his own would be too difficult. The other was on a trip to the Bristol Renaissance Faire. None of her friends had been interested, and when she asked her parents to come with her, they had looked at her as though she told them she was joining the circus. She ended up going alone and had a wonderful time, though she was sure it would have been even better with friends.

College seemed like the perfect place to meet people she could relate to. People who would join her in her nerdy exploits. If her classes hadn't been so overwhelming, she would have been looking at joining a tabletop role playing group on campus. There had just never been any time between classes and struggling to make sense of her schoolwork.

Lisa took a deep breath. She had been resolutely avoiding any thought about college since that morning. In her rational mind, she knew the dismissal notice was coming. She had never failed at something so completely before. The disappointment from her parents had settled into her bones. She would never forget the way they looked at her after they read the letter from the school. If they hadn't told her to leave, Lisa would have anyway. The tension and anger in the house had been stifling. She wouldn't have been able to stand it.

Logically, she knew it wasn't the end of everything. She could take some classes at the local community college, get her GPA back up, and apply to another school. There were still options.

Lisa kept repeating that to herself. She still had options, no matter what her parents might think.

After the sun fully set and Milwaukee was in her rearview mirror, time slowed to a crawl. Lisa had switched over to a bland playlist and tried to only focus on the empty road.

Zoning out was easy the further north she traveled. There wasn't much to look at beyond sprawling farmland and billboards on the roadside advertising the odd golf course or tourist trap. Before she knew it, she was speeding by the ethereal glow of a simple neon sign welcoming her to Door County.

Her playlist repeated for the third time as Sturgeon Bay came and went. She drove over the drawbridge and through the town. Starbucks and Target, the last vestiges of civilization, slipped away as Route Forty-Two shrank to two lanes. The navigation app helpfully reminded her that she had twenty-three minutes until reaching her destination. She breathed a sigh of relief, finally feeling her body begin to unclench.

The road was dark here. The sky had been overcast most of the day, and there were no streetlights to speak of. Lisa found it comforting. She could imagine that she was the only one in the world with no potential for disappointing those important to her.

The universe must have felt her finally starting to relax, because it chose that exact moment for her car to suddenly stall.

"Fuck," she swore and angled for the shoulder.

Lisa allowed herself a moment of despair with her eyes closed and her fingers clenched around the steering wheel. She would never be able to afford to fix a car, let alone hire a tow truck out here. She took a deep breath and reached for her cell phone. She started to type out a text message to her aunt, but stopped when she saw she had no signal. She threw it back down on the passenger seat, cursing it as it bounced into the footwell. Racking her fingers through her hair, she peered out the windshield.

"We could always just walk a bit down the road and see if we pick up a signal again," she said to the car. "Maybe? It isn't like it's pitch-black outside, and I have no idea where I'm going."

She fumbled for her phone and pushed against the car door. She stopped when a flicker of light caught her attention through the windshield. Her high beams were still on and illuminating the road in front of the car. Just at the edge of the shadow, two eyes were reflecting the light back.

Pulling the door shut, Lisa scrambled for the lock. The click of the mechanism did nothing for her nerves. Whatever was out there hadn't moved. It just stared at her. Lisa squeezed her eyes shut, hoping that exhaustion and stress had her eyes playing tricks on her. When she opened them, the reflections were gone. She sighed in relief, settling herself, only to be reduced to a screaming panic when something large slammed into the side of her car.

Lisa whipped around in her seat, squinting into the night. Nothing was behind her. She drew a deep breath in through her nose and dropped her head onto the steering wheel. She twisted the key in the ignition, willing the engine to life, but it remained silent.

She barely had a second to register that something else was very wrong before whatever was out there flung itself into the car again. She lurched violently sideways as the car popped up on two wheels before crashing back down. Her offerings to her aunt flung through the car.

Frantic, Lisa turned the keys again. She could feel the metal strain in her grip, and she worried that she might break the key off. The car refused to start.

A giant clawed paw slammed against the driver's side window. The glass strained as Lisa screamed. A snarling maw pressed next to the paw, biting against the glass. Spittle and blood sprayed against the window as Lisa scrambled with her seat belt. The car was small, but she needed to get as far as she could from this thing before it broke through. The stick shift stuck in her back as she scuttled into the passenger seat. She fumbled for anything that could be used as a weapon; a bottle of wine or the ice scraper, but she found nothing. She curled into a ball and willed the glass to hold.

Quickly as it appeared, the paw vanished from the window. A sickly yellow light flared beside her car, and Lisa could see the bulky, clawed murder machine that attacked her. The glow emanated from a woman standing on the blacktop. Her right hand was raised high in the air while her left twisted wildly. The creature gave a mighty bellow as the woman flicked her wrist. Her fingers formed another gesture, and the beast screeched loud enough to pierce an ear drum. Lisa pressed her hands against her ears and hunched over her knees, confused and terrified. The screaming cut abruptly with only the echo reverberating into the darkness.

Every piece of media Lisa had ever consumed screamed in her subconscious for her to get away, but dumbstruck, Lisa could only uncurl herself at the gentle rapping on the glass. The woman was standing there, waiting patiently for Lisa to roll down the window. The sudden calm had thrown Lisa for a loop. It took her a moment to readjust. She could feel the car vibrate back to life, the engine humming like nothing had happened.

Lisa batted at the window control until it finally rolled down. The autumn air was crisp and helped Lisa come back to herself. The woman was crouching by the window to meet Lisa at eye level. She was broad through the shoulders, at least from what Lisa could see under the dark long-sleeved shirt she wore. Her face was streaked with grime, and her black eyes absorbed the yellow glow. Her expression was schooled neutral, but she appeared struck when she saw Lisa's face. They stared dumbly at each other before Lisa broke the silence.

"What the hell was that?"

The woman cocked her head. "Which part?"

"I mean, all of it obviously, but let's start with the dire-bear or whatever that was."

The woman looked over her shoulder at the splattering on the road. "A black bear got possessed. Traveled farther south than it should have. Shouldn't be happening this early in the season."

"Is that...supposed to make sense?"

"Not if you aren't from around here," the woman said. She loomed closer, studying Lisa's face.

Lisa looked at the woman with a cocked eyebrow, waiting for some kind of explanation.

"I'm sorry," the woman said. "Are...are you related to Josephine Phines?" She winced as soon as Lisa's aunt's name was out of her mouth. "That's a weird question...I'm sorry."

Lisa pulled back further into the car.

The woman looked embarrassed. "Sorry. I'm...um...I'm a friend of hers. I'm Carie Waverland."

With no way to verify that, Lisa itched to pull her cell phone from her pocket. She figured she could wait until this woman left or killed her. Really, either seemed possible today.

"Does she know about all that?" Lisa pointed back towards the road.

"A bit of it," Carie said. "Maybe not all the details, but she knows."

Lisa wanted to either ask a million questions of this woman or never see her again. But someone who can tell she's related to her aunt by a quick glance must be very close friends. Or a stalker.

The awkward pause extended to an even more awkward silence before Lisa spoke again.

"Alright. Good talk. Nice to meet you, I guess."

Carie closed her eyes before snapping them back open. Her eyes glowed yellow for a moment, and Lisa felt the tension in her shoulders melt away.

"Just a little charm to get you home in one piece."

Instead of asking what kind of fairy godmother nonsense a charm was supposed to be, Lisa just said thanks again. They stared at each other for another moment before Carie stepped away from the car.

"I'll tell my aunt you said hi." Lisa watched something like panic, regret, and longing fight over the woman's facial expression. "Or not."

"Keep to the main road," Carie said after settling herself. "Those apps will want to avoid taking you through town, but just stay on Forty-Two until you can turn on E. Roll up your window, and I'll get you back on the road."

Doing as instructed, Lisa reflexively grabbed her cell phone. She cursed to herself, remembering that she wasn't getting service, but when she checked it appeared connected.

"Who knew that magic messes with the cell network," she said to herself before typing out a message to her aunt. A hysterical giggle forced its way through her teeth. Magic. What even was this day?

...Ran into some trouble on the road...Everything is fine...Back on my way...Do you know someone named Carie...

Three dots appeared and disappeared as the car lurched magically into the air. Lisa barely noticed as she watched with bated breath for her aunt's response. The car was gently set back on the asphalt when it finally appeared.

...Yes...

Lisa waited for more, but apparently the full story needed to be told face to face. She looked up to see Carie staring at her as if trying to figure out if something else was wrong. She tossed her phone down and waved before pulling away.

She kept the sudden revelation that magic existed tucked securely under her speculation about her aunt and this Carie person.

***

After speaking with Lisa, Jo went into hostess mode. This meant baking enough to feed a small army. With her phone back on the charger, she pulled together one of her more successful dough experiments from the last few weeks and set it to proof. It would be baked and ready to slice when her guest arrived.

The motions were easy enough to remember at this point; Jo had years of practice. She would receive a text from Carie late in the summer asking if the room was still available. Jo would tell her it was, and they would set a date for Carie's arrival. The weeks leading up to that day were a flurry of new recipes and deep cleaning. She always wanted the room to be perfect.

Jo remembered the giddiness in her chest last year as she refreshed the linens. After saying goodbye at the start of the high season, Jo spent the summer talking herself into asking Carie to stay permanently. Jo had filled her head with day-dreams of wandering the walking trails that crisscrossed the peninsula, catching a double feature at the Skyway drive-in theater, and watching the sunset on a rocky beach. She wanted more of the cozy evenings reading by the fire. Carie's work was important and strange and dangerous. Jo wanted to provide her with a safe place to rest her head. There were moments when Jo was so sure that Carie wanted it too. There were fond smiles over dinner and lingering looks when she thought Jo wasn't looking.

Jo had been so sure Carie would want to stay.

Tucking the sheets under the mattress, Jo ignored the familiar bite of tears in her eyes. The bedding was new. Jo hadn't been able to keep the old set. They had smelled too much of memory.

She'd been so sure.

But she'd been sure of things before.

She was sure her family would accept her choices and love her no matter what. She was sure they'd call eventually, or at the very least return her emails and texts. It had seemed impossible that they would write her off entirely.

It had taken so much of Jo to drum up the courage to ask Carie to stay. She'd been smiling and happy and so very sure.

Jo remembered the smile fading from her lips. The sting in her eyes. The stab in her chest. She remembered the confusion on Carie's face when she asked her to stay. The excuses. The things that were more important to Carie than Jo was. Carie had other duties in the summer. Other people needed her services. Carie only came up north to clear out the lingering paranormal beasts and odd possession to keep the beaches safe for the summer tourists. That was her job. That was the only reason why she came to Door County.

Maybe Jo should have pushed harder. She should have fought for what she wanted instead of saying something cruel and untrue. She shouldn't have been surprised when Carie fought back. She'd held the tears at bay until Carie left. They didn't speak about when Carie would return.

Jo came back to herself in the bedroom. She clutched the duvet tightly in her fists. She had been doing so well, ignoring the confused anticipation of an arrival that wouldn't be coming. She threw down the blanket and abandoned the bedroom. The lingering memories were too much. Her fingers itched with the need to create, so she started back to the bakery.

She opened the front door to the delivery driver walking up her driveway. He was kind and helpful. Jo led him across the property and showed him the space she had cleared. He carried the oven inside and made sure she knew how to install it. She sent him on his way with croissants that hadn't sold that day.

Eager for the distraction, Jo immediately set about roasting almonds for biscotti. She rifled through the pantry for other ingredients - some dried cherries and whatever kind of chocolate she had sitting around. She didn't bother with the stand mixer, just a wooden spoon and a wide bowl.

Jo scored her bread and placed it in the oven. She then moved on to forming the biscotti into a loaf for its first bake. She watched it puff slightly in her new oven when her phone buzzed on the counter. She frowned seeing the notification from Lisa. She couldn't help the punched-out gasp that escaped when she read Carie's name.

Because of course Lisa would run into Carie on the drive up.

Her initial inclination was to explain several years of a complicated relationship in a text. Jo started typing but stopped herself. If she offered any kind of explanation, it needed to be in person. Jo didn't want to talk about her sad and confusing love life with her niece. Or really with anyone. Not even herself if she was being honest.

Several long seconds passed and Lisa --and by extension, Carie-- were waiting on a response. She typed 'yes' and set her phone back on the charger. She hoped it would spontaneously combust.

Any hope of baking distracting her fizzled when Jo remembered that Carie was the type of person to escort someone in trouble home. She wondered if she had time for a shower, or if she had any concealer in the house. She'd hardly been living like a recluse, but she'd been sleeping terribly since spring. She needed a haircut. Her ends had split and gotten frizzy, but it hadn't seemed like a priority until just then.

Jo had tried not to imagine seeing Carie again, but in those moments where she was honest about lying to herself, she wanted to look her best. Effortlessly put together and with an easy beauty, Carie would realize in an instant what a mistake she had made. She'd hold Jo close in her strong arms and breathe in Jo's ear that she'd never leave her again.

Needy. Childish. Clingy.

That didn't stop her from plucking her phone off the counter as soon as the bakes were finished and racing back to the house. She charged into her bedroom to dig out clothes that weren't sweaty and dusted in flour. She tied her hair up in a messy bun and was comparing boxy, ill-fitting shirts she bought online and never returned when the doorbell rang.

Chapter Two

"I really should have grabbed a cooler," Lisa muttered as she juggled her tepid snacks.

She considered ringing the doorbell again. The house remained quiet with the porch and foyer lights on. The property was close to downtown Egg Harbor, but Lisa felt like she was on a little boat in the middle of a placid sea. It was just after eight thirty, and the likelihood of her aunt having fallen asleep seemed slim. Buzzing again would make her seem impatient, and Lisa didn't want to make a bad first impression. Impressions made as a child shouldn't count. If Auntie Josephine was nice enough to invite her to stay, Lisa imagined she hadn't been a terror as a child. Her parents wouldn't have tolerated that.

Muffled footfalls and the door pulling open stopped Lisa from spiraling about her parents. She stuffed those feelings down to freak out about later as her aunt appeared in the doorway.

Lisa remembered Josephine in the way she remembered a book she had been forced to read for school. Her aunt was just the barest memories held together by familiar sounding plot points and maybe a scene that was memorable at the time. The family never spoke of Josephine. Lisa's grandmother would mention her errant daughter after one too many glasses of sherry during the holidays, but she would quickly be shushed. Lisa remembered asking about it one year when she had finally been old enough to notice, but her mother only said that her sister had made some questionable decisions about her life that led her away from the family. Lisa considered that now, seeing how unfairly that statement was skewed. Hadn't she done the same thing? Would people ask after Lisa, only to be told that she had done something stupid her family hadn't approved of, so they no longer associated with her?

She shook her head as these thoughts threatened to overwhelm her. The woman that stood in the doorway was short and soft through the middle. She wore comfortable looking clothes that were dusted with flour. Her hair was dark brown and graying at the temples. She had it pulled back into a messy half ponytail. The family resemblance was definitely there. Her aunt looked how Lisa imagined her mother might look if her mother believed in aging gracefully. There was something sincere about Josephine. This was her. There wasn't anything to hide.

Josephine's gaze was aimed about a foot over Lisa's head as if she expected someone else on her doorstep. Lisa filed that away for later examination, though the flash of disappointment in her aunt's face twisted in her stomach. They stared at each other for a moment. Lisa contemplated apologizing for the whole fiasco and heading back to her car. This clearly was a mistake.

"Sorry I'm so late," Lisa finally said.

Josephine's eyes immediately lit up. "No apologies necessary! It's not even nine yet. I'm just glad you've arrived. Come in, come in."

She held open the door and waved Lisa into the foyer. Shuffling her grocery bags to grab her luggage, Lisa followed her inside.

"Do you need me to move the car?"

"We can worry about that in the morning. I'm not planning on going anywhere. I have a delivery coming, but he'll just be pulling up to the bakery. We can rearrange some of the junk in the garage to make space."

"Thanks, Auntie Josephine."

The older woman smiled warmly. "You can call me Jo, if you want. Josephine is so unfamiliar."

Lisa stopped herself from commenting on how they hadn't seen each other in years. It seemed like a rude thing to point out in the current circumstances, so Lisa only nodded.

"Are you hungry? I see you stopped on your way up."

"Oh," Lisa said as she remembered her haul. "Yeah, um, I didn't want to show up empty handed, so...you aren't vegan, are you? Because I don't think there's anything there that's vegan. Maybe the wine? No, there's honey in there..."

"I'm not vegan," Jo said as she pulled the bags from Lisa's grip. "I've actually got some fresh bread and biscotti I just pulled out of the oven. Did you want a quick bite? If not, I'm pretty sure all of this will hold until tomorrow."

Jo's eyes lingered and widened over the wine label before she looked back to Lisa. Lisa pretended she didn't see the mild horror on her aunt's face at the prospect of cherry wine sweetened with honey.

"I wouldn't mind a quick snack before bed."

"Excellent. The kitchen is just back this way."

Jo told Lisa to leave her bags by the stairs. They moved through a cluttered living space and into a warm kitchen. Lisa slowed as she took it in. Her parents' house looked like a newly built model home. No clutter was allowed. Her mother dusted, mopped, and cleaned on a near daily basis. Any indication that someone lived there was immediately frowned upon. Lisa couldn't help the smile that tugged at her lips. She could see herself in the mess. There were stacks of books and forgotten mugs on the coffee table. A knit blanket that clashed horribly with the couch was hung over the arm rest. Notebooks and loose papers with what looked like recipes scrawled on them were scattered over the couch. The walls were a gallery of paintings, but there were some open spaces here and there that used to be covered with frames judging by the faded paint. Two built in bookcases overstuffed with books flanked a large stone fireplace. A television a bit small for the space hung above the mantle.

Lisa's eyes landed on a smaller frame. It was tucked between a few larger ones on the mantle. The frame was simple and wooden. The photo was of two women. One was her aunt with a bright smile and love in her eyes. The other was Carie. Her black hair was blowing wildly. One of her hands held it back from her face. The other hand wrapped around Jo's waist. Lisa's smile softened. She moved closer to the picture.

"Lisa?"

She looked over and saw the horror on her aunt's face. "Sorry. Got a bit distracted. That's Carie in the picture, yeah?"

Schooling her features, Jo walked over and grabbed the frame. Something complicated flitted over her face. "Yes, that's Carie."

"I definitely wasn't expecting to have the existence of witchcraft confirmed in rural Wisconsin of all places, but after today, it's a nice distraction."

Jo huffed a laugh. "I thought the same thing when I first moved up here. It wasn't so immediate, but between meeting Carie and then the Witches of Door coming to pick up treats for their meetings, I started to catch on."

"You really can't say something like Witches of Door and just gloss over it without explanation."

Jo's eyes hadn't left the photo as she answered. "If you hang around the bakery long enough, you'll end up meeting some of them. Very nice, older ladies. And Archie, of course. They get ideas in their heads and start offering small spells for good health and shiny hair. You start to notice after a while when the local bridge club are muttering strange sayings each time you ring them up."

"Carie's one of them?"

Jo looked up from the picture. "No. Let's get you sorted with a snack. I'm sure that you're eager to get to bed. Driving always takes it out of me, and it's been a trying day for you."

Lisa watched Jo bustle back to the kitchen, taking the framed photo and shoving it into a drawer. Her aunt pulled a bread knife from her butcher block and started cutting slices from the loaf on the counter. Lisa made her way over, wondering if a glass of wine would loosen her aunt's lips about Carie. She had only been there five minutes and already there were plenty of distractions from her train wreck of a life. That photograph and Jo's reaction filled in several blanks in Lisa's mind about her aunt. For one, it finally solved the mystery of why Jo was estranged. Lisa had once commented on how pretty a girl at a school dance had looked, and her parents had jumped down her throat about how that path would lead to nothing good. Lisa hadn't even meant anything by it. She really didn't have any interest in anyone that way. She wondered if Jo's experience was similar.

That was too heavy a conversation for the first twenty minutes of their new relationship, and Lisa didn't want the specter of their family looming over them.

Lisa shook her head and moved to take a seat at the table in the kitchen. Her aunt brought over a wooden cutting board with fresh slices of bread, a small pot of butter, and a tiny bowl of flaky salt. She set out two small plates and a knife to cut the various meats and cheeses Lisa brought. The cherry wine remained unopened on the counter, but Jo did bring over a glass of water. She set it before Lisa.

"Did you want some coffee or tea, hon?"

Lisa shook her head and cut into a spicy soppressata, and then an aged white cheddar. "If I have any coffee after lunch, I can't sleep. Though I really don't think that will be an issue tonight. I'm wrecked."

The silence was interrupted by Jo grinding some coffee beans and heating water in her kettle.

"Caffeine never bothered me like that. If I'm tired, I can fall asleep just about anywhere."

"That's an amazing skill to have."

"Once I started working in the bakery, it served me quite well."

"You mentioned that before. You have a bakery?"

Jo smiled wide. "That's what that building is out front. It was one of the nicest things about staying up here permanently. My first job was in a kitchen and learning on the line how to cook. Baking was something I started doing in my spare time to relax. It was nice to discover a passion that wasn't really tied to anything back home."

Lisa nodded, looking beyond the cozy kitchen she currently occupied to the stark, white nightmare her parents had berated her in earlier.

"We really don't have to talk about any of it if you don't want to, Lisa." Jo said, picking up on her distress. Her fingers twitched on the table as if she wanted to reach out, but instead Jo wrapped her hands around her coffee mug. "We can leave everything down there, and let you figure out whatever you want here."

Lisa could feel the unwelcome bite of tears in her eyes. The offer of freedom was a gift that she could never hope to repay. She needed to figure out a plan and then she could present it to her parents. Business school just wasn't going to work. She needed something else, and they would have accept that.

Jo sipped her coffee, and Lisa took the opportunity to wipe her eyes. She grabbed a slice of bread, slathered on some butter, and sprinkled the salt over it. She took a bite and had to stifle the moan that tried to escape.

"Holy shit."

The tips of Jo's ears went a bit red. She wiggled a bit, preening at the reaction. "I've been messing with that recipe for a while, but honestly, it's all in the butter and the flakiest salt I can find."

"I'm pretty sure you could slather literally anything on this bread, and it would be delicious."

"If you want, I can show you how I make it. I usually take the off season to try out some new recipes."

"Oh...I'm not much of a cook. Mom didn't really bake, so I never really..."

Jo deflated a bit. "Well, if you do want to try, I'd be more than happy to show you."

Lisa didn't want to impose on her aunt anymore that she already had. She offered a quick smile before finishing up her bread and the cheese she had sliced for herself. Before she could ask after her room, Lisa's mouth pulled into a jaw-cracking yawn.

Jo began clearing the table. "Why don't I show you upstairs? We can chat more tomorrow."

She re-wrapped the meats and cheeses before setting them in the fridge. The bread she left out, presumably for herself. She moved into the living room and grabbed a keyring from the mess on the coffee table.

"You have your own entrance. There's a staircase on the side of the house that will take you right to the second floor. This key works for that door, and for the one up here."

Jo took Lisa's bag and started hauling it upstairs. She paused to unlock the door as Lisa scampered up behind her. The door opened into a cozy living space. To the left was a small kitchen with its own stove and refrigerator. The exit from the kitchen opened onto a small deck with stairs that led back down to the yard. To the right was a well-loved couch with a skinny bookshelf next to it. Around the corner was a queen size bed and a modest television mounted on the wall.

It was small, but Lisa fell in love immediately. She moved between the spaces with a pleased smile on her face, though her stomach flipped when she set down her bags. The events of the day were starting to feel real. Her heart stuttered in her chest. Jo was explaining how to connect to the Internet, but Lisa couldn't hear her. Jo noticed Lisa's thousand-yard stare and stopped talking. Her fingers twitched again, but she kept her hands to herself. Lisa wasn't sure if she'd welcome her aunt's touch.

Jo bit her lower lip. "If you need anything at all, please come downstairs and grab it. And if you can't find it, just grab me. I'll be up for a while yet, or I'll just be in my room."

Lisa managed a nod, and Jo took a breath again as if to speak. She shook her head and offered a smile.

"Good night, hon."

"Night, Auntie Jo."

Lisa listened to the door click shut and her aunt's steps recede back to the main floor. She stood in the small, perfect apartment for a long time before setting down her bags and immediately rushing for the bathroom. She sat on the toilet and pressed her hands over her mouth as a sob ripped out of her mouth.

What the hell had she done?

What the hell was she thinking?

Her stomach lurched and the tears she'd been fighting off all day finally fell.

She'd listened to her parents her entire life. Had they steered her wrong? She could have tried harder in her classes, couldn't she? Why did she have to open her mouth? She could have buckled down and finished school and found a job that she could learn to be happy with. Why did she fight with them?

She pulled her hair and snapped her mouth closed. She didn't want her aunt to hear her breakdown. They'd only just reconnected. Lisa didn't want Jo thinking she was a basket case on top of an ungrateful brat.

She squeezed her eyes shut, willing the tears to dry.

What the hell had she done?

What was she going to do for the holidays? She never missed Thanksgiving with her family. Never missed Christmas. Even if she apologized, would they let her come back?

She swallowed down the bile and blinked away her tears. She stood and turned the faucet on. Lisa splashed her face and avoided eye contact with her reflection. The towel hanging beside the sink was plush and felt soft against her heated skin. She wanted to take a shower, but the idea of even that little amount of effort seemed insurmountable. She left the bathroom, toeing out of her sneakers as she went. She didn't bother pulling off her jacket or jeans before dropping onto the bed. Burrowing into the blankets, tears stung her eyes again. The bed was comfortable, but painfully unfamiliar. She twisted her face into the pillows and let herself sob. Her shoulders heaved as she just let it all pour out. Exhaustion crawled up her back, wringing whatever strength she had left after the longest day of her life. The sobs quieted to whimpers, and in her little nest of misery, Lisa cried herself to sleep.

✎

Jo poured herself another cup of coffee as she tried to ignore the familiar sounds of a breakdown above her. She nibbled on another slice of bread. She focused on the crumb and texture instead of charging back upstairs to comfort her niece. As much as she wanted to, it wasn't her place. The woman upstairs was functionally a stranger. Lisa wouldn't want Jo to see her like this.

Jo remained in the kitchen, listening as the sounds above eventually petered out. She picked at the plate, watching the steam lazily drift off her coffee. A shadow danced in her peripheral vision, and Jo looked over to the stairs, half expecting to see Lisa. Nothing was there.

"You do really need to sleep, old girl," she told herself.

Sleep had been hard to come by that summer. Despite the busy days and the farmers markets and the endless special orders, Jo would lay down in her bed and stare at the ceiling for hours. When sleep finally did come, she dreamed of an endless expanse of dull color. She would be there, alone and silent. Sometimes she knew she was dreaming, other times she would run through the expanse desperately trying to find an escape.

As the peninsula settled into fall, Jo thought the nightmares would abate. But the empty apartment upstairs loomed in her mind, and a restful evening remained out of reach. So, she stocked up on coffee and set about finally organizing every recipe that she had ever saved. She could experiment with proofing times and the optimal spot in her kitchen for bread to ferment.

Tonight was no different, but at least she could tell herself that she was staying up just in case Lisa needed her. She topped off her coffee, rinsed the dishes before putting them in the dish washer, and settled on the couch. She tucked her feet underneath her before glancing back at the staircase again. She wondered if eventually the soft noises of another body in the house would settle her. She wondered if she could trick herself into thinking the strange footfalls upstairs were familiar, and that a beloved body would press against her on the couch.

Jo sniffled and dragged her sleeve against both her eyes. Eventually she hoped she'd be able to remember the good times without crying.

Chapter Three

L isa woke to the soft touch of an unfamiliar pillowcase on her cheek. She jolted up, wincing against the morning light streaming in through the blinds she forgot to close. Her face felt tacky with dried, salty tear tracks. She went back into the bathroom to wash her face again and drink some water from the sink. She began to plan out her day as she searched for her phone. It was on the floor near the foot of the bed, clinging to life with six percent of the battery left. She picked it up and tried not to feel anything about the lack of missed calls or messages. She needed to get some coffee and find a grocery store, not have another meltdown about how she'd ruined her life.

The kitchen in the apartment was well stocked with the essentials. Plenty of spices and seasonings, but nothing substantial. Lisa opened each cabinet, hoping for more than the very old packet of expired instant coffee she found. She would have to go downstairs eventually, but descending into her aunt's space would make this real. In the apartment, Lisa could pretend that she was just away for a weekend in a vacation rental.

"Stop being ridiculous," she scolded herself. "She invited you here. She wouldn't have done that if she wanted to be alone."

With a deep breath, Lisa unzipped her luggage and stacked her clothing on the bed. There was an empty dresser in the room that she would easily fill. For now, she left everything out. She pulled on the over-sized cardigan she was looking for and went downstairs. She braced herself for an onslaught of questions but quickly relaxed when her aunt didn't spontaneously appear in the kitchen.

There was a pot of coffee, a mug, and a croissant on the counter. As Lisa approached, she saw a notepad with an unfamiliar scrawl written on it.

Help yourself to the coffee and pastry!

I'll be in the bakery if you need anything.

~Jo

Despite her mood, Lisa felt her lips tug up into a smile as she filled a mug. She ripped the note from the pad and opened the garbage to toss it out. Three or four similar bright sheets of paper were discarded on the top. She didn't pull the notes out, but it made her feel better. Her aunt was on the same shaky ground as Lisa was. Neither of them was sure of what to do in this situation. She crumbled the note and tossed it in with the others. She was just about to bite into her croissant when the doorbell chimed. She chewed and swallowed too quickly, coughing and sputtering as she dashed for the door. She pulled it open and looked up to meet familiar black eyes.

"Oh," Carie said. "I...um...good morning."

The woman standing awkwardly on the porch was completely different than the one in the photo. The photo showed a woman relaxed and without a care in the world. Now, Carie's shoulders were near her ears. She hunched to make herself appear smaller. She looked like she was bracing for a fist to the face.

"Just...ah...wanted to make sure that you got here okay."

Lisa couldn't keep the smile from unfurling as she watched Carie's eyes lift to search the house behind her. "Took a little longer than I thought it would, but yeah, got in alright."

Carie clearly wasn't listening but waiting for someone else to appear in the doorway.

"Can't say that I've ever seen anything like that last night," Lisa said, raising her voice a bit.

Carie snapped her attention back to Lisa. "My job is to make sure that folks like you don't see things like that."

"On behalf of folks like me, thanks."

"Are you alright," Carie asked, sincerity in her tone. "Most people I've run across that have their world views destroyed don't take it as well. There's a fair amount of screaming. Had a pocket bible thrown at my head once."

"Oh," Lisa shrugged. "Well, I was already having a pretty shitty day. Things were already kind of falling apart, so...yeah...why not throw witchcraft in the mix? Might have a bit of a breakdown about it later."

"Is...it isn't anything with..."

"With Jo?" Lisa asked. "Oh, no. She's been amazing. I was actually going to head over to the bakery to see if she needs any help."

Lisa peered over Carie's shoulder and noted several cars parked haphazardly around the property. A forest green, rusted sedan was parked perfectly near the garage door. Carie spun quickly, as if expecting Jo to manifest behind her. Lisa huffed out an exasperated sigh. She really didn't want to pry, but there was no way that she wasn't going to ask her aunt about this.

"Just let me grab my shoes and my coffee. We can walk over together."

"No," Carie said too quickly. She let out a heavy breath. "No, I don't want to impose. I just wanted to make sure you were okay. Things like that bear don't usually appear until later in the winter."

"If I run into anything else like that, do you have a hot line I can call?"

Carie's mouth twitched. "Nothing so fancy. If...ah...if you do need anything, well...um...here."

She dug her hand into the tight pockets of her dark jeans for a moment before pulling out a crumpled business card. She held it between two fingers before waving her other hand over it. The paper straightened, but the creases were still visible. Carie held the card out for Lisa to take.

Carie Waverland

Freelance Witch for Hire

Exorcisms - Wards - Banishments

Nearly laughing at the mundanity of it all, Lisa flipped the card over and noted the phone number. There was no address.

"It's astonishing how many questions come to mind from a business card."

"I wouldn't worry about it," Carie said with a rueful smile. "If you're lucky, you won't see me again."

Lisa tilted her head skeptically. "Sure."

"Hm." Carie nodded once before stepping off the stoop.

"Should I bother asking if you want me to tell Jo you were here?"

The witch paused. Her body relaxed for a fraction of a second before pulling taut as a wire again. "I'll leave that to you."

"Well, I hope we do meet again, Ms. Waverland, Freelance Witch. If anything, you seem like you could use a friend."

Carie snorted and looked back with a smile before offering a quick wave. She stalked towards the car, which she quickly drove off the property. Lisa watched from the porch and tried to figure out a way to broach this topic with her aunt. This was a perfect distraction from her own problems.

Letting the door swing shut behind her, Lisa ducked back into the kitchen. She topped off her coffee and grabbed the croissant. Her own shoes were still upstairs, so she found a pair of well-loved flip flops by the door. They were a bit small for her, but they would work for a quick jaunt over to see her aunt. She stuffed the pastry in her mouth and closed the door behind her with her free hand. She dashed across the lawn with a careful eye on her sloshing coffee.

The aptly named Jo's Bakery sat on the front of the property, just off the road. There was a porch across the front, similar to the main house. Four sets of tables and chairs were set up. An older couple were sitting at the one set in the sun, both sipping coffee and reading the local paper. Lisa crested the steps. An older woman with a large pastry box smiled at Lisa as she pushed out of the bakery. She held the door open with her foot for Lisa, who slipped in with a quick thank you.

The yeasty smell of freshly made bread filled Lisa's senses as she entered. It was warm inside, just the perfect temperature for a fall morning. Behind the counter, Jo broke eye contact with the customer she was speaking with and offered a warm smile to Lisa. She pointed to an empty table which Lisa immediately sat down at.

This version of her aunt seemed perfectly put together. There was still an undercurrent disarray, but contained and charming. Between placing orders, Jo bustled over to Lisa's table. She refilled her coffee and set down a plate with a breakfast sandwich on it.

"New recipe," Jo said by way of an explanation. "Let me know what you think."

Lisa had barely opened her mouth to tell Jo that she'd already eaten the pastry left for her before Jo was back behind the counter. Shrugging -- she was *quite* sad after all -- Lisa took a sip of coffee and an experimental nibble of the sandwich. The bread was seeded and dense, the perfect thick rye slice. There was avocado spread over both pieces of bread with two thick slices of bacon, tomato, arugula, and a perfectly runny sunny side up egg. It was delicious, but the real star was the bread.

There was something comforting about sitting in the evidence that one could get by in life by finding something to be passionate about. Lisa's parents had always insisted on a practical approach. Get a degree in something that cast a wide net and make enough money that you could dig yourself out of crippling student loan debt with plenty of time to settle down with a nice man and start shoring up the population. That wasn't even an option for them. It was the only way.

But maybe that wasn't the way for her.

Lisa wondered idly as she ate the bacon that fell out of her sandwich. Her parents had seemed so immovable. Could she find something she could be successful at and present it to them as another option for her future? Did they know that Auntie Jo was a seemingly successful business owner? Why couldn't she picture a future without worrying about her parents' approval?

"Ms. Cambridge! I'm surprised to see you so early."

Lisa glanced up from her musings at the sound of her aunt's voice. An older woman with silver hair pulled into an immaculate bun and expensive looking hiking gear stepped up to the counter with an easy grin.

"Dottie, Josephine dear, please. Ms. Cambridge makes me sound like I'm ninety years old. Once I hit that milestone, we can discuss a change in names."

Jo chuckled and set a large coffee on the counter.

"Did you still want your biscotti? I made these special last night."

"I can't abide a cheat snack when I haven't had my hike," the woman sighed. "The park rangers have most of the trails closed up in Newport. Something about how the water level has been fluctuating and the waves are eroding the trails."

"Odd that they would close all the trails. Most of them are inland, no?"

"That's what I said, but they weren't interested in giving any straight answers. I didn't feel anything odd aside from the usual anomalies that we run into here and there. I just hope it isn't closed for most of the fall. As convenient as Peninsula can be, it does tend to get a bit crowded. Makes participating with nature a bit difficult. But I'll endure as I always do. There are some lovely trails down by Bjorklunden, Have you ever been to see the Shakespeare productions down there? Delightful."

Jo's expression stuttered for a moment before nodding. "A few summers ago. I did get to see Much Ado About Nothing."

Lisa made a mental note about that. She didn't know if she would still be here come summer, but if she was, that sounded like fun. She wished she had her cell phone to look it up.

"You must get out to see it again."

"Maybe next year."

Dottie hummed. "I'll be calling about catering for the next luncheon. We were just at Dandelion's this month, but for November, we'll definitely be needing your baking expertise."

Jo wrapped up a few of the biscotti that Lisa recognized from last night and set them on top of Dottie's coffee.

"I'll keep an ear out for your call. And maybe try Whitefish for some hiking. Though some of the trails are on the water, so maybe there's some weirdness going on there as well."

"I'll have to give that a try. Thank you, Josephine. Have a lovely day, dear."

The older woman turned from the counter and nodded to Lisa as they made eye contact. She paused for a moment as she reached for the door, looking back at Lisa with confusion on her face. The barest look of recognition passed over her expression before she left the bakery.

"That was weird," Lisa said aloud.

Jo came around the counter again and plopped down at Lisa's table. "Dottie?"

"I've definitely never met her before, but she just looked at me like she knew me."

Jo regarded her niece for a moment before reclining a bit in her chair. She looked as if she was trying to see what Dottie had seen, but after a moment, she stopped.

"She has a pack of grandkids that she comes in with over the summers. You might remind her of one of them."

Taking another bite of her sandwich, Lisa shrugged. She wasn't convinced, but she didn't want to press. She had a slew of other questions that she wanted to ask.

"Did you sleep alright?"

Lisa choked, coughing a bit before swallowing. "Oh...um, yeah. It...ah...it took me a minute to fall asleep, but once I did I slept pretty well."

Lisa chose to ignore the very guilty look on her aunt's face, She appreciated that they were both just going to pretend Lisa didn't sob herself to sleep.

Jo looked like she wanted to say something but jumped up from her chair. "Delivery's here."

As Jo hurried behind the counter, Lisa turned in her chair to watch a box truck pull up. She felt a swell of appreciation for the distraction.

"Would you change anything about the sandwich?" Jo asked. "I usually give Dan a little something when he gets here. "

"I thought it was super tasty. Might throw on some hot sauce for a little kick, but it was good."

Jo nodded, immediately lost in the sandwich assembly process. She grabbed a half empty bottle of hot sauce and squirted a dollop on the avocado spread. The sandwich had just slid into the oven to toast when the front door swung open again.

"Something smells good."

A sandy haired man walked into the bakery wearing an ancient baseball hat, loose-fitting black hoodie, and worn, comfortable looking jeans. His face was kind and pulled into a smile.

"You know, if you say that every time you walk in, it really starts to devalue the effect of the smell."

"Can't devalue the truth, Jo."

"What fantasy land are you living in?"

"I haven't settled on a setting for the new tabletop campaign, but soon as I decide, you'll be the first to know."

Jo held out her hand for the inventory list. "I'll hold you to that."

Lisa perked up immediately at the mention of a campaign. She couldn't be sure that he was talking about what she hoped he was talking about. She had always wanted to give role playing a try, but the opportunity never presented itself.

"Oh, Dan, this is my niece, Lisa. She'll be staying with me for a bit, so you'll probably be seeing her around."

Lisa waved.

"Give me a hand getting the stock in the back?" Jo asked. "Then you can try to sell Lisa on joining your game."

Dan lit up. "Do you play?"

"After, Dan. Some of this stuff is too heavy for me to lift."

"I don't," Lisa said. "But I've always been interested."

"After," Jo shouted as she moved into the back kitchen.

"I'll meet you around back, Jo," he shouted back, "but I definitely want to continue this conversation!"

Instead of sitting by herself and wondering if she'd be able to avoid the incoming onslaught of questions from Dan that would determine if she was nerdy enough to play with his group, Lisa pushed away from the table and followed her aunt. Jo seemed surprised.

"Well, I'm not going to sit out there while you're moving heavy stuff. I'm not an asshole."

Jo's expression turned warm. "Appreciate the help."

Jo opened the back door, and Dan wheeled in a stack of supplies with a hand cart. Lisa started pulling them off and looking to Jo for directions on where to put things. Dan chattered happily as they worked.

"So you're staying for the winter?"

"For a start," Lisa said. "Needed to get away for a while."

"This is the best place for that. Gets pretty quiet over the colder months, but if you know where to look, you can find plenty to do."

"Good to hear."

Dan leaned against the hand truck. He pulled off his hat and brushed his hair back before replacing it. He was clearly weighing whether to ask a question, and eventually seemed to decide he would just go for it with a little nod.

"So...did Carie decide to stay somewhere else this winter?"

Lisa could feel her aunt tense from across the room even before looking over to her. Jo had frozen in her tracks. Her arms shook from holding a heavy bag of flour. The moment passed, but Dan could tell he had asked the wrong question. He stammered, but Jo cut him off.

"I'm not sure where she's staying. I haven't really spoken to her since the spring."

Dan winced and shared a look with Lisa. Lisa shook her head in confusion.

"Um...well...sure she's somewhere..."

Lisa shot him an incredulous look and tried to diffuse the tension. "So, tell me about your game."

The awkwardness was immediately forgotten as Dan held up a finger. "Let me toss this back in the truck and we'll discuss!"

The front door opened again, and Jo wordlessly set down her burden and went out to assist the customer.

"I really need to hear about this Carie person," Lisa whispered.

"I didn't realize it was such a touchy subject still," Dan said apologetically. "She barely mentioned Carie all summer. I just figured they had been talking like normal, but I guess not. Must have been a bigger fight than I thought."

"She was over here this morning," Lisa said. She jutted her chin towards the back door. Dan went, and she followed him outside. "I just got up here yesterday, and I ran into a ...I'm still not really sure, but Carie got me back on the road. She showed up this morning to see if I was okay, but she was clearly looking for my aunt."

"They are maddening, let me tell you. I've been delivering to Jo for about five years now. Carie was in this bakery every Wednesday during the quiet season. Looked perfectly at home, and Jo was just...happy."

Lisa made a mental note to ask her aunt about Carie as soon as Dan was gone. "So, you play?" she asked.

Dan shook himself from the Carie discussion and started leading Lisa back around the front of the bakery. "I do! I mostly run the game. Curse of the forever game master. My group just finished a year's long campaign, and I'm getting ready to start up a new one."

Lisa swallowed and told herself to be brave. Dan hadn't started with the questions yet, so it was possible that he wouldn't at all.

"How would you feel about having someone who's never played before join?"

"Are you kidding? That would be great!"

Dan launched into a speech that he'd clearly given multiple times before about how new players don't have any preconceived notions of the game and that makes them more fun to run a campaign for. Lisa nodded politely, pleased as punch that she had finally come across someone who wasn't convinced they had to protect their beloved hobbies from interlopers and fake gamer girls. She paused a moment as they passed one of the bakery windows. She saw her aunt helping a customer, but Jo's smile had diminished. Lisa was determined to get to the bottom of it.

"So, I'll probably start with some pre-campaign sessions to round out characters and pick classes and all that. We can roll up your character stats then too."

"Just like that?"

Dan smiled like it was the most obvious thing in the world. "Yup!"

They exchanged phone numbers before Dan had Jo sign off on the inventory manifest. He waved goodbye, saying he'd see them next week. Jo thrust a can of soda and his sandwich bag towards him. Dan and the customer left, and Lisa decided to go for broke.

"So... I know haven't even been here a full day yet, but seeing as she's come up a few times, would it be weird if I asked about her?"

Jo looked up, her face the picture of misunderstanding.

"Carie."

"Oh."

"We definitely don't have to talk about it if you don't want to," Lisa hedged. "It's not my place to ask, but I don't want to keep stumbling into something that very obviously hurts you. We're only just getting to know each other, and I don't want to...I don't want to be like everyone else in our family."

Jo chuckled. "I'm glad you agreed to come up here, Lisa. And I'm glad you're understanding."

Lisa leaned against the counter, trying to look as open and understanding as she could. Her aunt sighed and crossed her arms, falling back against the counter behind her.

"There's not much to tell really. Carie used to rent the second floor over the winters. You've seen what she does. She only comes up for the off season. We met...I think it was my second or third winter up here. She was really hurt, so I helped her out. We met up a few other times. We started talking, and eventually I found out she was living out of her car, which is insane over the winter here. So, I rented the room to her."

A ghost of a smile danced over Jo's face. She shook away the memory and continued. "We got...close. Summers without her were...hard. She practices her craft all over, and I'm sure there are places and people that need her help just as much as we do up here. I should have remembered that last spring."

"What happened last spring?"

Jo shrugged. "I asked her to stay for the summer. I just wanted more of her time. That sounds weird...I wanted us to be together. It...um...it turned a bit heated, and we fought. And she left."

It was either the pity in Lisa's expression or the very clear follow-up questions that were bubbling to the surface, but Jo shook her head with a small, sad smile.

"Things would have come to a head eventually anyway. Maybe she could have stayed for a while, but then she would have had to leave. Or...or it just wouldn't have worked. It wasn't fair of me to expect her to change her entire life to suit mine. Especially when she has important work to do. "

"Auntie Jo..."

"It still stings, but it'll be okay. It's over, and we aren't pretending it was anything it never could be." Jo sniffed and discreetly tried to wipe her eyes. She shook her head and sighed. "I'm fine. I promise."

"I'm sorry that happened," Lisa said instead of blurting out that Carie had been there that morning looking to see Jo. That wasn't the way to fix this.

"Sometimes things just reach their natural conclusion," Jo said. "But I'm glad that I have the space for you this year. I don't think I got the chance to say it last night, but I'm so glad that you had my number."

Lisa smiled. "Me too. Would it be weird to hug? Is that a little too much too soon?"

A tear escaped from Jo's crinkled eyes. She opened her arms, and Lisa wrapped her aunt in a tight embrace. She felt Jo's body shudder at the contact and resolved to hug her aunt as often as possible.

"That Shakespeare thing sounded fun. Is it only over the summer?"

Jo pulled back. "Sometimes they have special events over the winter. We'll have to check if you're interested."

Lisa let her aunt chat a bit more about some of the other theater troops in the county. She nodded as if she was listening intently, but she was plotting out exactly how she was going to ignore her own problems this winter. She was going to do everything she could to get them talking again. Her aunt was clearly lonely and missed the companionship. And whatever the hell Carie was, Lisa was convinced that she didn't just randomly appear on a former friend's stoop in the morning just to check on things.

Lisa had space to figure out her own mess and a project. It was going to be an interesting winter.

Chapter Four

The next few days were a flurry of logistics. After Jo closed the bakery for the night and Lisa had washed off the previous day's travel in a scalding hot shower, they went grocery shopping. Lisa turned red as a tomato when her card was declined, but her aunt stepped right in with a quip about the banks in Illinois being incompetent. The cashier laughed it off, and Lisa had her own little stock of coffee, snacks, and even the odd vegetable. When they arrived home, Jo's phone buzzed. She went white as a sheet before closing herself in her bedroom to take the call. The house's walls were thin enough that Lisa could hear her aunt's side of the conversation..

"I'm not going to fight about this, Celeste. Please stop yelling. I wasn't...You would rather she had nowhere to go?"

Celeste. Mom.

"Celeste, that's a deeply flawed way of looking--"

"Look, she still has her phone. I can't make her answer, but you can..."

"I'm just trying to help. Lisa can stay here as long as she wants."

Lisa recognized her aunt's exasperated sigh as she ended the call. Her mother always had to get the last word in and when angry, would end the conversation before anyone else could retort.

Lisa braced for a flurry of furious text messages or a phone call, but her phone remained silent. Her mother had said her piece, and her father must have gotten tired of being the focus of her ire. Lisa tried to let the inattention roll off her back. She didn't really feel like talking to either of them, so she sat on the couch and pretended to look through the scattered recipes on the coffee table. They had already established that they wouldn't address how Jo could hear Lisa's meltdown upstairs, so why break precedent?

When Jo emerged, she was a little too cheery. She was performing. The conversation had clearly rattled her. Lisa pretended not to see her hands shaking as Jo started leafing through her recipes on the coffee table.

"What should we make for dinner, hon?"

Lisa had never been much of a cook. Between the meal plan at school and her mother's insistence that their home remain spotless, there wasn't much time to practice. She shrugged, still preoccupied with her silent phone. Jo suggested picking a recipe at random and then making it together. She moved to the bookshelf and started pulling down cookbooks. Jo presented the stack to Lisa.

"You have a look. I'll fix us a snack."

Jo sliced up the rest of the bounty from Lisa's arrival. They snacked on the nibbles until Lisa came back with a recipe for chicken piccata. Barring the capers-- which Jo didn't care much for anyway-- they had all the ingredients handy along with some spaghetti they could have on the side.

Jo showed Lisa how to slice the massive chicken breast into cutlets, then pound them out so they were of an even thickness. They dredged the chicken in flour, then an egg wash, then flour again. As they sauteed the cutlets, Lisa could feel a bubble of joy in her heart. The simple act of cooking a meal to enjoy with family wasn't something they did back home. Her parents seemed to resent the very notion of eating. Clearly, they had never felt like this.

Lisa glanced at her aunt as they cooked. Her heart warmed to see the tension from the phone call gone. Jo's eyes were twinkling as she watched the cutlets brown in the pan. They still barely knew each other, but Lisa never felt closer to anyone in her life. She let that feeling envelop her like a spell. She poured that love into the pan with the shallots and lemon slices. The chicken stock reduced, concentrating the love in the dish. When they ate the finished plate with their side of pasta and a glass of white wine each, Lisa swore she could taste the passion.

"Is this why your bread tastes so good?"

Jo's forkful of pasta stopped halfway to her mouth at that question. "Why?"

"Because you love doing it. You can taste that, can't you?"

Jo took another bite and chewed it thoroughly. "It is very good."

"It's more than good," Lisa insisted. "It's like magic."

Jo snorted fondly, savoring her bite.

"Can we do this again? We never really did the whole family dinner thing back home. At least, not like this."

"We can do this as often as you'd like," Jo said brightly. "I love to cook, but I don't usually have anyone to do it with."

Lisa stopped herself from asking if she used to cook with Carie. She promised herself she wasn't going to keep worrying at that string.

"Well, now you have me."

Dinner became a nightly ritual. Lisa would look through the endless pages of recipes that Jo had amassed over the years, and then they would make whatever she picked. Every night, Lisa could feel the joy and love in their preparation. She kept their favorites clipped together in a loose folio that she started calling their spell book. It grew thicker with each passing day. Jo dismissed the idea it was actual magic, but Lisa wasn't convinced.

They tried recipes from across the world in the weeks since Lisa arrived. Cooking was a wonderful distraction from the life-changing decisions Lisa was staring down. She tried to keep herself to a schedule, waking up around eight in the morning and doing online searches for Wisconsin cooking schools and creative writing classes. A few hits always popped up, but she needed to figure out how she was going to support herself if her parents truly were cutting her off. It wouldn't be fair to lean on Jo forever. Lisa was an adult. She could figure this out.

The tendrils of despair were never far those mornings. More than once, Lisa found herself staring at her phone. She could just call her parents and apologize and go back to school like they wanted, couldn't she? Wouldn't that be easier?

But then she remembered the swell in her chest when she cooked and the delicious taste of her aunt's bread. Those feelings were worth pursuing. She owed it to herself to investigate that path to happiness. She ignored her phone and got dressed for the day.

The weather had gotten cooler, so no one was sitting on the bakery's porch. Jo had asked Lisa to help her move the chairs and tables to the shed in the back. There were a few tables inside the bakery, though most customers that morning did not linger. Dottie Cambridge called the night before with a catering order, and Jo was showing Lisa how to adjust the weekly inventory to accommodate it when Dan arrived for the delivery. His smile was wider that day, and he approached the door with a spring in his step.

"I think I'm finally ready to kick off the new campaign," he shouted. He bounced excitedly up to the counter. "Are you free this Saturday?"

Lisa looked at her aunt.

"Did we have plans?" Jo asked.

"Oh...no. I don't think so," Lisa said. She felt her cheeks heat up when she realized she was looking for permission. "You didn't need me here?"

"I'm never going to say no to the help. Though we should discuss that. You've been doing a lot of work around here. I really should be paying you."

Lisa went a bit pink again. "You're also putting me up rent free, just bought me groceries—"

"We'll chat later about all that."

Lisa nodded and turned back to Dan. "Looks like I'm free."

"Amazing!" Dan pulled a thumb drive from his pocket and thrust it towards Lisa. "I'm assuming you don't have the player's guide, so here. This has all the books. Classes, feats, and all the supplemental material. Definitely acquired very legally."

"This isn't going to melt my laptop, is it?

"Last time I pulled files from it, mine was fine."

Lisa took the drive and held it like it was something precious. She didn't let the simmering anxiety about not having any idea how to use the information bubble up. She'd figure it out, and if she couldn't, that was what the internet was for.

As if sensing her sudden trepidation, Dan waved a hand in the air, scattering her concern. "Just give it a once over. Maybe think about characters that you've liked in fiction or in games or whatever. Use that as a guide and when you come by on Saturday, we'll roll up stats together. I'm guessing you don't have dice?"

Lisa did, but they were buried in her desk at her parents' house. She had bought them at the renaissance faire last summer on a whim. They were a swirl of blue and gold with bronze numbers painted on each side. When she bought them, she promised herself that she would use them. Foolishly, she felt like she was letting them down.

"Not with me."

"No worries," Dan said. "I have a ton of dice. You can use one of my sets until you can find your own."

And that was that. Lisa had entered a whole new realm of geekery, gatekeeper free. Instead of looking into cooking and writing, her morning internet searches were full of which character class was best for beginners. She took quizzes to find out what kind of role player she was best suited to be. She even watched a few videos of live sessions. It warmed her heart in the same way Jo's bakery did. Just more people who had found their joy and were making their way through life doing what they wanted. It made Lisa want to forget she had ever had a script to follow.

Instead of an elaborate dinner on Friday night, Lisa asked her aunt if they could bake something for her to take to the session the next day. Jo's eyes flashed with delight as they started flipping through the recipes looking at cookies, pastries, brownies, and all kinds of other sweets. Lisa set a few ideas aside for another day--puff pastry from scratch seemed a bit too try-hard for a first impression--and settled on an old classic: chocolate chip cookies. Jo let Lisa take the lead, offering suggestions along the way. Instead of semi-sweet chocolate chips, they hacked hunks from a bittersweet chocolate bar. Jo insisted they brown the butter to add a subtle nutty flavor. Fascinated, Lisa watched as the butter separated in the pan and the milk solids began to brown. They set it aside to solidify a bit while they gathered the other ingredients. Lisa felt the warmth grow in her chest again as she watched the dough come together. It was a high she would never get tired of.

In no time, Lisa had a tray of cookies for her group. Secretly, she had always wanted to be the friend who brought something to snack on. She hoped this would be her opportunity to seize that role.

The next day, Lisa found herself outside a modest house in Juddville, just north of her aunt's home. It was simple, but clean, and far from any other neighbor. It was nestled between two farms along the main highway. Lisa parked her car in the driveway and took a deep breath before she got out of the car. She wasn't one to throw herself into new social situations, but she didn't want to back out now. For all she knew, Dan was standing in the window waiting for her to approach. She turned down her anxiety to a low simmer and was ringing the doorbell before she could second guess herself.

Dan appeared in the doorway with a big smile on his face. He wore the same well-worn jeans and a t-shirt with an anime character Lisa was vaguely familiar with.

"You're the first here," he said as his eyes widened at the sight of her tray. "Did you make something?"

"I've been living in a bakery the last few weeks. I thought it would be weird to show up without anything."

"The best way into a new group's heart is through their stomach. I usually only have chips, soda, and beer."

"Well, now you have cookies too."

"Outstanding! Come on in. Folks should be getting here soon, so let's get you rolling."

The inside of the house reminded Lisa of a cleaner version of her aunt's place. It was lived in, but not as chaotic. Photos of Dan and his parents lined the walls, broken up with shelves of knickknacks and a painting of a small town on the water.

"We're set up in the basement. My parents are out at dinner, but they'll be back in a bit. We can get a little rowdy, so we're banished down here."

The basement was unfinished but still inviting. Dan had set up a long folding table with six chairs around it. The head of the table was piled with books and a short, four-sided screen with an elaborate scene of four adventurers fighting a fire-breathing dragon on it. Lisa picked a spot, and Dan immediately set down a few sheets of paper and a seven-piece set of dice.

"This is going to seem incredibly overwhelming, but I promise you that it's much easier than it initially seems."

Lisa nodded, pulled the foil off the cookies, and bit into one as Dan started running through rolling up a character. A shiver shot up her spine, and she was right back in the kitchen laughing with her aunt.

They had just decided that a melee class would be best when the doorbell rang. The screen door opened and slammed back shut before the sound of footsteps grew louder on the stairs. Dan and Lisa both looked up to see a round faced woman with short strawberry blond hair stride into the room. She waved to Dan, but her attention immediately focused on Lisa. She furrowed her brow for a moment before her face broke into a wide grin.

"Dan, I didn't know that you knew another witch!"

Lisa looked between the two.

The woman smiled with a commiserating air. "Oh, you don't have to hide that kind of thing here. I'm into chicks, and I can weave a bit of magic, no bigs."

She said it as if she was an expert. One look at Lisa, and she could just tell. Lisa stopped herself from saying 'just in the kitchen'. She was holding proof in her hand. The cookie seemed to buzz in agreement.

"What?"

"Kat, I don't know that she..."

"Oh shit," Kat slapped a hand over her mouth. "Was that...Did you not know? It's right out there... Fuck! I'm so sorry!"

"Wait wait wait," Lisa said. "What are you talking about?"

Kat looked helplessly between Dan and Lisa.

"It's part of my gift," Kate began to explain. "My weaving. I can conjure small fires, and I can tell if someone has that little spark of magic."

"I'm definitely not magical," Lisa said, though her tone betrayed her confidence in that statement.

"Don't sell yourself short," Kate said as she snapped her fingers. A red flame hovered over her pointer finger. "You definitely are."

"Kat, the smoke alarm."

"Shit, sorry."

Lisa looked down at her hands, as if proof would suddenly appear. The half-eaten cookie just stared back at her, reminding her of the conversation with her aunt after they made chicken piccata. That felt magical, hadn't it?

She remembered the woman in the bakery. Dottie, her name was. She had been talking to Jo about sensing things in the woods. She had also fixed Lisa with the exact same stare that Kat just had. Cooking felt like magic. Was that exactly what it was?

"Holy shit," Lisa gasped.

The doorbell rang again upstairs, distracting Dan. Kat stepped closer, looking contrite.

"Hey, we can definitely table this until later, yeah," she said. "I need to learn to control my big mouth. I'm so sorry."

"No, no...it actually makes a lot of sense," Lisa said with a laugh. "Maybe I should play a spell caster instead, huh?"

"What class are you going with?"

"Barbarian. A half-orc barbarian."

"Oh, no no no. You need to stick with that. It's easy to pick up for a beginner."

"I'll take your word for it."

Kat winked and gestured broadly. "I've been playing for a minute. Trust me. You'll have a blast. And if you don't, Dan will definitely let you roll a new character!"

Over the next half hour, the rest of Dan's friends filtered in. Michelle was a nurse at the local urgent care clinic. She had two kids under three and needed the outlet of role playing every few weeks. Jack sold farm equipment and lived with his wife and daughter. His wit was sharp and biting, but once Lisa got the rhythm of it, she found him quite funny. Max had a mop of red curly hair on his head. He was taller than anyone else in the group by at least a foot and had an impressive repertoire of height jokes. Lisa had never slotted into a group so easily. She remembered in high school being told by her guidance counselor that she'd find her people someday. She scoffed at the time but sitting at table arguing over stats and equipment with affable nerds, Lisa finally felt like she belonged.

Despite the distraction, Lisa found herself staring down at her hands throughout the night checking to see if sparks were flying out of her fingers. Every time she looked up, she caught Kat watching her. Once, Kat had taken a bite of a cookie and her eyes widened. She looked up at Lisa with confident recognition and nodded vigorously. It was an unspoken promise to talk about it later. Or the cookies were just really good.

Once all the back stories were sorted through and stats solidified, the group broke for the night. Michelle and Jack had kids to get back to, and Max had church in the morning. Lisa and Kat lingered, helping Dan clean up.

"So," Lisa started.

"So!"

Lisa tossed the used paper plates into the garbage and dusted off her hands. "I literally have no idea where to start."

"I still can't get over the fact that you're in your twenties and no one told you about this shit," Kat said.

"There's a very large chance that my parents do know about it and are just suppressing that knowledge because it doesn't fit into their perfect little world view."

"Weak. Magic is a blast."

"Fun definitely doesn't fall into that world view."

"Bummer," Kat said. "Weird that they live up here, but they've never run into it."

"They don't. Live here, I mean. They're outside of Chicago. I'm...ah...staying up here with my aunt for a bit, sorting some things out."

"Then surely your aunt knows about it."

"Yeah, she does. I don't know how much, but she definitely does," Lisa bit her lip before continuing. "She was close with Carie Waverland for a bit."

Kat's eyes lit up. "OH! Your aunt is the mysterious Josie?"

There was a pet name. No one called her aunt that. It was Jo or Josephine or Ms. Phines. Lisa couldn't help the grin that crept across her face.

"Yeah, Auntie Jo. I'm working at her bakery and staying with her for the winter."

"That would explain why Carie's been so quiet. Well, quieter. She was never super chatty. Dan mentioned they fought, but no one heard anything else."

"You're friends with her?"

"Not exactly," Kat said, twirling her hair with a finger. "I see her at tea sometimes."

"Tea? Please tell me that there's some kind of witch gathering. Please tell me that's a thing."

"Oh, it definitely is. The Society of the Witches of the Door! I tried to get them to make t-shirts, but most of the ladies are pretty old school. Archie said he'd wear one if I ever get around to it, but I think Ms. Cambridge would hex me."

"My aunt has definitely mentioned them now that I'm thinking about it," Lisa said. She raked her hands through her hair and sighed. "I swear to god, I should have flunked out of school sooner. This place just keeps getting better and better."

"You should come to the next meeting! At the very least, tell your aunt that you'll deliver the catering. Ms. Cambridge usually orders from the bakery for the lunches at her house."

"Is Carie usually at these things?"

"She doesn't normally stick around, but she stops by to talk with Ms. Cambridge."

"Then she'll have me go. Whatever happened she's still feeling pretty raw about it."

"It's been a rough season so far from what I call tell. Carie's been exhausted the few times I've seen her."

Dan came back down the stairs with beers in his arms. "Did you guys want to keep talking out here? We could get the fire pit going out back too if you wanted to hang around."

"I love that you're taking all this much better than I did," Lisa said.

"Oh, I think everyone here kind of knows about the magic stuff. Ask anyone and they can either tell you a story firsthand or they know someone who ran across something crazy in the woods. Whether they believe it all or not is up for debate. Kat's known about this stuff since high school."

"And my family comes up to the peninsula a lot. We stay down in Sturgeon Bay, but I'm up here most weekends. Dan and I hang out a bit, and I take classes up at the art school. That place attracts all kinds of bizarre shit. Remember that time at the reception? Carie came flying in there wrestling this ghoul looking thing. It was crazy. Most of that stuff stays pretty close to the knots. It's always weird when it strays."

"I'm going to need ghouls and knots explained," Lisa said. "But let's do it around the fire. Seems more appropriate."

They followed Dan outside, saying a quick hello to his parents. Dan stacked the firewood and crumbled old newspapers for kindling. He lit the papers and watched the fire catch. The slight breeze blew the smoke off into the fields around the house. Lisa tucked her hands in her coat pockets and looked at Kat expectantly.

"I don't know the ins and outs of this shit like some of the older ladies," Kat started. "I was up here with my parents one weekend years ago now. We popped into Dandelion's in Egg Harbor for coffee, and there were a bunch of these old ladies having coffee and chatting. One of them saw me, and she could feel that I had the same power that they did. I guess I always kinda knew. My parents are super low key, so they were just cool with it. They let me join the witches, though I think they see me as more of a mascot than anything. They aren't super powerful--aside from Dottie-- but they're capable enough to keep up the wards over the summer. It's Carie who really does the hard work over the winter."

"You're throwing a whole lot of information at me and I've gotta say that I don't know that you should," Lisa said. "I'm not from here. I could tell other people about this."

"Yeah, but you won't," Kat said with an easy grace. She smiled warmly. "You're one of us. Whatever's going on with them now, your aunt is close with Carie. And you don't seem like an asshole. I like to think I'm a good judge of character."

Dan nodded in agreement. "She really is."

Kat smiled smugly. "You're staying up here too. You need to know this stuff."

"Would probably be helpful, yes," Lisa agreed.

"You should really come to the next meeting. Be a lady who lunches. Or a dude. A dude who dines. Because Archie will probably be there too."

"I'll definitely be there, and if I've got some kind of powers or whatever," Lisa broke off there, dropping her head into her hands. "Fucking Christ..."

Dan popped the top off a beer and held it out to Lisa. It took a moment before she noticed it, but she tipped it back for a deep pull.

"At least you found out about it up here," Kat said. "There's people around who can help."

"Shit, if something like that happened around my parents, I could only imagine what their reaction would be. Jo knows Carie has magic. I hope she isn't too bothered by it."

"Listen," Dan started. "I've known Jo for a while now. I'm pretty sure you could tell her that you robbed a bank, and she wouldn't have a problem at all. She's the happiest I've seen her in a real long time."

"Been a bad summer?"

"I really don't know what happened, but it wasn't great."

Kat shrugged. "Carie's not exactly super chatty on any given day, but I don't think she's been doing well either."

"Well," Lisa said after taking another sip of her beer. "I think I can do something about that."

Chapter Five

It was cold.

But it was not dark.

It was very bright between the trees. Jo held up a hand to shield her eyes, but the light was coming from everywhere. Her eyes slowly adjusted, but she still felt off kilter. She heard the softest twinkling of the waves, broken ice shards lapping against the frozen shore. She kept one hand up to her eyes and the other stretched out in front of her. She felt for the trees and walked towards the sound. The foliage scratched against her shins. The loamy soil sucked at her bare feet. She could feel stones and roots stabbing at the soles, but the water was calling her. She pushed on.

The soil gave way to silt, sand, and then millions of tiny shells. The trees no longer tore against her body. She was clear of the forest. The wind whipped through her hair.

Jo dropped her hands to her sides. She was standing on the beach of a small bay. The waves were high and lapped at her shins. It was freezing, and the water was an unnatural deep indigo. The lake beyond smoothed out and met in a perfect line with the blindingly white sky.

She thought she had been there before, but she couldn't quite recall.

Jo blinked against the harsh light, and a misty shadow appeared hovering over the bay.

A voice whispered in her ear.

It's about time we met face to face. Jumping around in the shadows of your home feels so impersonal.

Jo spun, waving the voice away from her head. The shells cut into her bare feet.

It took me a while to realize just what you are, but once you were away from that witch, it became glaringly obvious.

Words bubbled in her throat, but Jo found them impossible to speak. She moved deeper into the water.

I'm surprised none of your other witchy friends figured it out. They aren't very powerful, so I suppose it makes sense.

Jo shook her head, chasing away the dark figures dancing in her peripheral vision. She felt the ghost of a touch on her cheek, guiding her eyes back towards the bay.

But Carie? She should know, shouldn't she? You spent so much time together. Unless, she was just there for a place to rest her head, some easy companionship...

Standing in water up to her knees, Carie was in the bay. She looked out into the lake. Her shoulders were heaving, as if she just ran a great distance.

You can call to her, but are you sure that she'll turn? You asked for her already, didn't you?

Jo tried to move her head. There was something just out of her range of vision; she was sure of it.

She won't turn, but that doesn't mean that you have to go through this alone. I still need a little time, but you'll wait, won't you? You been waiting your entire life for someone to see you, Josie. I can be that for you. I just need you to trust me.

"Auntie Jo?"

The sky shattered. Jo shot up from the arm of the couch with a sob. She frantically took in her living room when gentle hands touched her cheeks.

"Jo? Can you hear me?"

Lisa's face coalesced in Jo's swimming vision.

"Wake up. Wake up. I'm right here."

Jo reached out to touch Lisa's face. Another sob escaped her lips.

"It's okay. It was just a nightmare, yeah?"

"Y-yeah," Jo finally breathed. "I'm sorry. I was trying to stay awake to make sure you got home okay. I must have fallen asleep on the couch."

Lisa pulled her hands back, but the worry hadn't dropped from her face.

Jo blinked hard, willing her vision to clear. A tear rolled down her cheek, and she dashed it away with a quick wipe of her hand.

"I heard you outside," Lisa explained. "I couldn't understand what you were saying, but then you started to cry."

"Sorry...I'm sorry," Jo said. "I didn't mean to startle you."

"Do you want to talk about it?"

Jo choked out a laugh. "I...no...no I don't think so."

At a loss, Lisa could only nod.

Jo braced, expecting questions that she didn't have answers for, but Lisa just sat as her face ran through complicated emotions.

"Did...um...were you having nightmares before I came?"

"For most of the summer, actually. From what I can remember."

Lisa nodded. Her face twisted in concern.

"What's wrong?" Jo asked, her voice cracking with panic. "What's happened?"

"Oh, nothing," Lisa exclaimed. "Well, not nothing. It's actually a very big something. I just freaked out a bit when I heard you outside."

Jo grabbed the opportunity to swing the conversation away from her troubled sleeping. "Weren't you with Dan and his friends?"

"Yeah."

"What did he do?"

"Oh, he didn't do anything! None of them did. I had an amazing time. It all just...clicked, you know?"

"But something happened on the way back?"

Lisa looked confused for a moment.

Jo pursed her lips. "You look like you're carrying the weight of the world, hon. What's wrong? What happened?"

"It's...this is ridiculous. That woman, you know, the older one? Super classy? Always very put together?"

"Dottie?"

"Yeah, her," Lisa nodded. "The first morning I was here, she gave this weird knowing look as she left the bakery. Then before we started tonight, one of Dan's friends came in. She got that same exact look on her face. Then she said that I'm like her."

Jo leaned in, begging her to continue.

"That I'm... magic?"

"...oh."

"Yeah."

"That's...a lot."

"Imagine how I feel."

"Magical, I would guess."

Lisa guffawed before she could throw a hand over her mouth. Jo bit her lip to stop herself from laughing. They both dissolved into a fit of giggles. Jo forgot the sleepless bags under her eyes and the waning terror in the back of her mind. She shoved the idea that Carie would be able to help into the deepest part of her mind.

Taking a deep breath, Lisa tried to settle herself.

"I'm sure I already know the answer to this, but did mom or anyone in the family have anything...extrasensory?"

Jo dissolved into another fit of giggles. "If they did, they either repressed it so far that they ended up getting rid of it, or they were really good about hiding it."

Lisa bobbed her head. "So they were always..."

"Things like that don't really change," Jo said with a sad smile. "I've found that it's best not to dwell on them."

She left the *hurts too much* unsaid. Lisa was from the same family. There hadn't been any nights as loud as her first one staying over, but Jo had caught her niece looking at her phone as if expecting a call or a text, asking if she was okay. Even if Lisa left after a few months, Jo liked to think that they were forging a real connection. She hoped Lisa would see her as an actual person, and not just a refuge from her problems.

"You aren't...magical?"

"Not that I'm aware of," Jo said, choosing to ignore the nightmares and the odd dancing shadows she caught in the edges of her vision. They were talking about magic, not hallucinations. Totally different areas. "But that doesn't necessarily mean anything. Though, I would think the witches would have noticed by now. I've been up here for a long time, and they've been buying pastries from me for most of it."

"But...when we were cooking together," Lisa said, "it felt...well, it felt magical."

Jo had felt it too, but it seemed impossible that she could have such a special gift. She could only shake her head at her niece. Lisa looked disappointed, and it warmed Jo's heart. Even if the rest of the family didn't want her, Lisa clearly did.

"Either way, Kat--that was her name-- said that if I had any questions, I should meet up with the little salon that they hold. I think that Dottie woman is in charge of it?"

"She's the de facto leader of the whole thing. Though I think that's mostly because she has very strong opinions on everything, and the rest don't want to argue. It's more of a social club for them. They all just happen to be witches. And Archie. Though I don't think he'd mind being called a witch. I don't know that I've ever asked now that I think about it."

"Does everyone up here know about this?" Lisa felt she'd asked that question dozens of times since arriving.

"People notice what they want to notice," Jo said. "That's true in all things. Not just magic. My parents only saw what they wanted to. I told them one truth and that became the only thing they could see."

"You know that's wrong."

"What's that?"

"That you're only one thing," Lisa said. "You're lots of things. You're kind. You're a hell of a baker and a cook. You're, like, a pillar of the community up here. What would people do without your shop?"

Jo's eyes went teary, and she wrapped her niece in a tight hug. When she buried her face in the crown of Lisa's head, she tried to ignore the shadows flickering in the corners of her eyes. She just needed some more sleep, and they would fade. She had barely had any this week.

"Will you go to the next luncheon?" Jo asked after pulling away.

"I think I have to, right? If anything, I need some clarity on this shit."

"Do you need Dottie's number? I'm sure she wouldn't be mad about me giving it to you in this circumstance."

Lisa shook her head. She stood from the couch and yawned. "Kat said she'd introduce me at the next meeting. Said that if I didn't show, she would come here and carry me to Dottie's. I guess Kat was the last new witch they ran into and that was years ago."

"You get some sleep, then. I'll just--"

"Nope," Lisa interrupted. "You were sleeping, remember? You need to rest too."

Not bothering to argue, Jo took the hand Lisa offered and allowed herself to be pulled off the couch. Lisa didn't release her but led her to her bedroom door. She opened it and flicked the light on before looking back at Jo expectantly.

"I know the couch is comfortable, but the bed can't be that bad."

Jo stopped herself from saying anything and went inside. She was already wearing comfortable clothes, so she didn't bother to get changed. She sat on the bed and clasped her hands between her knees.

"It's probably all the caffeine that I've been drinking before bed. Never bothered me before."

The look Lisa gave her suggested Lisa didn't quite agree, but her niece didn't push it. Instead, she smiled.

"I don't know that I've said it enough, but I want to thank you again for letting me come stay with you. Tonight was the first night that I actually felt...felt like I found my people. Like I could belong with folks and just be me."

"I'm so glad that I could help you find that," Jo said. Her voice wobbled a bit, but she managed to stem the tide of tears. "And you know that you can stay here as long as you need."

Nodding, Lisa sniffled and quickly rubbed her sleeve over her face.

"I'll see you in the morning, hon. Good night."

The light switched off, and the door pulled closed. Jo reclined on the bed and blindly grabbed for her quilt. She wrapped it around herself and rolled over. The mattress and sheets felt foreign. When she let herself think about it, Jo really hadn't slept in the bed much since she shared it with Carie that one time.

"This is really getting pathetic, old girl," Jo whispered. "It happened once. You were both drunk, and then she said she didn't want to stay with you. This is your bed, and you really can't afford to buy a new one. You washed the sheets and the quilts. She's gone, and you're still here. You really need to just get over it."

Suck it up. It was the advice her family had always offered when she was feeling low as a child. The world was cruel, and a future employer or husband wouldn't tolerate a moody, broody woman. Shove it down and keep going. You have to be normal if anyone is going to want you, and constantly moping over what's passed isn't conducive to a prosperous future. Even though her experience in the world told her that her parents' viewpoint was very wrong, Jo found them still dogging her heels as she crept closer to forty. Still looking for approval from people who would never offer it no matter what Jo did.

This was why she didn't sleep in here. It was too dark, and it let her mind wander to places that should be avoided.

Jo almost got up, but she didn't want to worry her niece. Lisa clearly had enough on her mind without having to concern herself with her aunt's inability to move on from childhood slights. Instead, Jo kicked at the covers until they untangled. She squeezed her eyes shut and tried to ignore the feeling of eyes watching her in the dark. She could feel the heat of the bright white sun from that inky shore on her face. She fought against that pull, but exhaustion won out, and she sank deeper into the sheets and the mattress and the deep indigo water of that bay in her dreams. If she wandered those shores, staring out at the placid water, Jo didn't remember in the morning.

Chapter Six

"Ms. Cambridge lives here by herself?"

Lisa peered through the windshield of Dan's truck at a sprawling estate on the lake front. Jo had explained that Dottie lived on the quiet side of the peninsula where most of the permanent population of the county lived. The drive from the street had been shrouded with mostly bald trees from the biting winds off the lake, but when the forest gave way, a gorgeous log home came into view. Dan parked, and Lisa sent a quick text message to Kat.

"She has a pretty big family. Something like six kids and a whole pack of grandkids," Dan said. He opened the back door and pulled out the pastry boxes.

Lisa took the boxes from him, allowing him to grab the rest. She was giddy with anticipation at trying the goods. Jo had shown her how to make yeasted puff pastry the day before, and they had risen early that morning to turn it into all kinds of pastries. They had split a chocolate croissant while packing everything to go. She could taste the love between the flaky layers of pastry and wondered again if her aunt didn't have some latent magical power of her own that she was suppressing.

"No husband?"

Dan shrugged. "From what I've heard, he died shortly after she moved up here. Quite mysteriously, depending on who you talk to."

Dan and Lisa started towards the house. The massive front door swung open, and Kat bounded out. She was wearing jeans, a sweater, and a knit beanie hat. She looked far too casual for the scenery. She waved and held the door open for them.

"Right on time. Dottie will like that. She gets weird about folks being late," she said.

"Doesn't mind early though?'

Kat smiled smugly. "I'm an honorary grandkid, so I get special privileges."

"Witchy sweetheart of the peninsula," Dan chuckled.

"I'll get t-shirts made," Kat said. "Come on. Let's get this set out and then I can introduce you."

Kat led them through a two-story foyer with a wooden spiral staircase with intricately carved spindles. The foyer opened into a great room with massive windows that provided panoramic views of the lake front. They didn't linger there but moved through a butler's pantry and into the kitchen. Lisa tried not to be intimidated by the appliance package that looked like it cost what tuition had set her back last year. A large, quartz topped island separated the kitchen from the dining room. Kat stopped there and pulled the boxes from Lisa's hands.

"I think we have it from here, Dan."

"Did you need a ride back later?" he asked Lisa.

"Not as long as Kat's still cool with taking me home."

"I got it," Kat said. "Dan, you're tall. Before you go, can you grab the white plates from that cabinet?

"Sure thing."

"I'm not gonna lie," Lisa said as she opened the boxes. "I definitely thought this place was going to be a lot broodier."

"Dottie doesn't really do broody. These brunches aren't exactly all these old ladies clustered around cauldrons and hexing unsuspecting townsfolk," Kat said. "Honestly, it's mostly for them to gossip, knit, and see who's going to land Archie for that December romance. But jokes on them. I'm pretty sure that Archie has a husband named Ralph."

"Archie likes the attention more than anything. He gives just as good as he gets."

The trio turned towards the distinguished voice. The woman from the bakery stood in the doorway. Her gray hair was pinned back in an elaborate bun and she wore a shawl over her shoulders embroidered with flowers of all colors. Simple gold studs adorned her earlobes, and her makeup was immaculate. Her eyes were kind.

"You must be Dan and Lisa. I don't think we've been formally introduced. I'm Dorothy Cambridge, but please call me Dottie. Thank you for bringing the sweets."

"No problem, Ms. Cambridge," Dan said with an awkward little bow. His cheeks flushed as he gave a quick wave before heading back to the front door.

"He's not staying?"

Kat shook her head. "Not really his scene. But Lisa is."

"Ah yes," Dottie said. She moved gracefully into the kitchen, stopping just in front of Lisa and taking her hands in her own. "You do look so much like your aunt. She's a sweet woman. We worry about her."

"It's nice to meet you properly, Ms. Cambridge."

"Please dear, call me Dottie. You've come to visit and partake in brunch. We shouldn't be so formal."

"Of course."

"And from what Kat tells me, we do have much to discuss. Before all that, I must apologize. I'm sure my undignified staring when we first came across each other did nothing for your nerves. And to have no guidance while discovering your powers...well, that's not for me to apologize for, but I'm sorry nonetheless. Making these discoveries about oneself is hard enough when you have help."

"You don't need to apologize. Thank you for having me here, though."

"From what I've heard, you've made a nice little space for yourself. It's not a far reach to assume that you might decide to settle here, and we would be remiss if we didn't extend the hand of friendship to a fellow weaver."

Lisa didn't even have to ask the question. Her confusion was plain on her face.

"That's what they call themselves up here," Kat said. "Witches are weavers. There are threads of magic all around us, and we pull on those threads to make our magic."

She snapped her fingers and a flame appeared above them.

"If you're going to do that, light the fireplace, please. It's a bit chilly, and we don't need Evelyn and Mildred complaining about a draft."

Retracing their steps, they found themselves back in the great room. Lisa couldn't resist the draw of the picturesque landscape. She stood at the windows and watched the waves lap at the stony beach. Kat knelt at the fireplace and set the kindling alight.

Above the fireplace was a wood carving of the peninsula. Lisa pulled herself away from the view to look at it. At different points along the shoreline, there were several knotted designs.

"One of our old members was a woodworker. I commissioned that from him after I burned the portrait of my ex-husband that used to hang there. He did an excellent job of it."

"It's gorgeous," Lisa agreed. She pointed towards one of the knots. "What are those?"

"That's right, you wouldn't know," Dottie said to herself. "Those are the locations of the lighthouses around the peninsula. The Witches of Door aren't new. We've persisted for generations here. I'm just the first to take the initiative and gather us into a cohesive group. We really only have the oral history that's been passed down, but it is said that the lighthouses were built not only as beacons for the ships, but for weavers as well."

"I don't think that Lisa's been near any of them yet," Kat said.

"I didn't really feel anything until..." Lisa thought back through her entire history. She never felt any spark of power when she was home. She had felt something when she cooked with her aunt, but Jo insisted she didn't know about any magic in their family.

"I guess it really wasn't until I came up here," Lisa said.

Dottie considered her for a moment, her perfectly manicured pointer finger tapping against her lips.

"As far as I know, Door County is the only location of knots in the Midwest."

"You mentioned knots the other day," Lisa said, looking over at Kat.

"Oh, we call them knots, dear," Dottie explained. "Kat mentioned it earlier. Weavers use the threads to draw magic from, and the threads come from those knots. On the peninsula, we happen to have several knots, which is why many of us were drawn here in our retirement. It's also why we tend to have plenty of fantastical happenings up here."

"And that's a lot all in one place?"

"That's what makes this place so special. And dangerous."

"It's really not that dangerous," Kat said as she pushed up from the hearth. The fire caught, and the thicker pieces of wood started to burn. "If it was, we'd have a really big problem on our hands."

"It's dangerous enough. If a person with latent unknown magic like yourself wandered too close and didn't realize what they were doing, they could do immense harm by pulling on those threads. It could destroy one of the knots, and we've never seen what that can do. And that's not even mentioning the other entities that latch onto them."

Lisa thought back to the bear she encountered on her drive up. "But that's why you have Carie, right?"

Dottie looked confused for a moment, but then understanding dawned. "Ah, yes. She did mention that you ran into some trouble. Carie does freelance work for us over the off months. She keeps tabs on the knots and deals with the more dangerous creatures. We do what we can to keep it safe, but she's been an incredible help since she started with us. She comes from a family very strong in weaving. Her abilities far exceed our own. I was lucky enough to meet her mother some years ago when I was still performing. It's a connection I'm forever grateful for."

"You were a performer?" Lisa asked.

"I was a concert pianist for many years," Dottie said with a hand wave towards the grand piano in the corner by the windows. "There was a haunting at one of the venues I had a residency at. Carie's mother was summoned to exorcise it, and she recognized a fellow weaver. I can make mundane objects assist around the house. Being able to have a broom sweep up while cooking dinner for a family of seven was always very helpful. Helped in keeping an audience's attention on me as well. But that's enough about other people. Kat invited you so we can give you some guidance."

Lisa nodded. "Any answers you can give, I'd be really grateful. Though, I would love to hear you play."

"We'll have to wait for Archie to get here. He'll be cross if I play without him," Dottie said with a wide grin. She held her hands palms up between them and a burst of light flared from them. "Let's begin."

School had always been frustrating for Lisa. The practicalities of structured learning never seemed to stick. She did much better with a demonstration and then the opportunity to dive in on her own. Dottie didn't have any books for her to read, so the older woman took Lisa to the window and pointed across the bay.

"You can't see it very well from here, but on that island, there is one of the old lighthouses. Close your eyes and try to feel the line of the threads. There should be many from there. Do you feel them?"

Lisa did as Dottie asked and let her eyes slide shut. She wasn't sure how to reach out and felt a bit like she was fumbling for a light switch in a pitch-black room. Her cheeks burned in frustration, and she felt a bit stupid. But then she grazed against something. A shot like electricity zinged up her arm. She pulled back for a moment before steeling herself and reaching out again. She tentatively held it and opened her eyes to Dottie's smiling face.

"Got it?"

"I think so," Lisa responded.

"Now, slowly, pull on the thread."

Lisa nodded and plucked at the invisible line. She felt the power up her arm again and looked eagerly over to Dottie.

"Excellent," Dottie said, her eyes sparkling. "Hold up your hand and will the power from the thread there. Let's see how it manifests."

Lisa cupped her hands, staring at her palms and directing the power there. A small light flickered to life, quickly coalescing into a shining ball of blue flame. Delighted, Lisa looked from the ball to Dottie's proud face.

"That's a great start. We can definitely work from there."

Shortly after the lesson, the rest of the ladies filtered in. Kat had been right about Archie. Lisa saw him exit a car, stroll over to the driver side window and kiss the handsome, gray-haired man sitting there before heading towards the house. Each of the weavers fussed over Kat as they entered. They pinched her cheeks and tugged at her hands so they could comment on how skinny she was getting and demanding that she stop by their houses for a decent meal. She seemed pleased to have another younger person in the vicinity to redirect the busy bodies. Lisa smiled through their attentions and enthusiastically answered their questions even though they were the same ones over and over and over again.

The praise didn't stop once they got to the pastries.

Dottie produced an ancient steel coffee carafe and fancy glass mugs and made everyone wait for coffee before they dug into the catering. Once the coffee was ready, the witches descended. Lisa preened at the pleased noises they all made as they dug in. She looked to Dottie for her reaction and was surprised at the considering expression on her face.

"We must speak with your aunt," Dottie said after taking another bite of a bearclaw. "Now that we've had a chance to explore your magic a bit, I can distinguish it in here, but there's something else as well."

"A bit shocking that we didn't catch it before, though," Archie chimed in. He was cutting croissant with a knife and fork and had a linen napkin tucked into his shirt to avoid crumbs. "We've all been patronizing the bakery for years. Not to mention that Josephine has catered our little affairs as well. No one else has been making the pastries."

Mildred rolled her eyes. "You know as well as we all do that when we're around each other our powers can amplify. If we were to cast something all together now, it would be stronger than anything else we've ever done alone. It's possible that having Lisa there drew out whatever latent talent Josephine has. Kat, dear, can you please put another log on the fire? There's a dreadful chill in the air."

Lisa bit her lip as Dottie rolled her eyes. She had cracked open a window not long ago because the thermostat had soared into the eighties.

"Weaving tends to run in families," Dottie said. "It would be odd that her power hadn't manifested until now, but not unheard of."

Lisa kept herself from launching into their family history. She had been having such a nice time, and really didn't want to bring up the past. It also felt like a violation. Jo's story was hers to tell. She couldn't help but wonder if her aunt wasn't hiding her magic without knowing it.

Archie furrowed his brow and plucked at his napkin, sending crumbs flying. "You would think then that with Carie having been so close--"

His eyes went wide, and he shoved the rest of his pastry into his mouth. Lisa followed his gaze and found Carie looming in the doorway. Her dark hair was pulled away from her face but fly away strands stuck out from her head. She wore a button up of deep crimson, black jeans, and heavy boots that made her a few inches taller. She had clearly heard them talking about Jo, but she schooled her face into a neutral expression as she continued into the room.

"Ms. Cambridge," she said. "Sorry I'm a bit late. There was--"

Carie stopped herself when her eyes landed on Lisa. Instead of engaging in the staring contest, Lisa placed a bear claw on a plate and held it out to Carie.

The witch cocked an eyebrow before picking up the treat and taking a large bite.

"That's delicious." Carie chewed for another second before her expression went considering. She held the half-eaten bear claw to her face, starting at it hard before looking back to Lisa. "That's not just you though, is it?"

"Apparently not."

"That's Josie."

Lisa clamped her mouth shut, stopping the goofy smile from spreading over her face upon hearing the nickname. She just nodded. "The witches seem to think so."

"We have a few more members of the knitting circle that we weren't aware of, Carie dear," Dottie said. She took the empty plate and replaced it with a steaming cup of coffee. "Lisa here has come to learn a bit more about herself."

"Welcome to the club," Carie said.

"Who knew rural Wisconsin allowed for such self discovery?" Lisa sighed.

Dottie patted Lisa's shoulder before gesturing towards the kitchen. "You had something you wanted to discuss, Carie?"

The freelancer switched into business mode immediately. She straightened her shoulders and wiped the besotted look from her face. "If you have a few minutes."

The two women moved out of the room, and Lisa discretely followed. She stopped just outside the doorway and tried to lean beside it as casually as possible.

"Is everything alright?" Dottie asked.

"You wanted me to let you know if I ran into anything unusual."

"And I'm assuming that you have?"

"The possessions are getting bolder. Lisa was barely out of Sturgeon Bay when her car was attacked. I thought it might be a fluke, but I've tracked several other entities along Route Forty-Two heading that way. They weren't hard to dispatch, but it's more than I've seen this time of year before. The oddest part is they weren't heading for the lighthouse. At least, they didn't appear to be."

"Has anyone been hurt?"

"Lisa was the only one that made contact. They may have been called to her."

"We can make sure she learns how to ward herself. She and Jo--"

"That's not the only thing that's worrying me," Carie interrupted.

Dottie took a deep breath. "The knots?"

"You asked me to look into them, and the wards I cast have held up for the most part. I'm heading into the state park after I'm done here. There's something trying to get through. I need to make sure I'm there to stop it."

"Is there anything you need?" Dottie asked. "What can we do?"

"I'm just going to post up in my car. Keep an eye out until whatever it is shows itself."

"Please be careful, dear. If you need any help, call me."

"Of course."

"Take some pastry with you."

Lisa could hear Dottie bustling around the kitchen. She leaned into the doorway and saw Carie sadly staring at the pastries. Pulling back before she could be seen, Lisa looked around the room trying to find Kat. She was tucked into the plush couch next to Archie and Evelyn. Archie was playing a game of solitaire and moving the cards with a flick of his finger. Evelyn was crocheting a scarf, but the needles were moving on their own. She offered Archie opinions on his possible moves. He did his best to ignore her. Kat caught Lisa's eye and dashed over.

"Theoretically, how would you feel about driving me to Peninsula State Park?"

"And why would we be doing that this late?" Kat asked with a wry twist of her lips.

"I may want to follow Carie."

Kat's expression shifted to concern. "Is that a great idea?"

"No, but I'd still like to do it."

"Lisa..."

"Listen. I know it's a very stupid idea, but she needs someone looking out for her. If something were to happen to her, I can at least call for help."

Kat shot her a skeptical look.

"If you won't drive me, I'll just call for a cab, or I'll walk which isn't ideal, but I'll do it."

"Fuck. Fine."

A throat cleared, and they both turned to see Dottie hovering behind them.

"Lurking in doorways is terribly unbecoming, ladies," she said.

"Sorry, Ms. Cambridge," they both said in unison like scolded school children.

"However, if you leave now, she won't have too long of a head start."

Kat and Lisa shared a look.

"You don't mind us following her?" Lisa asked.

"If what she just told me is true, Carie is spread quite thin even for a witch as powerful as she is," Dottie's expression went from concerned to deadly serious. "I'm worried enough about her, so do anything foolish. Stay back, and let her do her work, but if she runs into trouble, call me immediately. I'm not nearly as skilled as she is, but we should be able to perform an exorcising ritual should it come to that."

Kat and Lisa quickly said their goodbyes to the witches. They were followed outside by well wishes and invitations for the next luncheon. Dottie's home was in Baileys Harbor on the opposite side of the peninsula from the state park. Kat squealed onto County F and floored the accelerator, passing one pokey pick-up truck on their way. The sun had set by the time they pulled into the park's entrance. Kat flipped the headlights off when she pulled over about a half mile from the lighthouse.

"Thanks for the lift."

Kat looked at Lisa like she just said she was going outside to await her alien brethren to beam her off planet. "Do you honestly think that I'm not going to wait here?"

Lisa bit her lip. "I did kind of think that you were going to go."

Kat rolled her eyes with her whole head. "Yeah, no. I'll be staying right here. Mostly because I'm still not very clear on what exactly your plan is here. Are you just going to sit in the dark until Carie sees you and drives you home?"

Lisa blinked.

Kat sighed. "You know she's going to see you immediately, right?"

"I hadn't actually thought of that."

"Not to mention that it's very much not warm out there. Freezing in the dark until either Carie finds your or some beast attacks doesn't seem like the best plan."

"Would it make you feel better if we drove a little closer, and I hung out in the car for a while?"

"Hey, you're an adult. I just want to make sure that you've thought this shit through. I really like your aunt's food, and I don't need her banning me for life because I didn't stop you from doing something stupid."

A warm feeling settled in Lisa's chest. "You know, she probably would do that. And I gotta say, it's nice to think that I have someone in my life like that."

Kat's expressions softened. "Didn't before?"

"Coming to realize that I didn't."

Kat leaned over the center console and rested her head on Lisa's shoulder. She looked up at Lisa through her bangs. "Well, you've got a few now."

The corner of Lisa's mouth tugged up. She dropped her head onto Kat's.

"We should go to the renaissance fair with the group next summer," Lisa said. "I've always wanted to go with a people."

"I think we can--"

They both shot up as a shrill scream pierced through the forest. Lisa flung the door open and peered out into the forest. Another shriek lanced through the night.

"Get in the car," Kat shouted.

Lisa ignored her and slammed the door shut. She pulled her phone out of her pocket and flipped the flashlight on.

Another scream. This one was human. The voice was familiar. Pained.

Unbidden, the image of her aunt's face crumbling as she was told Carie died flashed through Lisa's mind. She wasn't much of a runner, but she started sprinting north towards the lighthouse. She could hear Kat start the car over her own labored breathing. The headlights flashed on and starkly illuminated the pitch-black forest. Ahead, a sickly green light flashed against the night sky.

Deep in her stomach, Lisa could feel that same magic bubbling within her. It felt stronger this time. More tangible. They were close to a lighthouse. Lisa could hear Dottie's words in her mind. She reached out for the threads, easily making contact this time. The tips of her fingers tingled with possibility. She shoved her phone back into her pocket and pumped her legs harder.

"Lisa," Kat shouted from beside her. "Get in the fucking car! We can get there quicker."

Lisa stopped only long enough to shout, "Stay here!".

The engine shuttered and died. She heard Kat swear. A car door swung open, and Lisa could hear driving footfalls behind her. She ignored them and urged her own legs faster.

The Eagle Bluff lighthouse was built of tan brick with faded forest green shutters and a sun-bleached red roof. It rose over a modest home, and the light oscillated over the forest and the water below. As she approached, Lisa could feel the threads tangling around her fingers. She skidded to a stop before bending over and gasping for breath.

"Lisa, what the shit," Kat angrily shouted. "Running towards the shrieking horrors in the woods is not--"

Kat stopped short, her eyes pulling wide. From out of the nearby woods, a massive beast stepped into the clearing. A large buck, it stood at least seven feet tall. The antlers stretched above its head like the boughs of a dying tree. They were seeping with a black ooze. It plopped to the ground in sickening puddles. Flies buzzed around its blood-matted fur. Its eyes stared down at the girls, reflecting red. With a snort, it pawed the ground. The ooze splashed up around its hooves.

Lisa felt Kat at her arm and yanked at the threads spilling from the knot. The power flashed at her fingertips. She willed it to protect them. The air shimmered around them and solidified into a clear wall. Lisa held her hands out, pouring what strength she could into the barrier. Movement at the tree line pulled her attention. She looked over and saw a familiar dark-haired figure staggering out of the woods.

Carie lurched forward, heavily favoring her side. Her eyes were wild and furious. Her shirt had been torn and twigs stuck out wildly from her hair. Her shoulders heaved with every breath she took.

Glowing with the same sickly yellow from the highway, Carie slapped her hands together. She gritted her teeth as she pulled them apart. A golden bolt of light appeared between her palms. She took hold of it, swung it down to her side, and charged the creature with murder in her eyes.

The creature rushed before Carie could get to it, slamming against Lisa's field and bellowing with frustration when it couldn't get through. It turned just in time to see Carie throw her golden light like a javelin. It pierced the creature's side, spraying black ichor against Lisa's barrier. It sputtered and fizzled against the magic. The buck screamed in pain. It rounded on Carie, who was moving her hands frantically. Whatever she was summoning was taking too long. She looked up at the beast, panic flashing in her eyes as she abandoned her spell and managed a thin ward of protection. The creature shattered it instantly, shaking its mighty head and piercing Carie with its sharp antlers. The witch screamed through clenched teeth but took the opportunity to summon another spear. She stabbed the beast in the head. It staggered, struggling to right its footing before shaking Carie off. The witch fell at its feet.

The beast reared up on its hind legs, ready to crush Carie beneath its hooves. Lisa dropped her barrier and thrust both her hands in front of her. Bolts of blue light coursed down her arms and through her fingers. They lanced out and struck the beast in the chest. The lighthouse shook with the power of its death screech before the beast toppled backward and dissolved into a sickly puddle of ichor. Little bolts of Lisa's light flickered in the pool. The echoes of the battle faded into the night, and only the crash of the waves on the bluffs below filled the silence.

"Fuck," Kat breathed. She rushed to the puddle and immediately started muttering. Lisa glanced over as she charged to Carie's side. She could swear she saw the pool sputtering and growing, but whatever quick ritual Kat performed settled it.

"Carie?"

The witch's eyes glowed with residual magic. Blinking, she shook her head to dispel it. She groaned as Lisa pulled at her arm, flopping her onto her back.

"Carie?"

"I'm here. I'm fine. Just a... just a scratch."

Lisa cast her eyes down the witch's form. It was too dark to accurately tell if she was lying or not, but Lisa had seen the buck charge. She'd heard Carie scream. Her clothes didn't move right against her body. The fabric should slide against skin, but Carie's stuck.

"Yeah, I don't think so."

"I think this thing is exorcised," Kat shouted. "That's not really my thing, but Mildred showed me a simple rite when I first joined. Are you two okay? I've never seen anything like that before. Whatever Dottie is paying you should be doubled, Carie, because holy crap!"

She paused long enough to see Lisa frozen in panic. Kat rushed to her side.

"Carie, we're going to get you up. If you can help, great," Lisa said.

Both girls braced a hand behind Carie's back and gently shoved her to a sitting position. Carie pressed her lips together, clearly trying to keep her pain hidden. They each draped one of Carie's arms over their shoulders and after a count of three stood up. Carie couldn't keep quiet. She wailed as they stood. Lisa opened her mouth to offer comfort, but she felt herself swoon.

"Lisa, you still with us over there," Kat said from a thousand miles away.

"Yeah. Yeah, I think so."

Their brutalized group jostled as Kat dug into Carie's pockets. She found her keys and readjusted her grip.

"I just need you to get to the car, alright? That's goes for both of you. We can get in there, and I can take us to Dottie's."

"Josie...go to Josie's," Carie muttered.

Kat faltered under their weight, looking over to Lisa. She clearly wasn't prepared to make the decision.

"It's closer than Dottie's," Lisa managed between labored breaths. "She used to stay there. Auntie Jo might know what to do."

Kat shrugged as best she could and dragged them towards Carie's car, one slow step at a time.

Chapter Seven

Jo couldn't repress the shiver that ran up her spine. She had closed the window above the kitchen sink as she waited for her tea to steep. Tugging her cardigan tighter around her shoulders, she took her mug and settled into the couch. She kicked her feet up on the coffee table after shoving aside a few cookbooks with her toes. With a well-loved paperback at the ready, Jo settled in for a quiet evening.

Jo had gotten used to Lisa's presence over the last month. After being re-signed to a lonely winter, she let herself enjoy the company. She had done the paperwork to hire Lisa officially in the bakery. They argued about it a bit, but Jo had insisted. She loved having Lisa in the apartment upstairs, but she never wanted her to feel beholden to her aunt. Her niece shouldn't feel monetarily bound to anyone but herself. If Lisa ended up wanting to move or start another job, Jo supported that fully. She'd miss the company, but she'd been working on telling herself that Lisa wouldn't just drop out of her life.

Unlike her parents.

And others.

Jo huffed at herself for even letting her thoughts wander before even getting through a paragraph of her book. She'd been doing such a good job of not thinking about Carie.

Which was an enormous lie that she told herself daily.

Of course, Jo fantasized in her quieter moments about calling Carie and reconciling. Her phone sat heavily in her pocket as she rested her novel on her chest. She stared into the middle distance, wondering what she was so scared of. Nothing was stopping her from picking up the phone right now, but Jo didn't think she could handle being rejected again. It was better this way. If Carie wanted to talk, she knew where Jo lived. She had Jo's number.

After the way they left things, Jo was foolish to expect anything.

Jo had spent a week making sure the evening would be perfect. She had a special meal for two all planned out with drinks from the fancy winery just down the highway. She hadn't bothered with makeup, but she did put on the dress she wore when fell into bed together for the first and only time. When Carie had arrived from a day of hard work, Jo was sure she could hear her heart thudding against her breastbone. They ate, and Jo tried to act like everything was normal. Carie could pick up on her anxiety, so Jo asked her question. Would Carie stay with her that summer? Carie's eyes had gone wide with panic and then confusion. She schooled her face into a painfully neutral expression as Jo felt the floor drop out beneath her.

It only devolved from there. They fought, both hurling hurts with pinpoint accuracy. Carie had slammed the door at the top of the stairs and locked it for the first time in years. When Jo woke the next morning, the upstairs bed was made, the kitchenette cleaned, and Carie's car was gone from the driveway. There was no note, no text message. Carie had left, and Jo was alone.

With a sigh, Jo turned back to her novel. She shivered and looked over her shoulder. The kitchen light was off, and Jo squinted into the dark. She knew she had closed the window, but she couldn't confirm. Something shifted in the corner of her eye. It was just the shadow of the tree outside, shifting in the wind. But then it moved with purpose and precision. Jo stood from the couch to investigate closer when her living room was bathed in bright yellow light. A car turned into the driveway. Jo went to the front door and looked out the storm door. Her eyes widened at the sight of the familiar rusty sedan.

Immediately, Jo panicked. Her mind flashed through every possible thing that could have happened for that car to appear in her driveway. She was halfway across the yard before even realizing she'd moved from the porch. The back door flung open, and a familiar figure dragged herself out of the car. She leaned heavily on the door, her shoulders heaving with the effort.

Jo's fingers clenched in the cardigan around her shoulders as she moved towards the car. With great effort, the figure lifted her head. Familiar eyes resolved under a mop of dirty hair.

"Auntie Jo?"

A sob caught in Jo's throat as she lurched forward. She pulled her niece into her arms, burying her face in the rat's nest of her hair. "Are you alright? What's wrong? What happened?"

"I don't know that you'd believe us if we told you, Ms. Phines."

Jo looked towards the voice over the roof of the car.

"I don't think we've had the pleasure of meeting. I'm Kat. I'm a friend of Lisa's and Dan's."

"Are you hurt?" Jo asked.

Kat shook her head, but she nodded to the back seat of the car. "I'm not, but she is."

A jolt shot through Jo's heart. Carie was hurt. A stranger was driving Carie's car because she was hurt.

"Let me get Lisa inside. I'll come back and give you a hand."

Shuffling as fast as she could, Jo guided Lisa inside. She kept her lips pressed tightly together. Her thoughts were jumbled with thousands of questions.

They got inside, and Jo managed to maneuver Lisa to the couch. Her niece was muttering something. Her breath puffed irregularly against Jo's cheek.

"What's that, hon?"

"I'm magic," Lisa said with a tiny smirk. "I'm special."

Jo's eyes went hot immediately. She pressed a kiss to Lisa's forehead. "I don't care what happened tonight or since you arrived here. You were always magic, no matter what anyone else told you."

Jo didn't wait for a response. She pulled a blanket from the couch and tucked it around Lisa. The younger woman was sinking into the cushions and struggling to keep her eyes open.

"I need you to stay awake for just a few more minutes, hon. We need to see if you have a concussion."

Lisa shook her head. " 'M just tired. I pulled too hard. Never done anything like that before..."

"Just for a few more minutes, sweetheart. I'm going to help your friend."

Back outside, Jo could hear Kat muttering as she struggled with Carie in the backseat.

"How are you this heavy," Kat hissed.

Jo approached and stopped dead. Her eyes homed in on the familiar boot Kat was pulling on. It had made its home beside her own ratty sneakers over the last ten winters.

Without a word, Jo moved next to Kat and reached into the car. Her hands found purchase on fabric, and she pulled. Carie's unconscious form flopped forward into Jo's waiting arms.

"What happened?" Jo demanded, panic pitching her voice high.

"It was at the lighthouse," Kat said. She grabbed one of Carie's arms and helped Jo finally pull her out of the car. "We followed her to Eagle Bluff and there was this huge deer...beast...thing. It had been possessed by...something... something that I've never seen before. Dottie's been saying that the possessions are getting stronger. Carie was really banged up when we got there, but then Lisa...she was amazing."

Jo was hardly listening. She'd wrapped her arm around Carie's middle and could feel the congealed mess of blood and ichor on her clothes.

"When we get inside, I'll take Carie back to the bedroom. Go in the bathroom, under the sink, and get the black medical bag. Not the red first aid kit. Though if you bring that out too, we can make sure that there's nothing Lisa needs patched up either."

They crested the porch, and Kat scrambled to open the storm door. It slammed shut behind them, startling Lisa awake from her stupor on the couch. She tried to push herself up to help, but Jo fixed her with a venomous look. She fell back into the cushions, her eyes fluttering again.

Jo nearly faltered under Carie's weight as Kat broke off for the bathroom. She steadied herself and slowly lurched the rest of the way to her bedroom. Toeing the door open, she all but collapsed onto her bed with Carie partially on top of her. She forced the memories from her head.

"Josie? We need...I need to get to Josie..."

Jo let herself wallow for just a moment and tucked her face into Carie's neck. It wasn't fair that her former...whatever should come to her quiet little sanctuary in the heart of Wisconsin. She had built a life for herself up here. She wasn't happy, necessarily, but she was satisfied. And so much more so than when she had been with her family. She was self-sufficient here. She had a business. She baked for a living. She did what she loved. How many people could honestly say they had that same thing? But now, pressed into the mattress by the woman that she tried to give her heart too, Jo didn't want any of it. She wanted to run into the fields behind her house and scream until her throat went raw.

Before they fought, Jo and Carie had fallen into bed just like this. Carie's cheeks with flushed with lust and too much red wine, but she smiled down at Jo with unguarded love. It felt like a promise. It felt like a vow. It felt like permission. They kissed each other silly, tossing each other's clothes about the room until they could get their mouths on bare skin. Jo's skin sang as Carie breathed her name into the private nooks of her body.

Josie...Josie...Josie...

It was someone that Jo could only be with Carie. She had pulled her hair out of its messy tie, letting it fan across the pillows like a halo. Carie ran her fingers through the strands, whispering Jo's name over and over. They pressed themselves together, finding their mutual pleasure with shared breath and sweet sweat. Jo hadn't washed the quilt for weeks after. Once Carie had gone, seemingly for good, she wanted to have a fleeting reminder of the one night that she had everything.

But reality crashed back down. The quilt had since been washed, but now Carie's blood was rapidly seeping into it. Her breathing was shallow and too quick. Jo had seen her cast healing spells before, but only when she was lucid.

Gently as she could, Jo pushed Carie onto her back and stood from the bed to turn the light on. Visibility did nothing to alleviate her worry. Carie was pale, dirty, and bruised. Her fingers twitched. Her eyes fluttered behind her closed lids. Her clothes were a total loss, torn and splattered with gore, both Carie's and whatever beast she had fought. The mess mingled together in a fast-spreading puddle on the bed.

"Is this what you were looking for?"

Jo came back to the world as a black bag was held out to her. She took it with a nod, and immediately set it on her dresser.

"You know how to check for a concussion?" she asked Kat.

"No, but I can look it up on my phone."

Not ideal, but it would have to do.

"Look it up and make sure that Lisa doesn't have one."

"I don't think she does," Kat said. "I was with her the whole time, and she didn't hit her head."

"Just humor me, please," Jo said, a hint of desperation clouding her words. "If she's fine, get her some water and let her sleep. You're one of Dottie's witches?"

"I like to think that I'm my own--ahem--yes, yeah, I can cast a bit."

"Know any healing spells?"

"Not really, but..."

Jo stared at her, pulling out antiseptic and gauze from the bag.

"But Lisa might be able to?"

Jo paused and took a deep breath. "Then please go see to her. We might need her help."

Kat left the room, and Jo could hear her murmuring to Lisa as the door swung shut. She turned back to the bed. Carie's eyes were fighting to stay open, but her gaze was far away. Jo took a deep breath to steady herself and got to work. With the scissors from the bag, she cut away the tattered shirt, revealing a quilt of purple bruises on Carie's right side. A puncture wound still oozed blood at the center of the bruising. She grabbed a trauma pad and ripped it out of its packaging.

"This is going to hurt, but I can't have you bleeding to death before we get a chance to talk to each other again."

She didn't wait for a response. She pressed the pad down hard, doing all she could to ignore the pained, choked off scream from Carie. Working as quickly as she could, she poured the antiseptic over the wound and wiped away the mess. She called for Kat, asking the girl to fetch her some warm water and towels from the linen closet. While she waited, she opened another pad and pressed it over the first one.

Kat arrived with her requests, her face pale with worry. "Lisa seems to be okay? She's just exhausted."

"Weaving threads...," Carie muttered under her breath.

Kat shrugged at Jo. "What she said."

Jo didn't want to ask a clearly exhausted and inexperienced weaver for help, but Carie was getting paler by the minute.

"If she's up for it, can you have her come in here? I can only do so much, but if she has a punctured lung or some other trauma, we need a little magic."

"She's been asking after Carie since I sat down with her. I'll get her up."

Jo waited until she was gone again before wetting a towel and squeezing out the excess water. She gently wiped the grime from Carie's torso, cleaning as best as she could while keeping pressure on her wound.

"It's going to take a lot to get me to forgive you for this. I do hope you survive this. I'll feel like an asshole if I'm mad at a dead person."

"...Josie..."

"I'm here. You're home."

Lisa limped into the room with Kat hovering two steps behind her. "Auntie Jo?"

"I need you to answer me truthfully. Can you help without hurting yourself? I won't be able to handle losing you both in the space of one night."

Lisa looked down at the mess of her aunt's bed and lied. "Yeah, I can try."

Kat looked skeptical. "You've already got magic baking powers and defensive magic. It would be insane if you can heal too."

"Let me try. If I can't do it, call Ms. Cambridge. Someone from their circle must be able to heal."

"Little things, like a scraped knee or a paper cut."

"Well, then let me try."

Jo held out a hand to Lisa, steadying her as she moved to sit on the edge of the bed. Her body tingled under the touch, and Lisa gasped in surprise. She looked at her aunt.

"I can do this."

Lisa didn't break contact with her aunt. She moved her hand over Carie's hurts and closed her eyes. Jo watched her face for any sign of strain but found none. If anything, her niece seemed to glow. Translucent tendrils of light pulled from the air and swirled between Lisa's fingers. Jo looked from her to Carie's prone form. She held her breath as the bruising faded from deep purple to pale, barely there green. The swelling around the wound receded. Jo itched to remove the dressing, but she kept her hand entangled with Lisa's.

Lisa broke off with a gasp before the bruising was gone, but Carie's breathing settled. Jo felt her worry abate. It felt like swooning.

"I think her lung was punctured," Lisa said dreamily.

Kat stared at the scene with a slack jaw. She held her phone out in front of her, ready to dial for help.

"Josie?"

Jo's attention pulled back to the idiot witch lying in her bed. "Here. But you need to sleep, now."

Carie's eyes glazed over again and her lids slipped shut.

"You're still a bit hurt. Sleep so you can fix yourself up when you wake."

Sweaty warm fingers found her own and squeezed. Jo shifted, so she could thread their hands together. She forced down the hurt and the anger and looked into Carie's face.

"I'm right here. Go to sleep."

The grip relaxed, and the tension in Carie's body melted into the sheets. She slept.

Jo took a deep breath and leveled a look at her niece and her friend.

"You two go back out to the kitchen. I'm going to try and clean her up best as I can. Kat, get a kettle going. We'll have some tea, and you can explain to me in excruciating detail what happened."

"Jo--" Lisa started.

"I'm fine. I just need a few minutes."

The girls left, and Jo grabbed the least gore-covered pillow. She pressed it against her face and screamed until she ran out of air. If anyone else heard, they were either asleep or too polite to comment. Jo threw the pillow as hard as she could at the wall. It knocked a painting askew, then plopped down to the floor. The painting followed a second later. Jo stared at it, contemplating whether ripping it to shreds would make her feel better.

She drew in a deep breath and held it for as long as she could. She relished the burn in her lungs. She let it go and set about wiping Carie's face clean. Jo was thankful she was unconscious. Because as soon as Carie was able to look at Jo with lucidity, Jo would run right back to her and beg to be taken back as whatever Carie wanted her to be. Lover? Friend? Landlord? It didn't matter.

She'd missed her so much.

⁓ ◆ ⁓

"I'm genuinely not sure if she's going to yell at us or not," Kat said, staring at the bedroom door.

"She's not much of a yeller," Lisa said.

Silently, both women decided to ignore the muffled screaming.

Lisa flexed her hands again. She hadn't been able to stop since she touched her aunt. Before, she had been exhausted, but now she felt like she had just had eight hours of perfect, uninterrupted sleep. She could still feel the charge of magic in the tips of her fingers. That feeling was all the confirmation that Lisa needed. Her aunt clearly had some spark of magic. Mildred had mentioned witches joining together to cast stronger spells. That would explain why she felt so refreshed. She hoped her aunt felt the same.

It warmed Lisa's heart that she had this deeper connection to her aunt, but it raised questions about their family. Did they know? Had that been part of the reason that Jo had been kicked out of the house, or were they just so repressed that they ignored and dismissed anything out of the ordinary? Had Jo repressed her magic because unconsciously she knew she'd be rejected for it?

Lisa decided then and there that it didn't matter. She felt like she was becoming the person she was meant to be. Her parents could either accept that or not.

"Tonight would probably be a solid night to start," Kat said. She peered at Lisa while Lisa studied her hands. "I know you haven't been around witches much, but you've got to know that being able to weave three very different threads is super rare. Dottie's going to lose her mind when she finds out."

"Jo mentioned that Carie used to heal herself. She can do multiple things."

"Yeah, and she's the powerful freelancer they hire. I don't think any one of the ladies can do anything like that. Dottie, maybe, but..."

"Maybe I can ask Carie about it when she wakes up."

"She's not the most chatty, but I'll bet your aunt can get her to talk."

"If a near death experience doesn't get them talking, then nothing will."

"Do you know what happened?"

Lisa shrugged. "Only a bit. My aunt...well, our family kind of sucks. Not her, obviously. How many people are just going to ask their estranged niece to stay with them while they figure shit out? But my grandmother and my mom...they make love seem like a competition. Or like something you have to be constantly earning. And if you aren't what they want you to be, then you aren't worthy of their love. My dad isn't as bad, but he just kinda goes along with whatever my mom says. I think my aunt still looks at love that way. She has such a big heart, but she's so scared that if she does something wrong, she'll lose everyone she cares about.

"She told me a little bit about what happened, but not the whole story. She asked for something, and I don't think Carie was ready to give it. There was some miscommunication, and I think they fought. Carie left for the season, and they hadn't spoken since."

Kat immediately looked guilty. "Maybe we should have just brought her to Dottie's."

"I don't know. Something about being here...it helped. Jo says she isn't magic, but I could definitely feel it in her. I don't know if I would have been able to do that without her."

"This shit is bonkers."

"Tell me about it."

The kettle whistled, and Lisa jumped up to pour hot water into the mugs she had set out. Her aunt's bedroom door opened, silhouetting her for a moment before she slipped the light off.

"She okay?" Lisa asked over her shoulder.

"We'll see when she wakes up, but it looks like you fixed the worst of it."

Jo pulled a chair out from the table and collapsed into it. Her shirt was dark with blood. "It's very late, and this has been an emotionally exhausting evening. I don't have the energy to ask all the questions I very much want to ask. So we're going to drink our tea, and then you two will go upstairs and sleep. Is there someone that you need to call, Kat?"

"I've already texted my parents. They know I won't be home."

Jo nodded. "Good. Then we'll talk in the morning."

"Do you want the bed upstairs, Auntie Jo?"

"I'll be fine on the couch after a shower."

"There is one thing we should discuss..." Lisa said. "The pastries we made..."

"I don't think I have the energy to discuss Mildred's issues with the flake on the palmiers."

"It's not that. The witches could taste my magic in the pastry. And it wasn't just mine there."

Jo stared at her niece, trying to parse the information she had just been given.

"Auntie Jo?"

"I don't think I can process that just now, hon."

"I just...I didn't want to wait to tell you."

With a tired smile, Jo said thank you.

Silence fell over them as they waited for their tea. Jo stared into the middle distance, while Kat and Lisa made pointless small talk.

Once the tea was steeped, drank, and the mugs placed in the sink, they adjourned to their separate rooms. Lisa paused at the top of the stairs, watching her aunt turn out the lights and move to the bathroom.

Kat had already snuggled into a ball on the left side of the bed. Her eyes were closed, and she was snoring softly. Lisa peeled herself out of her dirty clothes and managed a quick shower. She sat on the couch and stared out the window, waiting for the sun to come up.

⁓ℓℓ⁓

Magic. She had magic. Her food tasted of magic.

The water was hot enough to be painful as it rained down in the shower. Jo stood under the spray for several minutes, staring at the mold starting to form in the grout. She tapped it with her finger, willing it to vanish. Nothing happened.

No shower cleaning magic then.

It had been quite a night already. Jo hadn't been prepared for another life-altering revelation. She was exhausted, so she couldn't stop her mind from spiraling. How could the family not know? Lisa and Jo both had a spark of magic. That couldn't be coincidental.

Jo combed her fingers through her hair, noting it was much too long. She wound some strands around her fingers and willed it shorter. She raked through again, but it felt just as long as before.

Just food magic then.

Had Carie known before she left? She was so attuned to the magic of the peninsula it seemed impossible that she would have missed magic right under her nose. Was Jo so inconsequential that she hadn't noticed?

"You need to stop," Jo told herself.

She didn't have all the information. Lisa might have more for her in the morning. She needed to calm down.

Jo had never felt magical. She held out her hands, flexing them under the water. They were raw and pink from the scrubbing. She managed to get most of the blood off, but her fingers still felt tacky. Somethings would never wash off properly.

She lingered under the shower until the water turned unbearably cold. With her body on autopilot, Jo towel dried her hair then wrapped the damp towel around her body. She pushed out of the bathroom and into her own room, pausing when she heard the soft, whistling breath from her bed. Jo fumbled around in the dark, pulling any clothes from her dresser to wear for the night. She paused at the door, looking back at Carie's sleeping form.

Carie had never kept her own magic secret. When Jo found her on the side of the road all those years ago, Carie had a small creature tailing after her. It had made eye contact with Jo when she stumbled out of her car, inclined its head ever so slightly, and vanished into thin air, confident that Carie was in good hands. Jo had been catering for Dottie and her witches, so she knew about the odd happenings over the winter. Dottie had even mentioned the freelance witch they hired to help. Jo never anticipated meeting her, much less helping her to safety. Soon as she was lucid, Carie healed herself and then apologized for the intrusion.

Magic was part of everyday life to Carie. Jo had to believe that if Carie knew, she would have told Jo about any spark she saw in her.

Jo left the room. As she settled on the couch, she found one calming notion in the back of her mind. The magic was something that she shared with her niece. In the years in exile, Jo had wondered if she would ever reconnect with her family. Having Lisa with her and discovering this secret truth about themselves, it felt like a thread worth clinging to.

Jo pressed a hand to her chest as it warmed under that idea. Whatever great family tapestry she had been cut out from, she still had that one connection. She would keep it close to her heart and protect it with all that she was.

Jo fell asleep that night able to ignore the lingering shadows that haunted her thoughts, but the shadows still watched, hungry and intrigued.

Chapter Eight

When the morning light hit Lisa's eyes, Kat was still wound tightly into a ball on the bed. Lisa didn't want to wake her. She stretched and made her way back downstairs, softly closing the door behind her. Her aunt was gone, and the blanket she'd been using was draped over the back of the couch. Lisa started making coffee and was startled when Carie stumbled into the kitchen. She held a bundle of sheets, dyed with gruesome whirls of dried brown blood and indigo ichor.

They stared at each other for a moment.

"Coffee?"

Carie shrugged. "Couldn't hurt."

Lisa eyed Carie as she opened the closet near the bathroom. As if she knew exactly where everything was, Carie pulled out the detergent and stain remover. She turned the washing machine on and moved back into the kitchen. She plopped into a chair.

"How are you feeling?"

"Like shit," Carie said bluntly. "I've been through a lot of fights, and that's gotta be one of the worst in recent memory. If you didn't show up when you did--which you shouldn't have done--that could have been bad."

"What the hell was that thing?"

"Something very similar to the bear you ran into. Just older, and a bit stronger."

"A bit?"

"Well, maybe more than a bit," Carie said. "I don't usually see creatures like that until my wards around the lighthouses have had a chance to wear down. And the colder it gets, the worse it'll get."

"That's not encouraging."

"It is what it is. I'm paid to handle it, so I'll handle it."

"Again. Not encouraging. Maybe you could use some help?"

Carie met her eyes.

"I'm not going to act like what you did last night wasn't impressive," Carie said. "It definitely was. I've never seen anyone that can weave all those different threads. That's not even mentioning that you've only just realized you can weave. I've managed to pluck one or two different ones, but feeling the love you put into your food and then seeing you knock a possession out like that isn't something you run into every day. You wove a defensive ward, an offensive spell, and then cast a healing spell. It's...it's extraordinary."

"The way you and Kat talk about this, I'm starting to worry I'll end up some curious witch's lab experiment."

Carie stood from her chair so quickly she knocked it to the floor. "I wouldn't let that happen."

Lisa raised a challenging eyebrow, noting that witch labs were apparently a thing. "Because I'm Josie's niece?"

Sinking slowly back into her chair, Carie let a sad grin tug at her lips. "Obviously."

"You going to talk to her?"

"After bleeding all over her house, I don't think I can avoid it."

"She's over in the bakery, I think. Been up early making pies for the Thanksgiving rush this week."

"So cold up here, and it's not even the end of November yet," Carie muttered mostly to herself. She looked up at Lisa. "You clearly have potential. Like I said before, not many can do what you do. If you're interested in honing that talent and if Josie is okay with it, maybe I can help you. We can keep it quiet too. Dottie will be able to tell, but she'll make sure it doesn't leave her little coven."

"Well, I am an adult, so I can make that decision without my aunt's approval."

"I won't do anything that would cause her undue distress. Jos...Jo needs people around her. I know how lonely she can get, and if something were to happen to you after you two just reconnected? I don't think I'd be able to forgive myself."

Lisa pictured her aunt sitting alone at the kitchen table, picking at breakfast on a bleak winter's morning.

"That's a fair point," Lisa conceded. "But even if she doesn't want me going out to hunt those things, you should still teach me more about weaving. It probably isn't safe for me not to have a handle on it. I don't want to accidentally hurt anyone."

She poured coffee and unwrapped some bear claws she had made the previous morning. She set them on the table and ate to distract herself from asking questions she really shouldn't. Carie had referenced a wider world of witches, and Lisa wanted to hear everything. It was superfluous in the moment.

The silence went on just long enough to become uncomfortable, so Lisa asked one anyway. "Where do you go over the summers?"

Blinking, Carie tilted her head. "What?"

"Just curious," Lisa shrugged. "Must be pretty important."

It was a pointed question. Perhaps a bit too cruel. She felt a stab of guilt when she saw Carie flinch.

"My line of work is dangerous," Carie said after a moment of consideration. "I go many places over the summer. Sometimes, I go see my brother, Chase, but he isn't always keen to see me."

"Family can be hard," Lisa said.

"Yeah, but Chase not wanting me around is my own fault."

"Oh, I didn't mean..."

"It's okay," Carie said. "He's got a wife and kids. He doesn't want anything to happen to them, and I tend to attract trouble. Magic calls out to other magic. Weavers can usually sense that spark in each other. Chase is the only one in my family who can't weave. I think he likes that. My parents leave him alone, and he doesn't have to worry about ending up like Ethan."

"Ethan another brother?"

"He was," Carie said, looking anywhere but Lisa's face.

Lisa wanted to push, but she had a feeling Carie had shared more than she was comfortable with. "So you don't see Chase often?"

Carie shook her head. "Mostly I'm following jobs. In my spare time, I look for better wards to protect the knots up here."

"You couldn't do that research here?"

Carie huffed a quiet laugh. "You know, it is weird that the very secretive magic cabal hasn't digitized their dark and powerful spells for the internet age."

Lisa had to concede the point.

"But there are places...archives with stockpiles of useful information. They're all over the world. They act like knots, and they attract all kinds of entities to them. I've done summer work at a few of them in exchange for time researching in their stacks."

"So, you don't really have a home base?"

Carie waved a hand. "Honestly, it never seemed important. My work is never in just one spot. I travel all over."

"But you stay here for months at a time."

"Part of that is work."

Lisa looked out the window towards the bakery. Neither of them bothered saying what the other part was.

"Everyone needs a place to rest for the winter," Lisa said. "And honestly, with the work you do to protect this place, you deserve one more than anybody."

She pushed away from the table and moved so she was standing at Carie's side. She tugged on Carie's arm, pulling her out of the chair.

"Go talk to her," Lisa demanded. "I think she deserves that."

Carie downed the rest of her coffee and allowed Lisa to guide her towards the door. She walked down the porch steps and was halfway across the yard when she stopped dead. Lisa had been about to close the front door but paused when Carie went stone still. Lisa looked towards the bakery, and saw her aunt frozen by the garbage cans. She let the storm door close but couldn't repress the urge to rubberneck. She kept the front door open and tried to remain hidden.

~ele~

Jo had always needed an outlet for her more explosive emotions. Kneading dough soothed her nerves. It required just enough attention that the mind couldn't wander and enough physical force to work out some stress. It was the same with pie dough. Jo kept focused on the feel of the butter. It needed to be cold as possible for a proper flake to the pastry. The fillings didn't require as much babysitting, but Jo always made little tweaks to the recipes as she went. More ginger with the apple or more maple with the pumpkin. She had a large bubbling pot of cranberry sauce reducing on the stove. It was a new thing she was trying this year, so it pulled much of her focus from the large, unresolved mess back in the house.

She finished crimping the crusts for their blind bake and loaded them on the baking racks for a trip to the walk-in cooler before they hit the oven. She labeled her fillings in large plastic containers and moved them into the cooler as well. After checking the heat on the cranberry mixture, Jo took off her apron and slipped it on the hook by the door. Sighing, she pushed into the cool November air. She stretched, and her back popped loudly.

"Age," she sighed, running her fingers through her hair, then tucking them under her arms. She breathed deep, trying to alleviate the tension in her shoulders.

Seeing Carie again and learning she had magic was doing nothing for her aches and pains. Though, weirdly, last night was the first restful sleep she had in ages. No odd dreams of vaguely familiar bays. No shadows set deep in the corners of her vision. She woke easily from the couch with only a crick in her neck to show for it. She genuinely forgot what a good night of sleep did for the next day.

Jo woke, didn't bother changing, and dashed to the bakery without disturbing anyone. She kept her head down and took great pride in ticking items off her to do list. It was going to be a productive day.

At least, it would have been until she spotted Carie stalking across the driveway.

Soon as they made eye contact, Carie stopped dead in her tracks. Jo felt her face flame red. Before she realized what she was doing, she was striding forward. She grew angrier with each step. Carie's eyes grew wider and wider, but she didn't move. She was rooted to the ground. Jo stopped inches in front of Carie, glaring up into her face with her hands fisted on her hips.

"What the hell were you thinking?" Jo demanded.

Carie's mouth flapped open, but no sound came out.

"What are we going to do if something happens to you, huh?"

Carie just stared.

"Why would you go charging into a situation like that?" Jo yelled. "You must have known it would be dangerous even for you. And then you get Lisa involved?"

"She followed me," Carie finally managed to say. "I didn't ask her along."

"You didn't notice her following you?" Jo challenged her. "I'm supposed to believe that?"

"Josie, I wouldn't--"

"Don't call me that," Jo snapped. She felt her eyes sting, but she managed to reign in the tears. "What would I do if something happened to her? How would I explain that to my sister? She already hates me."

Carie just stared.

"You've already left me all alone. Isn't that enough? You put her in danger and then almost get yourself killed?"

Carie winced as the force of the words hit her full on. She hunched, trying to make herself small as possible. She looked back at Jo, and her hands raised involuntarily when she saw the tears in Jo's eyes. Furious as she was, Jo craved her touch. She'd missed that familiar warmth on her skin.

"You can't do that to me," Jo said quietly. She sniffled and immediately hid her face behind her hands. "It's bad enough--"

A sob ripped through her words, and once the tears started, Jo couldn't stop them. She pressed her hands hard into her eyes, willing the ground to swallow her whole. She could tell she was making Carie uncomfortable and that just made her cry harder. How in six months had they grown so far apart?

"I'm sorry," Jo managed to say. She turned away and rubbed at her eyes. "I don't...I don't mean to make you uncomfortable. I'm just...I'm sorry."

The wounded noise from Carie's mouth almost made Jo turn back, but she didn't. If she did, she might do something stupid, like throw herself at Carie's chest and soak her shirt with her tears. With a deep breath, she tried to pull herself back together. She tried to take a step further away, but the familiar weight of a hand on her shoulder stopped her.

"Josie..."

Jo squeezed her eyes shut. She loved the sound of her name from Carie's mouth. It was teasing and warm and everything that she wanted but couldn't have. She went where Carie moved her, pliant and willing, and found herself cocooned in a warm embrace. She felt lips against her hair, not a kiss, but close enough for Jo to pretend. She didn't care how desperate she looked. She tucked herself in tighter and let herself cry.

"I'm sorry," Carie whispered. "I didn't mean to worry you."

"I thought you were dead. I thought Lisa was dead."

"I never meant for Lisa to get involved, I swear. She was amazing out there, Josie, but I would never put her in harm's way. Especially not knowing how much it would hurt you."

Jo managed a nod.

"I'll be more careful," Carie promised.

"No, you won't."

"If you ask me to, I will," Carie said. She pulled away a bit and tilted Jo's chin up so they could look at each other.

Jo immediately missed the gentle touch of Carie's fingers, but she stared into Carie's black eyes. Her voice was rough when she demanded, "Please be more careful."

"I will. I'll turn my phone back on, and if I get into a spot, I can always call Dottie to send back up."

Jo furrowed her brow. "Why isn't your phone on?"

Her cheeks reddened, and Carie averted her gaze for a moment.

"I...um...I didn't want to...it hurt to not see missed calls or texts from you. I thought...I knew you were mad, and I didn't want...It was easier to just turn it off. Remove the temptation to call, and then I didn't have to see that you hadn't reached out."

Jo fixed her with a flat look. "That's very stupid."

Carie answered quietly, "Yes, I know."

Before she could stop herself, Jo found herself blurting, "I've really missed you."

She was rewarded with a small, sad smile from Carie.

"I've missed you too," Carie said. She pulled Jo back in tight. "I'm sorry for keeping my distance."

"Seems fate thought we were both being stupid."

"Rude of it to use your niece to pull us back into orbit."

Jo hummed into Carie's shoulder. She closed her eyes and breathed in her familiar scent, a homey combination of warm sage and rich soil. She'd missed it dearly.

"Can we be friends again?" Jo asked. "It doesn't...we don't...I just...I want to go back."

Carie pulled back again. Her expression was calm.

Jo pushed the rising tide of memory aside. She wanted twisted sheets and Carie's breath hot against her neck, but more than that, she just wanted Carie in her life. She would take whatever she was given.

"We were never not friends, Josie," she said.

Jo melted further into Carie's arms. She tried to memorize the feel of the embrace.

"Maybe she could stay with us for a bit?"

Jo and Carie pulled away from each other to look at Lisa who was perched on the porch steps.

"Dottie said something about you staying in your car," Lisa said.

Jo whipped her head back to Carie. "You said you wouldn't do that anymore! It's freezing up here in the winter, and your car barely runs. Dottie has a huge house, and I know she would have offered you a room. You could have stayed with her!"

Carie opened her mouth, but Jo immediately held a hand up.

"I won't hear any arguments," Jo declared. "You'll stay here. Lisa is staying in the apartment, but you can either take my bed or the pullout sofa."

"I don't want to put you out."

"My insomnia's flared up a bit again anyway. Truth be told, I slept better on the sofa last night than I have in my bed for weeks."

She ignored Carie's concerned look and glared at her niece. "That storm door is hardly soundproof."

Lisa blushed and shrugged. "Honestly, Auntie Jo, I just wanted to make sure you two weren't going to start screaming at each other. Didn't want to have to call the cops. Though I haven't seen a single cop car since I've been up here, so I'm not sure they exist."

"I have enough parking tickets to prove that they do," Carie said.

"Enough about your shitty car. I have some pies to fill and get in the oven."

After a split second of hesitation Carie asked, "Can I help?"

Jo should have said no, but she couldn't help herself. It was so easy to slip back into old routines. She shoved aside memories of holding up a heaping spoon of her latest concoction to Carie's lips, waiting for her to taste. She wanted Carie close, even if it made Jo weak in the knees.

"Of course. The extra hands would be very much appreciated."

Jo looked back to Lisa. "See if your friend is awake. I'll brew some fresh coffee, and we can have some breakfast in the bakery while we wait for the pies to bake."

"And talk about that other thing," Lisa said.

Jo took a deep breath and avoided Carie's inquiring gaze. "Yes and talk about that."

Carie's eyes burned the side of Jo's head, so Jo turned with a heavy sigh. "Turns out I have a bit of magic too."

"I know."

Jo felt her insides freeze. She had known, and she still left without mentioning it.

Carie continued, aware of Jo's distress. "I mean, I could taste it in the pastries yesterday. I never had before. I would have said something. Josie, of course I would have said something."

With a heavy breath, Jo thawed herself out. "I know...I just...I know."

Carie clearly wanted to follow that line of conversation, but Lisa had walked over. She gave Jo a look promising they would talk about it later.

"We need to give Kat a ride back to her car," Lisa said. "We left it in the state park."

Carie winced. "I'll bet it's been towed. If you're lucky, they just gave you a ticket."

"We definitely left it in the center of the road."

"I'll give the ranger's office a call before we have breakfast. We can probably get them to tow it here once I explain what happened."

"Much appreciated!"

Jo looked up at the opened window on the second floor. The sash was thrown open, and Kat was hanging out of it. She'd clearly been enjoying the show as well. Carie's cheeks reddened.

"You can work off the cost of the tow truck by helping with some pies," Jo shouted up. She looked over to Carie and smiled.

"C'mon. It's warmer inside."

Carie nodded. Soon as the storm door closed behind Lisa, she reached out and caught Jo's hand.

"You don't have to put me up if you don't want to."

"I want to," Jo assured her. "And we've got the holiday coming up on Thursday. If I'm worrying about you freezing to death in your car, I won't be able to enjoy my turkey."

Carie chuckled. "Wouldn't be fair to you or the turkey."

"And I know you would have said something," Jo said. "If you knew about this nonsense. It's been a stressful day--"

"You don't have to justify anything," Carie said. She bit her lip and squeezed Jo's hand. "We'll work on it together."

Chapter Nine

They spent that Sunday morning and most of the afternoon baking pies. Jo's heart felt as full as her bakery. Kat claimed not to be much of a baker, so she offered to work the cash register while Lisa and Jo made the pies. Carie kept the coffee carafes full while helping Kat with orders. She stole into the bathroom once to press healing wards into her wounds. Folks came in for their usual Sunday orders or grabbed a frozen pie for Thanksgiving. Dottie had even stopped in for a word with Carie, which turned into a very one-sided dressing down on the porch. Carie was much taller than Dottie, but the older woman drew up to her full height and waved her finger in the air between them. Carie only nodded a few times, but Jo could see her eyes getting misty when Dottie rocked up on her toes and kissed Carie on the forehead. With the care of a grandmother, Dottie frisked Carie's arms and led her back inside.

"Josephine, please promise that you'll keep an eye on this one," Dottie called when they re-entered the bakery.

"I'll do my best, Ms. Cambridge."

"And I don't mean to be too forward, but if you'd like some guidance with your magic, please do not hesitate to reach out. The Witches of Door look after our own."

"Thank you," said Jo. "I'll keep that in mind."

Before leaving, Dottie had then ordered an apple and cranberry pie that she would pick up before the holiday. She cast a warm wink at Lisa as she walked out the door.

After the morning rush, Carie and Kat tried to clean the back of Carie's car. Neither had the magic to just will the mess away, so they made do with elbow grease. Jo and Lisa ignored the smell of burning polyester as they finished up on the orders for the day.

"So..."

Jo looked up from the dishes she was washing.

"You really didn't know that you had magic?"

Rinsing out the last bowl, Jo set it on the drying rack before turning to her niece with her full attention.

Lisa fiddled with a biscuit cutter as she spoke. "Yesterday. The witches and Carie mentioned it. She tried the pastries we made together. Said they could taste my magic, but mine wasn't the only one there. And I felt something too when I was healing Carie. From you, I mean."

"Dottie mentioned something when she stopped in," Jo said. She let herself chuckle a bit. "Maybe that's why everyone likes my pastries."

"I don't think magic can account for how good your baking is," Lisa said. "But maybe that gives it an extra little kick?"

"Maybe."

"Must run in our family."

"Could you imagine mother," Jo cackled.

Lisa laughed. "Or my mom? At the first sign of anything weird, she'd flip the fuck out and start blaming my dad."

"The Phines have a long, proud history of ignoring things that don't line up with their narrow world view," Jo said. "Mother and Celeste could be brimming full of magic, and they'd just brush it off."

It wouldn't do to think of the alternative. Jo could see her mother and sister gathered around an ancient family heirloom, whispering spells to chase away their gray hairs and wrinkling skin. It was possible they knew about the magic, but just horded it for themselves. Jo had been easy enough to cast off. Why share any magical knowledge they may or may not have?

"Fuck 'em."

Jo's head popped up so fast she could feel her neck creak.

"Seriously," Lisa said. "Fuck them. If they want to ignore it or keep it secret or whatever, let them. We've got people up here that can teach us. Carie, Dottie's witches, and even Kat can show us a few things. The rest we can figure out together."

Jo covered her mouth with her hand. She felt all she was doing was crying these days, but she couldn't help it. Hearing Lisa include her. Hearing 'we' and knowing that she was part of it made her weep.

Lisa noticed the tears immediately and panicked. "I'm sorry!"

Shaking her head, Jo stepped up to her niece and took her hands in hers.

"You have nothing to be sorry for," Jo said as earnestly as she was able. "I'm just a bit overwhelmed. After...I just thought that I was going to be alone up here. It felt like they were right about me."

"Who?"

"Our family. And if I had just listened to them, settled down and found a husband and a job they approved of, I wouldn't have to be alone. I was choosing that loneliness."

"Auntie Jo..."

"I know," Jo said. She squeezed Lisa's fingers tight. "It's just nice to have my choices validated."

"I'm so happy that you asked me to come up here."

"And I'm so very happy that you took me up on it."

They finished cleaning the bakery once Carie had given up on getting the stains out of her back seat. She said she would ask one of the witches to weave it away for her. She had also called the ranger's office at the state park and arranged to have Kat's car towed to the bakery.

Jo didn't mind the extra company for dinner. She had recipes she wanted to try for a crowd, but never wanted to risk making that much food in case she ended up not liking it. She roped Lisa in to help pick, and they landed on bacon and sauerkraut pierogis, breaded pork cutlets with homemade gravy, and potato pancakes. Kat and Lisa made a quick trip to the store, while Jo insisted on Carie having a lie down while they waited. She supervised the witch weaving away her hurts again until the bruising was a faded yellow fog against her skin.

When the girls got back, everyone pitched in with dinner. Carie peeled the potatoes while Jo pounded the cutlets. Lisa and Kat worked on the pierogi dough before moving on to the fillings. The cutlets were coated in breadcrumbs and fried in the reserved bacon fat Jo had in the fridge. They boiled the pierogis, then finished them in butter before patting down the potato pancakes for a pan fry. They stacked the dishes to deal with later and feasted on their meal.

There was magic in every bite of the food. Jo could taste her niece's enthusiasm and Kat's excitement at learning something new. She could taste Carie's quiet care in the potatoes. She picked up another nuance, which she assumed was her own love for cooking and the people around her. She watched them linger on each bite with a small proud smile. Carie would close her eyes after each bite she took. Jo wondered what her love tasted like to Carie. Was she even picking it up? Jo made sure to quickly look away each time Carie opened her eyes. She didn't want to be caught staring, but she hoped Carie could taste it, even if was only a trace.

Kat's car finally arrived while they were finishing the dishes. She hugged Lisa tightly, telling her she'd see her at the next session of their campaign, and then kissed both Carie and Jo on the cheek. She thanked them all for dinner, saying that next time they got together they should avoid anyone almost dying. Lisa locked the door behind her, then scampered upstairs to get changed. Carie had brought her duffel bag in from the car. Jo shook her head at the meager luggage. She was already in leggings and an over-sized sweater, so she plopped down on the couch with a heavy sigh.

"I can honestly say that's been the most stressful twenty-four hours I've experienced in years."

Carie looked at the couch as if she was waiting for an invitation to sit, but after a moment she sat on the opposite end.

"It's definitely in the team photo," Carie said. She wrung her hands in her lap before speaking again. "Thank you for offering me a place to stay."

"This is the only way I can keep an eye on you. Someone needs to make sure you won't go running into the woods to get murdered."

"Well, I'm glad either way."

Lisa came pounding down the stairs. "Is it okay if I leave my stuff upstairs? I haven't used all the drawers, and I've pushed most of my crap to one side of the counter in the bathroom."

"Of course," Carie said. "I don't have much."

Jo scoffed. "We'll make a trip to the store at some point. You're down an outfit, and if you start washing everything you own every other day, it'll be threadbare before you know it."

"I don't--"

"If you don't come with me, I'll just end up buying you a bunch of frilly, brightly colored shirts that you'll hate, but you'll still wear because you feel bad that I spent the money on you."

Carie's cheeks went pink as Jo shot her a smug look.

"I won't keep you from the horrors in the woods for more than a few hours."

It was like slipping right back into a familiar routine. Jo could see her niece grinning wildly out of the corner of her eye. It was a welcome reprieve from the shadows that usually lurked there.

"Do you mind if I throw something on, Auntie Jo?"

"Not at all," Jo said. She sunk deeper into the couch and stopped herself from tucking her feet under Carie's thigh. "Honestly, I'll probably fall asleep here. One of you take my bed if I don't make it there."

Remote in hand, Lisa plopped into the armchair and started flipping through the streaming options. Jo felt her eye lids drift closed. She stretched out her legs and crossed her arms over her chest. Her breathing evened out, and as she fell under, she could feel a welcome touch to her ankle.

When she woke with the sun the next morning, Jo was tucked lovingly in her bed. Her sleep had been peaceful. The sheets were freshly laundered, and her quilt—blood free-- was pulled to her chin. She started her day with a smile, her steps a bit lighter as she went to open the bakery. She clung to that feeling as long as she could.

⸻ ℓℓ ⸻

To her great surprise, Carie acquiesced and took the upstairs bed. Lisa was convinced it was because she didn't trust herself to not curl up next to Jo, but either way, she was pleased it didn't turn into a quiet fight. The couch ended up being much more comfortable than it had any right to be. She resolved to start napping on it whenever possible, though the next few days were going to be a frenzy of baking and meal prep for the holiday. Jo had lit up like a supernova when Lisa asked if they could prepare a proper Thanksgiving dinner. Jo had herded her into the car and sped to the supermarket so they could pick their bird. She had only ever made a turkey breast for the meal. Lisa couldn't help but be warmed by her aunt's excited chattering about brines and getting to make stock with the turkey carcass.

The longer she stayed in Door County, the more Lisa found herself resenting her parents and grandparents. Seeing her aunt bloom in the last few months had been a gift. How could they just decide she wasn't worthy of their attention? How could one perceived infraction of unspoken rules be worth throwing away a relationship with this kind woman? She often wondered if they thought of Jo at all.

With the holiday coming up, Lisa was wrestling with whether she should call her parents. She hadn't spent a holiday away from them ever, but with each passing day that her notifications remained free of her mother and father, Lisa leaned towards letting the day go unmarked. As far as she knew, her mother had only called once, and it was to yell at her aunt. Jo hadn't mentioned the conversation, so Lisa didn't bother bringing it up. It must have been painful for Jo that the only reason her sister would reach out was to yell about her niece.

Could she make a clean break from the family?

Though, it wouldn't be a completely clean break. She still had her aunt.

The week was so busy that Lisa didn't get a chance to bring up Carie's offer. She figured a little distance from the weekend's chaos couldn't hurt either. She had stolen away a few times with Carie to practice wards, which she was finding much more difficult. It was frustrating because she had been able to easily throw one up around her and Kat when they were on Eagle Bluff.

"That's because we were so close to one of the knots," Carie explained one evening.

Jo had gone to bed early, and Lisa had begged to practice a bit. Carie took her outside and showed her the hand maneuvers to pluck the threads of magic from the air. Lisa had only managed a weak dome around herself. Carie tossed a rock easily through it.

"Dottie brought up the knots, and she showed me a bit about pulling on the threads. I didn't have a lot of time to practice, and anything I did at Eagle Bluff was all just luck."

"Luck or innate ability," Carie said. "All the threads that crisscross the world gather together in random spots that we call knots. Lighthouses mark their location. There are five here that attract all kinds of nastiness. It's the main reason that Dottie keeps me on retainer."

Lisa lifted her hand and could feel the invisible strand as she plucked it.

"The knots have an incredible concentration of power. Enough to supply all the weavers across the world with the means to cast. They work as anchors too."

"Anchors to what?"

"Other places. Other worlds. Other dimensions."

Lisa's eyes flicked up to Carie's.

The witch shrugged. "It's a bit narcissistic to think we're the only creatures out there. The possessions that happen are usually spirits from those other worlds. Most times they're just really confused about where the hell they are, and they think that the knots can help them get home just because of the sheer amount of power radiating from them. Every now and again, you'll get an actual entity that falls though a rip or a tear in the dimensions."

"You mean like that stag we saw?"

"I would guess that was a possession. Normally, I would try to exercise it and let the host go on its merry way, but that wasn't in the cards that night. When you see something that doesn't belong in this world, you'll know."

"We shouldn't mention that to my aunt."

"We're going to give your aunt all the information she'll need to have an informed opinion on the matter. I know that you're an adult, but I'm not about to piss her off."

Lisa wanted to argue, but she stopped herself. Carie moved them swiftly off the topic of Jo.

"I'm going to throw up a ward around myself," she said, quickly flicking her wrist and drawing the magic around her. "I want to see if you can cast that offensive spell again."

Looking unsure, Lisa flexed her fingers.

"I don't know that I could. That really felt like...like a 'holy shit, you were about to die and I really didn't want to have to be the one to tell my aunt that I saw it happen' kind of thing."

"Humor me."

With a shrug, she adopted her best orchestra conductor pose before throwing her hands towards Carie. She could feel the threads around her, and she tried to pluck them like Dottie had shown her. There was a charge that zipped through her fingertips. It felt like the shock of touching metal after walking on carpet in fuzzy socks. It was hardly the entity killing death blow it had been a few nights ago.

"Feel anything?" Carie asked from the security of her ward.

"Yeah, I can feel it."

"Excellent. You're making a connection, and that's the hard part."

Lisa relaxed her hands and closed her eyes. She tried to picture the threads around her.

"Try this. I find it helps me. You can feel the thread, right?"

Lisa nodded.

"Picture traveling along it like an electrical charge. Each thread connects to the knots. That's where it gets its power from. See that energy flying through that connection and pull on it. Make it yours and weave your spell."

Carie powered up her ward again, making it a bit opaquer than it had been before. Lisa appreciated the vote of confidence. She clung to that feeling as she found her thread again. She tried to picture all the jolts of magic spilling from the tangle at the lighthouse. She closed her eyes and gave the thread a metaphorical tug. The charge started up in her fingertips again. Smug, Lisa began to release the thread to cast her spell, but she felt something else tug at her attention. When she opened her eyes, she wasn't standing in her aunt's front yard.

Lisa was on the shore of a small bay. The water was calm, and the horizon was a stark line in the far-flung distance. It seemed like nighttime, but the sky was blindingly white. A twig snapped behind her, and in the space of a blink, Lisa was back before Carie. She could feel the buildup of magic in her hands and recognized it would obliterate Carie's ward. With a grunt of effort, Lisa flung her hands skyward, and the energy exploded above them like low-hanging fireworks. Her brief glimpse of the shore was forgotten.

Wincing, Carie dropped her ward and jogged to Lisa's side.

"I probably should have mentioned that the longer you pull on that thread, the more powerful the spell."

Lisa absently nodded. Her knees felt weak beneath her. She barely registered that Carie took hold of her arm to keep her upright.

"Pulling a thread that hard will take it out of you too. Just like the other night. Let's get you inside."

"Not gonna argue with that."

They both turned back to the house but froze in their tracks. Jo stood on the porch in a loose-fitting tunic and leggings that stopped at her calves. Her feet were bare. Her arms hung limp at her sides.

"Josie?"

Lisa steadied herself as Carie released her to run up to her aunt. She took a moment to make sure she wouldn't collapse before she trotted after.

Carie had Jo by the shoulders and was peering into her face. She shook her gently as Lisa approached.

"Is she sleeping?"

Carie hummed. "I think so, but I don't remember her ever sleepwalking before."

"I haven't seen her do it either, and I feel like I would have heard her if she's done it. This house is so creaky, and the walls are thinner than crepe paper."

"Josie, wake up."

"Auntie Jo?"

It took another gentle shake before Jo's eyes flickered back to wakefulness. She blinked rapidly, swaying to one side before catching herself. Jo looked between them.

"Why are you outside at this hour?"

Carie huffed out an incredulous laugh. "I think we could ask the same thing."

Lisa could see the calculation in her aunt's eyes. She tried to pull a lie from the sleep-dulled depths of her mind, and she came up empty.

"Bad dream," Carie offered.

"No," Jo said with a little laugh. "I've actually been sleeping soundly the last few days. Peaceful dreams, mostly. The beach. A quiet bay."

Recollection tickled at the back of Lisa's mind, but she worried if she chased it, she might keel over.

"We were heading back inside to get to bed," Lisa said.

"That's an excellent idea," Carie agreed. She gently turned Jo around and guided her back into the house.

Lisa lingered by her aunt's bedroom door, trying not to eavesdrop as Carie set her back to sleep. The witch closed the door behind Jo and crooked an eyebrow at Lisa expectantly. Lisa had a thousand questions to ask, but her mouth chose the oddest one to blurt out.

"Would it be bad if I don't call my parents to wish them a happy Thanksgiving?"

Carie chuckled. "Not sure what I was expecting."

Lisa let her grin turn shit eating. "I mean, I can ask about other stuff if you'd prefer."

"That's alright."

"So?"

"I'm not good with parents," Carie said. "I'm not particularly close with mine, even when Ethan was still alive. And they were hardly typical. They can weave too, and they work freelance gigs like I do. Though their work tends to be a bit higher end. We don't really talk. But I can remember Josie mentioning talking to her sister maybe once or twice in the ten years I've been coming around. I don't know much about your family, but if they haven't reached out, then why should you be the one to bridge the gap?"

"Honestly, I thought you were going to give me the 'be the bigger person' bit."

Carie waved her hand dismissively. "I know better than anyone how hard it can be to lose someone you love, but assholes who cast you aside for making a mistake aren't worth fretting over. That's not to say you can't have a reconciliation in the future, but from what I understand, you didn't murder anyone."

"I lied about flunking out of school."

"And why did you lie about it?"

Lisa shrugged. "I was...I guess I didn't want them to be disappointed."

"I think that you were worried this exact thing would happen. Jo told me a little bit about your whole situation, and yeah, maybe you should have told them sooner, but their reaction shouldn't have been how dare you not be good at this thing I want you to be good at, and then kick you out of the house."

"So, don't call?"

"I can't tell you what to do, Lisa. All I can say is that if you do reach out, don't expect something different than what you know is going to happen. If you get a different reaction, then great, a nice surprise. You don't want to ruin your holiday."

"Maybe I'll just text them."

"Sure," Carie agreed. "And it's not the end all be all. Maybe you can talk more another time."

"Yeah."

"Hey," Carie put her hand on Lisa's shoulder. "No matter what happens with them, you've got Josie, right? Kids aren't a commodity, and they shouldn't be exactly what their parents want. And a witchy, table top playing, baker-in-training sounds a hell of a lot more interesting than an accountant or whatever the hell future they had mapped out for you. Not that there's anything with accountants. I'm sure they are very nice people."

"Thanks, Carie."

"No problem. Now go to bed. If your aunt isn't completely against it, you can come check the wards with me tomorrow after you finish with the Thanksgiving orders."

Chapter Ten

Jo didn't dream of the forest anymore. When she remembered a dream, she was ankle deep in the cool water of the crescent bay. The sky was still white, but it wasn't as blinding. Sometimes Carie was further out in the water. Sometimes Jo could hear her struggling through the foliage further inland. Carie's presence was a soothing balm against the burning touches of the shadows that play in her periphery. Voices, low and incomprehensible, competed with the gentle lapping of the waves. They had been growing clearer with each dream. The different tones coalesced into a soothing lullaby that called to Jo from the horizon.

It begged her to stay.

It was peaceful there. Easier. Why not stay?

It needed her, desperately. Why wouldn't she come to them?

The first night the voice rang out clear and powerful over the water, Jo awoke outside. The dream was gone like an unimportant memory soon as Jo opened her eyes to Carie's concerned face. She could feel a fleeting frustration, but she shrugged it away at the warm touch of Carie's hands on her shoulders.

Jo told herself it was the stress of the holiday. Since Lisa had arrived, business at the bakery had picked up considerably. Whether it was their dual magic enhancing the flavors of the pastries, Jo's decade of honing her craft, or some combination of the two, the bakery was busy in a way that Jo wouldn't have been able to deal with alone. Carie would even pop in on occasion to help at the register.

That was nice.

Less welcome had been the conversation with her niece about making rounds with Carie to the wards around the peninsula.

It was a delicate balance. Jo was not Lisa's parent, but she did feel a compulsion to protect her niece. She also trusted Lisa to make her own decisions, and she said as much the night before Thanksgiving. She felt like a fisher's wife as she stood on the porch, watching Carie and Lisa drive away to protect the peninsula.

It was selfish in part too.

It was only a few days since Carie had crashed back into her life. They had reconciled and agreed to be friends again. Jo knew it would never be enough, but she convinced herself she could train her heart to live with what it was given. Carie had been nothing but considerate and kind, but Jo had told herself it was foolish to expect any more than that. Carie staying in the house was a temporary arrangement for the winter. She would be gone in May just like every year.

And what if she took Lisa with her? What if Lisa got a taste for Carie's work and started traveling with her? Jo wanted nothing more than for the both of them to thrive, but she didn't think she would survive being left behind again. She worried that asking Lisa what her plans were would drive her away, so Jo kept quiet.

Instead of dwelling on things that hadn't even happened yet, Jo tried to focus on all the happiness that she had in her life at the present. Thanksgiving had been exactly what she wanted it to be. She made dinner with the two people dearest to her. Knowing she possessed some little bit of magic, she tried to infuse it in her food purposefully. She imagined every grain of salt shimmered with her love and care. She willed the spices and herbs in the stuffing to deepen, dancing with the sausage and the apple. When Jo sampled the food, it sung in a way it never had before.

It had been easy enough to panic about whether her cooking was any good without her magic. Food was something she had always found solace in. It gave her comfort in the years after she had been kicked out. It boosted her, showing her that she had a path forward outside of her parents' influence. Knowing it might just be a fluke hurt deeply. Watching Lisa grow more comfortable with her magic helped Jo to realize that it didn't matter. Her magic was a part of her, and Jo would use it to her fullest ability to make the best food she could.

Dan had made the normal delivery that week and happened to mention that they were having a quiet holiday at home since his dad had just got over the flu. Jo invited them over to the house, not expecting they would accept, but was very pleased when Dan called her later that day saying the three of them would stop by after dinner. They had a football game on in the background, though no one really cared for the sport. Dan's father would make a point to comment on a play call every now and again, and Carie would grunt her agreement. They both took to criticizing both quarterbacks though neither of them ever played a down of football.

Dan's mother had insisted on turning off the game after a bit. They ended up playing cards and drinking too much wine. Jo reveled in the gentle touches from Carie throughout the evening. A hand on her knee while they played rummy. A bump of the shoulder doing dishes. A head on her shoulder after telling a terrible joke that had everyone cackling.

She still went to bed alone that night, and Jo had never felt colder in her life. That night, she was back at the bay. The voice was low and strong, and it begged her to come below the waves.

When she woke, Jo had made a path through the dusting of snow on the ground. Her feet were numb, and her hair damp. She managed to get back in the house without waking Lisa, who had polished off at least a bottle and a half of red wine over the course of the dinner while enthusiastically regaling everyone with tales of her barbarian's exploits. If Carie heard anything, she didn't come down to inspect. After towel drying off, Jo changed into warm clothes and snuggled back into bed. She plied herself with excuses for not telling anyone about her sleepwalking. She reasoned that both Lisa and Carie had seen her do it once already. If they were concerned, they would ask again.

After all, it wasn't anything to worry about. They had enough on their collective plate. Jo didn't need to say anything.

When she was young and before she realized just how different she was from her family, Jo's favorite part of the holiday was the weekend after Thanksgiving. The Christmas creep hadn't completely overtaken November and October yet, so she enjoyed watching the transition in the neighborhoods and the store fronts. Her parents never went out shopping on Black Friday--they saw it as something that poor people did--but once she was old enough to drive, Jo enjoyed getting an early coffee and people watching at the mall. She loved the local Christmas parade the town threw the day after Thanksgiving. It was a time to rest and regroup before the final push to the holidays.

When Lisa pushed up from the couch with her hair sticking up at all ends and lines from the cushions pressed into her cheek, Jo felt that fondness for the holiday rekindle in her chest. Jo set a cool glass of water on the end table and sat beside her niece.

"Aspirin's in the medicine cabinet if you need it."

Lisa groaned and chugged the water down in one gulp.

"If you see me even looking at red wine again, please just slap me right in the face."

"I think the hangover should be enough of a deterrent."

"Maybe I'll go wake up Carie. She cures things. She can cure a hangover, right?"

"Can't hurt to ask. Let her sleep, though. I'm surprised she stayed up as late as she did yesterday. Usually, she doesn't do well around people she doesn't know."

Lisa ran her hands over her face and through her hair.

"She did it because she knew it was important to you," Lisa said. "You light up when you get to cook for people, and she likes to see you happy."

Jo fixed her niece with a withering glare.

"You can look at me like that all you want," Lisa said, not bothering to meet her gaze. "Doesn't make it any less true."

Lisa pushed off the couch and went to put some coffee on.

Jo prayed with all her might that Carie was still sleeping. Sound carried in the house, and feelings were balanced precariously. Jo didn't want things to crash.

"How busy are you usually this weekend?" Lisa asked as she waited for the water to boil.

"Weekend after Thanksgiving is a breather before the Christmas onslaught. We should be getting a call from Dottie about catering her holiday party. That's the big kick off in the sprint towards the end of the year."

"There's something kind of hilarious about a bunch of old witches having a holiday bash."

"It's more of a nod to an old pagan thing. Yule, she calls it. She has a huge bonfire on her property for the solstice. But it is an excuse to have everyone get together before they scatter for Christmas."

"That sounds fun."

"There's no way you won't be getting an invite. Your friend Kat will make sure of that."

"Think that Carie will get invited?"

Jo thought for a moment. "Probably. Though big gatherings aren't really her thing."

"If you went with her, I'm sure she would go."

Jo sighed heavily.

"I'm just trying to help," Lisa said with a sparkle in her eye. She ground the beans and dropped them in the filter. "You clearly need a little nudge, and that's what I'm here to do."

"We spoke a bit," Jo said. "I don't want to push."

Ignoring the look on Lisa's face, Jo clapped her hands on her knees and bounced to her feet.

"But speaking of Christmas, what is your tolerance for decorations?"

"Oh...well, Mom and Dad always hired someone to decorate the house."

Jo couldn't help the incredulous expression that fell over her face.

"Dad never wanted to bother with it, and Mom was more concerned with the aesthetic than the actual bonding activity, so I usually just left them to it."

"Then, we're definitely going to decorate. We're going to need a tree. I'm pretty sure the Fir Farm will be open."

The stairs creaked, and Carie appeared in the same clothes she was wearing the day before. Her hair was pulled back in a messy bun at the top of her head, and her expression was tight around the eyes.

"Looks like we may not have a miracle hangover cure after all, Lisa," Jo said. She tried not to stare at Carie, but her eyes couldn't help but follow her. Having her sleep-worn and hungover and home warmed Jo's heart.

"I can definitely cure hangovers, but I didn't want to cast it multiple times. Let me see that pot of coffee, Lisa."

Carie stepped to the counter and took the carafe. She muttered a soft incantation, and soothing violet strings of magic laced like knit-work from her fingers and slowly faded into the warm liquid. She poured out three cups, leaving one for Lisa at the counter. She walked the other to Jo and handed it to her with a soft smile. Jo felt her stomach flip. She ignored her niece's dancing eyes over Carie's shoulder.

"This takes about twenty minutes to re-hydrate you, so you should be good for your errands."

Lisa scoffed. "Our errands? You're obviously coming with us to get a tree."

"If you'd like to join us," Jo added. She swallowed and bravely added, "Obviously, we'd love if you did."

Carie sipped her coffee, hiding some expression that Jo didn't want to parse.

"Of course, I'll come. Where were you heading?"

"Auntie Jo mentioned the Fir Farm."

"Just outside of Fish Creek."

Jo could see Carie calculating just how far that was from Eagle Bluff.

"Well, if we run into anything, that'll be a great test of your wards, Lisa."

With a grin, Lisa waved a hand and a blue bubble radiated around her. It blew the papers on the kitchen table to the floor.

"I really need to get a proper book for all these recipes." Jo slipped to her knees and gathered up the papers. Lisa dropped her spell and knelt to help her.

"You've been saying that since I first came here," Carie said as she grabbed a few of the loose pages. "The binder was a good idea, but it didn't really help much, huh?"

Jo laughed as she got back up. "I'll find something that works eventually, dear."

She froze as soon as the endearment was out of her mouth. Avoiding Carie's face, she straightened her papers, snatching the ones that Lisa held out to her.

"Great," Lisa said. "I'll go get washed up, and we can head out once you two are ready."

Her niece scampered upstairs and pulled the door closed behind her. No footsteps creaked on the floorboards, so Jo figured she was eavesdropping.

"I...um"

Jo jumped when she felt Carie's hand on her shoulder. She spun to face her, shifting her arm so that the hand slipped off.

"It's okay."

"What?"

Carie sighed. "We said we wanted to go back to the way it was. You used to call me dear all the time. I don't mind."

Jo wished she could control the blazing flush that spread like a wildfire across her cheeks. They had said that, hadn't they? They were friends again. Friends called each other dear, right?

"Josie?"

Carie kept calling her that name. And Jo could hear it whispered in her ear as the sheets bunched around their hips while they moved together on the bed.

But that's not really an option anymore, is it?

Jo shivered as if the voice had tittered in her ear. It was distantly familiar, like a half-remembered dream.

Carie was looking at her with concern. "Josie, are you okay?"

"Yes, sorry...I just...got caught up for a moment."

Carie frowned and raised a hand to her forehead. The fresh scent of her magic permeated the air between them. Jo leaned into the touch and let her eyes drop closed.

"Holidays are always a bit tiring," Jo offered as an excuse.

"You should make sure that you're getting enough rest. Lisa and I can handle dinner the next few nights. You've been running yourself ragged for us."

Jo looked up at Carie through her eyelashes. "I like taking care of you. And Lisa."

The corner of Carie's mouth tugged up. "And we'd both like the chance to take care of you."

Would take two. You are such a terrible burden after all.

Carie frowned as if she had heard the words. She wiped her thumb across Jo's brow with a word that Jo didn't catch. She felt the voice sink into the void, and her head was quiet again.

"Finish your coffee," Carie said, her expression still furrowed in concern. "Lisa will be down soon and then we can go get some fresh air."

~ele~

Silence reigned over the entire trip to the tree farm. Carie said she would drive, and she grabbed Jo's keys instead of her own. The backseat of her car was still a bit of a nightmare. Lisa slid into the middle seat so she could follow the conversation and have easy access to the radio should she need to veto any song choices. Carie flipped on the classic rock station and kept the volume low. She stole worried glances over at Jo who had fallen asleep with her head tipped against the passenger window. Lisa was desperate to ask what was wrong, but she didn't want to wake her aunt.

"I'll show you the sleep ward," Carie said.

Lisa met her eyes in the rear-view mirror.

"I don't know what it is," Carie continued, "but I can feel something wrong."

Lisa's fingers dug into the faux leather of the backseat. "What does that mean?"

Carie sighed. "It could just be exhaustion catching up to her from both the bakery and from tapping into whatever magical ability she has."

"From when we're cooking together?"

Carie smiled as she said, "She's been trying to use it. You can taste it in everything she makes. It's not typical casting, but it is still spell work. She hasn't been taught the efficient ways to wield it."

"Makes sense. Even after those few minutes that we've practiced, I've definitely crashed hard."

"We just need to keep an eye on her."

With an empathetic nod, Lisa relaxed back into the seat and watched as snow began to fall. She was glad she thought to grab her coat and hat when they left the house. When they arrived and parked, she burst out of the car with a twirl. She tipped her head to the heavens and shivered at the feel of the snowflakes against her skin. She watched her aunt stir and smiled as Carie rushed over to the passenger side to open the door for her. Jo rolled her eyes but stepped out and dropped into an indulgent curtsy. Carie snorted a laugh, but her smile dropped as Jo shivered. She unwrapped the scarf around her neck, and looped it around Jo's, tying it and letting it fall against her coat. Lisa turned away when she saw her aunt's eyes go wobbly.

It was appropriate that they were at a tree farm. The pining was getting a bit ridiculous.

They stopped at the front office, rented an ax because they forgot their own, and started off into the rows of trees.

Something immediately felt wrong.

Lisa was new to her magic, but she reached to tug on a nearby thread. It vibrated under her touch, jumping as if someone else was pulling on it. The sensation surprised her, and she stumbled a bit. Carie noticed her step hitch and tensed.

"Are you alright?" Jo asked.

Carie looked at Lisa. "Did you feel something?"

Lisa reached out again and felt that tension on the thread. "It's like something else is pulling."

"Well, you can't expect that the threads are exclusive to your witchy uses, girl," a silky voice purred.

Carie grabbed Lisa's arm and hauled her next to her aunt while throwing up a ward around them. Lisa grabbed for Jo's wrist. She could feel the tension in her aunt even through her gloves.

"Please, Carie. I hardly think that's warranted."

Lisa peered around Carie's side. Beyond the ward was a shivering mass of shadow. It billowed widely before pulling together and resolving into a vaguely humanoid shape. Its head tilted, regarding them without eyes.

"I don't think I've been introduced to these two," they said.

"And you shouldn't expect to be, Aldred."

"Well, that just hurts my feelings," Aldred pouted. "And here I was so worried about saying hello when you hadn't been up to see me at all this year."

"Still a bit early in the season to be refreshing the northern lighthouses."

"And that's why I decided to have a bit of a wander."

The entity called Aldred floated to the side, trying to get a better look. Lisa stumbled as Carie pushed Jo back with a protective arm. A ripple went up through the shadow.

"You're only making them more enticing, witch. Are they the reason why everything seems so interested in heading south?"

"We've enjoyed a peaceful sort of truce all these years, Aldred," Carie hissed, furious. "Don't make me reevaluate that position."

Aldred laughed and lazily floated over the ward. They settled like a cat curling up in the sun. Two vortexes swirled in the shadow, giving the vague impression of eyes.

"An apprentice, perhaps?" Aldred asked. They slipped a bit, looking at Jo hungrily. "Though she seems to be a little bit of something too, eh?"

"I'm Lisa, and apprentice isn't too far off."

Carie tensed, but Lisa didn't care. Aldred wasn't looking at her aunt anymore. They were focused on her.

"New in town?"

"Yes," Lisa answered.

"Rather more ghosts and goblins than you're used to?"

Lisa shrugged. "Still better than where I came from."

"I don't want to interrupt your outing any more than I already have. It's nice to see Carie mingling. She works entirely too hard up here for very little credit. She deserves a treat every now and again."

They slipped off the ward into a puddle of smoke on the ground. They leapt a bit father before looking back to the group.

"I'll be seeing you, Carie. Perhaps you too, Lisa. Don't be a stranger. It's lovely up north this time of year."

Their eyes flickered back to Jo for a second before their entire being swirled into nothingness. The oppressive feeling of being watched lifted, and Lisa felt Carie unclench. The witch's hand had slipped from Jo's arm to her hand. Their fingers were interlaced and white from the force of the grip. Jo's eyes were wide as she stared out to where the being had disappeared.

"Popular up here, huh," Lisa said.

Carie let out the gasp of air she had been holding, slumping a bit as she did.

"Oh yeah. I'm huge with the interdimensional entity set."

"I didn't realize that they could talk," Lisa said.

"Most don't," Carie responded. She looked at Jo, who was still staring out at nothing.

Carie tugged on her hand. "Where did you go?"

"I'm here," Jo said, finally looking over to Carie. "I promise, I'm here."

They didn't take long after that to select a tree. Lisa could tell her aunt wanted to browse a bit more, but Carie wanted to get back to the car.

"You're worried," Jo said about an hour later. They had the tree tied to the roof of the car and been talked into hot chocolate by the owners of the farm. The warmth felt nice between Lisa's palms. Jo had been chatting about the Christmas decorations she thought she might still have in the garage when she noticed neither Lisa nor Carie was listening to her.

"I'm not," Carie said, not taking her eyes off the road.

"You don't have to lie," Jo murmured after a sip of her drink. "You were always shit at it."

The steering wheel groaned under the sudden pressure from Carie's grip. Lisa had tucked herself into the seat behind Carie, hoping to fade into the background of their conversation. She wondered how many times in the past her aunt had asked after Carie's business and been stonewalled. Lisa could see the familiar routine playing out. Jo had stared at Carie for a second or two after speaking, and then turned to look out the window with a soft sigh. Carie's shoulders hitched up to her ears, and the quiet in the car became stifling. Lisa considered alleviating it, but it was Carie who spoke again.

"This winter..." she started. "This has been the hardest it's been before a solstice since I've been coming up here."

Jo jolted herself from watching the fields fly by outside the car. She turned her full attention to Carie.

"And I keep asking myself what's different this year," Carie said.

Lisa swallowed. "Me."

Carie met Lisa's eyes in the rear-view mirror. "Both of you."

Jo kept her eyes forward. She held herself perfectly still. "I hardly think making food tastier is summoning anything sinister."

"Don't do that," Carie said. She kept her eyes on the road, but after a moment's hesitation, she moved one of her hands to Jo's knee. "Don't belittle your magic. It's a difference. We need to keep it in mind."

"We should speak to Dottie and the witches about it," Lisa suggested. "Maybe we can come up with some kind of containment ward? Be a bit more offensive then defensive? "

"Do you have any idea of where they could be coming from?" Jo asked. "Could there be a way to stop them at the source?"

"It's a rare occurrence, but there must be a tear. A miniscule space between realities. Normally, I cast a seeing spell to check. The threads will thrum with power when it happens, but I haven't felt that this year. I've been pulled in a thousand different directions the last few months. I could have missed something. It's possible some of these entities are like Aldred."

"A friend of yours," Jo said with a smile.

Carie snorted but returned her grin. "Hardly a friend. Aldred's been haunting the peninsula for decades, maybe even a century. Tried to exercise them my first winter up here, but it didn't work."

"What does that mean?" Lisa asked, leaning up between the two front seats.

"Just what I said," Carie said. "Used the proper spell, but Aldred didn't disappear. Either means that their home dimension is gone, or something else. A ward? A banishment? Something like that. I made the mistake of asking about it, and I thought they were going to take my head off. As long as they keep to themselves, I tend to leave them alone."

"Is that safe?" Jo asked.

"Has been so far," Carie said with a wink. "I can handle Aldred if need be. So don't worry. I'll protect you. Uh... both of you."

Lisa fell back into the backseat, failing to hide her laughter. Jo looked out her window with a pleased look on her face as Carie cleared her throat.

"Regardless, I don't hate the idea of going on the offensive," Carie said. "If your friend would want to help, we could cover a fair amount of ground."

"Kat?"

Carie bobbed her head.

"She did a good job that night at Eagle Bluff. I vaguely remember her casting a simple exorcism spell, but it did the job."

"I'm sure she'd love to help. I'll text her right now," Lisa said as she reached for her phone, "Honestly, Dan would probably be down to help too."

"Does Dan weave?"

"Dan drives."

"Then Dan doesn't help."

Lisa made a mental note to work on that point. Dan was organized and a great planner. His filing system for his notes during their campaign was very impressive. He could at least help behind the scenes.

Chapter Eleven

It hadn't taken long for Lisa to wear Carie down. Jo said that as long as Dan helping them didn't interfere with his deliveries or helping his parents, she didn't mind. Lisa ended up bringing Carie to their next campaign session so they could chat. She also slid in to take Michelle's place for the night as a guest character. Michelle had managed to finagle the holidays off to spend with her family, but she was paying for it in extra shifts and favors that kept her from the game. Dan didn't like holding sessions if someone couldn't make it, but the holidays always tested his resolve. It was either run a game missing a party member or two or not play a session until deep into January. The dice always called to Dan, and in the end, he always broke.

Carie took the game in stride. She delighted in the magic system, making comments about how weaving was so much less convoluted than the game made it out to be. She chortled in disbelief when Dan told her she couldn't cast certain spells unless she had the correct components. Max and Jack traded incredulous looks, while Kat tried to egg Carie into showing them how magic was really supposed to work.

For Lisa, it just solidified that she was going to set down roots here. She could feel the threads around her tremble as she had that thought. It didn't matter what was tugging at them, or what was struggling to get to the knots. She had found a home up here with a little family, and she would do whatever she had to do to defend it.

"She's more than welcome to join us every week if she wants," Jack had said on his way out. Max nodded his agreement, waving to the group as he pulled out of the driveway.

"So, I understand that you need a driver?" Dan asked with a glint in his eye.

Carie looked over at Lisa. "I think that's a bit reductive."

"But it's definitely part of the help we'd need," said Lisa.

"My car drives fine," Carie insisted.

Kat shrugged. "Sure, but Dan's got a truck. More room. And the backseat doesn't look like someone exploded all over it."

"And," Lisa added, "we really should have someone that's just dedicated to driving. If Kat wasn't up to it at Eagle Bluff, we would have been stuck there."

"I've driven in worse condition," Carie said.

"And I'm sure my aunt would love to hear about that so she can harangue you until the day that you die about it."

"Traitor."

"I'm just saying," Lisa continued. "Dan's a solid driver. And he already knows about all this stuff."

"I also do deliveries all over the county," Dan offered. "I know this place like it's my backyard."

They moved the conversation back inside, after a quick hello to Dan's parents who were enjoying whatever regular people enjoyed on television late on a Saturday night. They barely spared a glance for the odd group parading through their living room and back into their basement.

"Dan can also keep track of places we've had sightings," Lisa said. She looked at Dan, prompting him to spill the credentials they shored up for this conversation.

"Oh, yeah! It's just like tracking deliveries," he said a little too enthusiastically. "I can make a spreadsheet!"

Kat snorted, trying desperately not to laugh. "Fighting the forces of evil with the drudgery of Excel!"

"If evil can be banal, why can't the solution be just so?"

"It's really not fair to call the possessions evil," Carie started.

"Yeah, but when Dan eventually turns this into fodder for his campaign, it won't matter," Kat explained.

"Alright," Carie huffed. "If you want to use a spreadsheet to keep track of sightings, that's fine. And if it will keep you from telling your aunt what I said before, sure, he can drive us. But only sometimes. I'm not going to be dragging him to the lighthouses in the middle of the water. And he's definitely not coming if it's something we know is going to be dangerous."

"Seems like those are the times you'll definitely need a driver," Dan said.

Lisa smiled. This was going perfectly.

Kat jokingly insisted that they come up with a name for their group to stencil on his truck, which was catnip for Dan. They huddled together, trading increasingly ridiculous names. Lisa sidled up to Carie.

"I mean, it is a role playing group. You really should have been expecting this."

"I suppose so."

Lisa sighed. "Look, if you don't want them involved, I can tell them after we leave."

"It's not that. Kat has that exorcising spell. We'll definitely be needing that. And not having to worry about getting to safety if something goes wrong isn't a bad thing either."

"But..."

Carie sighed. "But it's dangerous."

"If we didn't get involved back before Thanksgiving, I don't know that you'd even be alive to have this conversation."

"It's not that I can't see the reasoning," Carie said. "It makes sense. I get it. I just worry. I don't want anyone to get hurt."

Like Ethan, Carie didn't say, but Lisa heard it all the same. She almost stopped herself from saying anything else. She would feel terrible if Carie blamed herself for something happening to one of them, but if she kept trying to deal with everything alone, something worse was going to happen to her. Lisa found herself feeling very protective of the witch in the last few weeks. As far as Lisa was concerned, Carie was family. She would do whatever she could to help.

"We know what we're getting into," Lisa said. "Well, Kat and I do. Dan just needs to know where to take us and then any data we want to throw at him."

"Doesn't change the fact that there's risk involved."

"Well, sure, but there's risk involved with everything. Any time we walk outside there's a risk. And when you involve other people, you don't have to bear it all yourself."

Carie worried at her bottom lip as she watched the others argue. "It's not always as simple as that."

Lisa shrugged. "I think it is."

"I know it isn't."

"I wish that I could promise you that what happened to Ethan won't happen to us, Carie, but you have to trust us."

"It's not about trust," Carie started. "I thought I was helping him. We chased around the world looking for more and more dangerous jobs. We thought we could do anything, but honestly, I think we did it more to prove ourselves to our parents. Mom and Dad were so busy with their own work that they rarely paid attention to each other, let alone us. We wanted to stand next to them and prove that we were worthy of their attention. Better than any shiny bauble they might find digging through the magical hordes of weavers in Europe.

"We had no business trying to stop that thing out on Mount Rainer, but dozens of hikers had either gone missing or showed up with their minds' hollowed out. If we couldn't stop it, who could? We camped out up on the Paradise trail. There's a powerful knot up there. The wildflowers were all in bloom, drawing their vibrancy from those threads. It was beautiful, until that thing appeared. We thought we had it. We were strong. Ethan even more so than I was, but I wanted the killing blow. I wanted to send it back. Ethan had it distracted, and I rushed up to exorcise it. It saw me coming a mile away. It turned to face me, ready to tear me apart. Ethan shoved me out of the way. He managed to exorcise it before it tore him in half. It had a hold of him when the spell went off. Ethan was banished with it. I didn't even have a body to bring home. I ended up burying his journal with his finest set of clothes.

"I won't let that happen to anyone else that I care about," she finished.

Lisa was silent for a moment, letting Dan and Kat's conversation fill the space between them.

"I get it, Carie, and that's exactly why we're going to help. We don't want you to end up like Ethan. We can keep each other safe. Watch each other's backs."

Carie bowed her head and breathed deep through her nose. Lisa gave her the moment to compose herself before reaching out and patting her arm.

"Jo's not the only one that cares," Lisa smiled. "Sorry."

With a cut-off laugh, Carie finally met Lisa's gaze. "Then you'll make sure that they listen when I tell them to go. Dan needs to stay in the car unless we give him the all-clear. Same with Kat. We call her in when we need an extra hand, but I don't want her out there if things get violent. I'm still having a hard time reconciling you being out there."

"Someone needs to watch your back," Lisa said. "It would hurt Jo terribly if you didn't come home."

"That goes double for you. Triple, even."

"Well, then we just both need to make sure we're careful."

Carie grunted.

"That thing...Aldred...really rattled you, huh?"

"More what they represent. Aldred isn't something worth getting all worked up over, but it's very early in the season for them to be wandering. It's rare to see them during the day."

"You think I might be...I don't know, calling to them somehow?"

"Possibly," Carie said. "You're a new player pulling on the threads. And when you do draw on them, you've been taking a lot more than say Archie or Mildred with the witches. Even Dottie only really pulls on the threads with any strength once in a while. You've only been here a few months, and you're making a splash."

"We'll figure it out," Lisa said before clapping her hands on her thighs before leaning in conspiratorially. "So..."

Carie crooked an eyebrow. "So?"

"Did you ask my aunt to Dottie's solstice thing?"

"We're not in high school."

"Yeah, but I think she'd really like to go."

"You think she wants to come to a party with the biggest busy bodies in Wisconsin, who all have an obnoxious interest in our friendship?"

"With you? Absolutely."

Carie rolled her eyes.

Lisa took a deep breath and was about to launch into a tirade, but Kat squealed loudly with laughter.

"We can't call ourselves the Entity Busters. That sounds like some kind of gastrointestinal problem."

"It's recognizable," Dan insisted.

"Yeah, because it's based on a very popular, very beloved eighties property."

"Come up with something better then."

"The witchy avengers!"

"Now who's being derivative?"

Carie patted Lisa's shoulder before standing up. "We don't need a name. The work speaks for itself."

Kat and Dan looked at her flatly before glancing sideways at each other. They barely nodded, and silently agreed to continue the discussion elsewhere.

Lisa laughed to herself before pushing off the sofa. "Kat, you'll be at Dottie's?"

"Yep! I'll be bringing my parents too. And Dan if he wants to come."

"Good. We'll run this all by Dottie and then figure out a night to try out this new configuration."

⸺ ✦ ⸺

"It's always tripped me out how dark it gets up here," Lisa said to the passenger side window.

"If you want to see dark, we'll have to go up to the dark sky park in Newport," Carie said. "There's no light pollution, and if the night's clear you can see the Milky Way."

"Hard to believe it could get much darker than a corn field with dim farm houses every mile or so."

"You'll see when we go to the northern lighthouses. They're on islands in Death's Door strait. You have to take a boat. Being on the water with only your own light to mark the way feels like being in deep space. It's peaceful, but unsettling."

Lisa hummed and pressed closer to the window. It was cloudy that night, so she couldn't see the stars.

The rest of the drive home was uneventful, but they didn't arrive until close to midnight. The living room lights were on, but Jo was not on her usual perch on the couch. She always made an effort to stay awake until Lisa or Carie arrived home. She'd be tucked into a corner of the couch with a blanket over her lap and a novel on her chest.

Carie noted the empty sofa with a furrowed brow and walked back to the bedroom. Lisa was putting her coat away when the witch reappeared in the kitchen with a stricken look.

"She's not in the bedroom."

"Check upstairs?"

With a wild look, Carie took the stairs two at a time. Lisa listened as she tossed the apartment. She moved to the kitchen to check for a note, but there was nothing. Jo's car was still in the driveway, and her shoes were by the door.

"She's not here," Carie said, panic bubbling up in her voice.

"She could be in the bakery," Lisa reasoned. She tried to keep her own concern locked down. They both didn't need to be freaking out, but Carie's worries were echoing in her head.

"The bakery," Lisa said again, more for herself than for Carie. "She must be there."

Neither remarked that the building was dark when they pulled up the drive, but until they were proven wrong, Jo was safe in her kitchen. They pushed out the door when Jo appeared in the front yard. It was cold that night, and the snow from the last few weeks had begun to accumulate, assuring the peninsula of a white Christmas. Jo's hair was falling out of a ponytail, sloppy from being blown about by the biting December wind. She wore flannel pants and a hooded sweatshirt with the bakery's logo on it. Her feet were bare, wet, and dirty.

"What the hell are you doing out here?"

Jo didn't seem to notice them until Carie was scooping her off her feet. Her eyes focused, and she arrived back in the present.

"I thought I heard something."

"It's freezing out here," Carie all but shouted. Her tone was incredulous. Her shoulders shook. "Why wouldn't you put shoes on?"

Jo shrugged. "I didn't think I'd be out there for that long."

Lisa held the door open for them. She didn't know if Jo thought they forgot her sleepwalking right around Thanksgiving.

"Josie, you're frozen through," Carie said gently. She ignored the couch and took Jo right into the bedroom. Lisa didn't follow but lingered in the hallway. Carie hadn't closed the door.

"You don't need to fuss."

"Your toes are blue. I'm going to fuss."

"I really wasn't out there that long."

"It doesn't matter! It's December! There's snow on the ground! You're freezing, but you aren't shivering. That's not good! That's really fucking bad!"

"Carie, it's really--"

"You know that there's things out there that are dangerous. You know that! Things that I can't stop without help. I don't care what you hear outside. Please don't go wandering into the cold without shoes if you hear something. Just call me or Lisa and we'll check it out."

"You make it sound like I'm completely helpless."

"That's not what I'm saying at all. Stop wiggling and just put your head down."

"I've lived up here alone for a long time," Jo said, her voice a bit muffled. "I can take care of myself."

"That's not in question, Josie, but there's nothing wrong with letting other people help."

Lisa couldn't help but roll her eyes. She filed the exchange away for the next time Carie tried to talk her out of helping.

"Like a scarf in the cold," Jo said.

"Yeah," Carie's voice had softened, her anger fading. "I like to keep you warm."

Lisa flushed and dodged the floorboards that squeaked the loudest. She busied herself with heating up the leftovers from the lasagna they made the other night. As she watched the plate spin in the microwave, she wondered if Carie and her aunt had finally admitted their feelings for each other. Lisa could see it in the casual intimacy they shared. Carie had wrapped her scarf around Jo to keep her warm. She would move Jo's feet into her lap while they sat on the couch, her hand resting gently over Jo's ankles. Jo always offered seconds and thirds when she fed Carie. If the witch fell asleep on the couch, Jo would be sure to turn off the lights and cover Carie with a warm blanket. There was care there. There was love. Lisa saw it when Jo finally replaced the photo she snatched off the mantle early in her stay. It sat next to a picture of the three of them that Dan insisted taking on Thanksgiving.

Lisa knew that if they did talk about it, she would only hear it accidentally through walls that lacked for insulation. It really wasn't her business. She just wanted them both to be happy. She tried to figure out if there was a way to nudge them even closer as she burned her fingers on the steaming plate. She dropped it a bit quickly on the counter and resolved to let it sit there to cool. She walked back to her aunt's room, knocking gently on the door. There was no answer, so she pushed it open so she could look inside.

Jo was wrapped in her thick duvet. Only her head stuck out, and it was tucked gently into the crook of Carie's neck. She was shivering a bit. Carie had both arms wrapped around Jo's bulk. Her leg was draped over Jo as well, pulling her close as possible. Carie's nose was buried in Jo's hair, and they both appeared to be asleep.

Maybe it didn't matter if they said anything. Lisa flipped off the light and pulled the door closed. Their actions spoke volumes. She tucked into the still steaming lasagna.

Lisa set an alarm on her phone and settled in to sleep on the couch. Christmas was only a week away, and they had many orders to fill. She wanted to be close to wake her aunt up for work in the morning.

Chapter Twelve

Jo had always loved Dottie Cambridge as a customer because she ordered as if she was preparing to feed the entire National Guard and their extended families. Her orders kept the bakery flush and Jo with plenty to do in the weeks leading up to them. Having Lisa on full time in the bakery now was a huge help. They had finished the bakes and had everything packaged up in the early afternoon of Dottie's Yule party. Lisa begged off to get ready, though Jo spotted her shoving Carie out of the house. Her niece meant well, but she really didn't want Lisa hounding Carie about anything.

Jo had just been about to say so as Carie walked into the bakery. The witch's expression was mildly panicked, and Jo snapped her mouth shut when she saw Carie. She hurried around the counter.

"What's wrong?"

Carie blanched, her expression going pained. "What? Why?"

"You look like you're on the verge of a panic attack."

"Oh, um...I'm fine."

Jo studied her with a disbelieving look. Was this it? Was the other shoe about to drop? Carie had been staying with them for weeks, but Jo still wasn't convinced Carie wouldn't just pick up and leave. The witch's panic fed Jo's anxiety. Jo's chest tightened. She bit the inside of her mouth to stop the spill of words, begging Carie to reconsider, to stay.

"Um...I came over here to..."

Jo bit her cheek hard, drawing blood. "You're tied up in knots about coming to talk to me. Is everything okay?"

"I'm sorry," Carie said quietly.

Jo braced for the worst. Carie wasn't meeting her eyes. The witch blushed, just a light dusting of pink high on her cheeks, but it was impossibly endearing. Why did she have to be so easy to love?

Some are easy. You clearly aren't.

The voice had become a mainstay in the back of her mind. It always seemed more forceful when Carie was close.

Her consternation must have shown on her face. Carie frowned and stooped to look Jo right in the eye.

"What was that?"

Jo waved it away with a small smile. "Just a bit of a headache. Nothing a little aspirin won't help."

"Maybe you should stay home tonight, then."

Jo looked up at Carie. "What?"

"I...um...I wanted to ask if you'd like to come with me tonight."

"To Dottie's thing?"

Carie nodded.

"Will they mind?"

"Of course not," Carie said. "Dottie adores you. Dan's going too. And you have a bit of weaving ability. You're more than welcome."

"As long as I'm not crashing."

"Not at all. You'd be my guest."

The voice scratched at the back of her head, but Jo ignored it. Carie was staying. Relief flooded her chest.

"Yes. Thank you for asking me."

Jo watched as Carie let out a held breath. Clearly, she had been worried Jo might have said no. Jo tried not to look further into that. In the month since they'd reconciled, Jo had made an effort to keep herself in check. She didn't want to come on too strong and scare Carie off. She'd already done that once. She would do anything she could to avoid it happening again.

But then summer is right around the corner, isn't it?

The march of time was relentless. No matter how long the winter days seemed, eventually they would be standing at another impasse. Jo had spent many a night sitting up on the couch, staring into nothing, wondering if she could find a way to not talk about it at all. Was it foolish to expect Carie to just know Jo wanted her to stay? It felt like she knew. When Jo woke up tucked against Carie, buried under blankets and blissfully warm that felt like understanding. Carie had worried for her. She wanted Jo to be safe. Wouldn't she want to stay to make sure?

But every other winter had been the same way. They had slept together last winter. They were drunk, but it had happened. Jo wanted nothing more than the opportunity to provide Carie that haven all year long.

Foolish of you if she doesn't want that.

Carie frowned again as she studied Jo's face. "We should get you something for that headache. Smoke from a bonfire won't help with that."

"I must say that I'll be very disappointed if Dottie hasn't found a way to weave the smoke away."

"She'd love to be able to, but unfortunately, weaving doesn't really work that way. Dottie's very adept, but not in banishing minor inconvenience spells."

"Well, let's get ready. Dottie also strikes me as the kind of person who will never forget if you're late."

Carie chuckled.

The weather was ideal for the start of winter. A blanket of snow had accumulated since the first flurries at the end of fall. It insulated the world, making it seem a bit warmer than the temperature read. Low, gray clouds moved slowly across the sky, letting the slim crescent of the waning moon slip through.

Lisa dressed in layers, not bothering with her heavy coat. She wore earmuffs to avoid having to wash the smoke smell out of the hat later. She watched Carie fuss over her aunt, insisting she bring her coat just to be safe. Jo ran cold and tended to suffer in silence. Carie pulled on a heavy, dark purple sweater. The cold didn't seem to bother her much.

The smoky scent of a bonfire hit the group as soon as they pulled up to Dottie's house. Red and orange colors danced against the shadows of the nearby trees. The lake was smooth as a looking glass, and the moon's reflected light danced over the water.

"Ladies!"

Dottie, highlighted by the dancing flames of the bonfire, rushed over and pulled Jo into a tight hug.

"It's lovely to see you all. I'm so glad you could make it."

"Well, at the very least we had to deliver your order," Jo said.

"Jo, you should know that you're always welcome to my little parties. And you should join us for lunch the next time we have everyone together. Have you been practicing your weaving?"

"Not with any kind of skill, I assure you."

"You were always too modest, dear, but that's what we're here for. I've walked Lisa through the basics. I'd be happy to help you too, though I think that Carie would be a suitable tutor."

Dottie took Jo's arm and led her over to the canvas tent that housed the catering and the bar. Lisa and Carie tagged along behind, balancing the pastry boxes in their arms.

Lisa couldn't help the gasp that escaped as she stepped into the tent. Dottie had gone all out on the decorations. A chandelier hung from the apex of the tent's roof. Fairy lights were draped from the light fixture to the corners of the tent. A handful of tallboy tables were deliberately placed about the space with linen tablecloths and towering centerpieces of pine boughs and poinsettias There were no waiters behind the bar, but Lisa could see a wine bottle uncork itself and generously fill a wine glass for Evelyn, who waited patiently for her drink.

Carie placed her boxes down then took the ones Lisa was holding. She arranged the pastries on the provided cake stands. She stacked them just how Jo did in the bakery. The attention to detail made Lisa smile. Dottie still had Jo companionably by the arm as she listed the litany of reasons why Jo should consider joining the Witches of Door. At least half of them included some variation of getting to spend more time with Carie, which had her aunt blushing furiously. It turned out the witches were very invested in their freelancer's and caterer's love lives. Lisa wasn't the only one listening in. Though she was trying to hide it, Carie was very clearly straining to hear the conversation.

"I'm glad you asked her to come," Lisa said. "She really doesn't get out of the house enough."

Carie hummed. "She's always been a bit of a home body. At least, she was when I was around."

Lisa tilted her head and tapped her finger against her pursed lips. "Wonder why that was?"

"Shut up."

"You know," Lisa continued with a shit-eating grin. "You could see what she's like over the summer."

"That's a bit complicated."

"But it really doesn't have to be."

"Lisa..."

"I'm not saying you have to stay glued to her side the whole summer. You work, she gets that. I'm pretty sure there's an airport down in Green Bay. You could get where you need to go."

Pressing her lips together in a tense line, Carie shot Lisa a biting look.

"There's ways to make this work, is all I'm saying."

"Carie, dear!"

They both turned to see Dottie dragging a very red Jo in her wake.

"I've told Josephine that she's welcome at any of our events, but I wanted to reiterate that with you. Now, we have plenty of food and drink to keep everyone warm and full for the evening. There's chairs set up around the fire, and I have blankets in a basket just outside of the tent should you get cold. We'll weave the ritual of protection once we're a little deeper into the evening. Not too late though. Archie has one too many snifters of brandy and the whole thing will be too sloppy to hold. Please, enjoy yourselves!"

Dottie gave Jo one last squeeze before darting off towards the other guests slowly trickling in. Carie offered an apologetic look. Jo waved it off.

"I've been filling orders for Dottie for years, dear," Jo said. "I know just how enthusiastic she can be."

"Still...I feel like I should have asked her to tone it down a bit."

"That would have just pushed her further. She's excited to have something other than her hiking and my baking to chat about. And honestly, I wouldn't mind a little social interaction, even if it isn't your average bridge club."

"Since when do you know how to play bridge?"

Jo batted at Carie's arm. "Better than you know how to play rummy."

"You play the wrong way."

"Hardly my fault you learned the wrong rules."

"Easy to call the rules wrong when you always lose playing that way."

Jo laughed loudly, her eyes twinkling.

Lisa let them walk ahead of her, watching with a hopeless smile. Since she'd been staying with Jo, Lisa wouldn't help but see her aunt's life as a possible future. She wondered what her aunt might have become if she had someone to welcome her to a new life with open arms. Without the support system her aunt provided, Lisa was positive that she would have tried to go back to her parents with her tail tucked between her legs. She would have tried to cram herself into the template that they had ready for her, and she would be diminished. That path would have ended in a lingering unhappiness. Her aunt had clearly had that choice, and she picked loneliness instead of unhappiness.

Things between Jo and Carie were clearly better, but there was still a rift between them that neither sought to cross. Carie had provided a bit of insight that night at Dan's, and Jo was just terrified of being denied again. Lisa didn't know what Carie would say if Jo asked her again to stay. Now that Lisa had a glimpse into the life that they could have if they chose each other, she didn't understand why they didn't see it as worth the risk.

Lisa wandered away from the fire and tried to spot the lighthouse across the harbor. Dottie had pointed it out the last time Lisa had been at the house and Carie had run through the locations of each of the knots on one of their first drives together. The Old Baileys Harbor Bird Cage lighthouse was one she wanted to visit without the threat of possessed fauna attacking. It was a bit too dark now to be able to see it, but on a clear sunny day, she wondered if it was visible among the trees.

"Never took you for much of a brooder."

Kat sidled up and hip checked Lisa from her thoughts. Dan stopped on her other side, drink in one hand and hand pie in the other.

"I think it's hard not to when faced with such a scenic vista," Lisa said. She crossed her arms and straightened her spine, affecting her best brooding posture. Her giggling ruined the entire effect.

"You really need to go check out the drinks, Lisa," Dan said. "Ms. Cambridge has an invisible butler back there or something. You just order a drink like normal, and the bottles just all come together and make it perfectly."

"I've told Dottie a thousand times that she's the luckiest witch in existence," Kate said. "She's a lady who lunches who's weaving manifests in ways that make her the perfect host."

"Did your parents end up coming, Kat?"

"Sure did!"

Kat pointed across the yard to the far side of the bonfire. A man and a woman were bundled in huge coats. They clutched large mugs of steaming hot chocolate while chatting with Dottie.

"They just take this all in stride?" Lisa asked.

"Dad seems to think that mom has a bit of ability. He said he's never seen anyone program a macro faster in Excel than mom can, but I think he's just trying to be supportive."

Ignoring the ping of jealousy in her chest, Lisa reminded herself that she was carving a little family up here for herself. There were people who supported her, and if her own parents didn't want to be a part of her life, that was their own affair.

"Alright, Lisa?"

She shook herself from her thoughts and found both Kat and Dan staring at her. She tossed her head, raked her gloved hands over her face, and reminded herself how lucky she was to have found these two.

"Yeah. Let's go check out that bartender. Help me come up with a complicated drink order. I want to see just how refined Dottie's weaving is."

Dottie's spell work was impressive as always. Lisa and Dan had pulled out their phones to search for the most elaborate and complicated cocktails. Nothing phased the spell, but the sheer number of drinks they ordered began to show in their rosy cheeks and incessant laughing. Kat had driven Dan, so she stayed sober for the evening. She made her own fun by positing increasingly ridiculous questions and then stepping back as they argued. Lisa planned to ask Carie for a sobering spell before they started the ritual, though every time she looked for the witch, she found Carie sitting increasingly closer to her aunt. If she didn't know any better, she would swear that they were cuddled on one of the benches near the fire, tucked under a blanket and talking quietly.

"I want you both to know it's taking all of me not to shout something at them right now," Lisa declared in the loudest whisper ever.

Kat looked over her shoulder. "They're adorable, and they'll get there on their own. Us shouting at them won't help matters at all."

Dan swayed as Lisa leaned against his shoulder. She felt tears bite at her eyes.

"They've both done so much to make me happy up here. I just want that for them."

Kat's attention snapped to Lisa when she heard the wobble in her voice.

"None of that," Kat said as she wiped the errant tear that escaped down Lisa's cheek. "You two keep each other propped up. Dottie's been shooting us those disappointed-at-the-holiday-dinner grandma looks for the better part of an hour. I'll go grab Carie and see if she can't sober you the easy way so you can help with the ritual."

"You guys have too, you know," Lisa said. "I didn't really have my people before coming here. Getting to nerd out with people who get it...I never got to do that back home."

"That isn't home," Dan muttered.

"What do you mean?"

"This is home now. Here. With Jo and Carie and whatever the hell they are. With the campaign. It's here. Not with your parents. You're ours now. And we're yours. And we're very very drunk, but that doesn't matter."

Lisa let herself lean heavier on Dan's shoulder. She twisted to try and kiss his cheek, but she missed and ended up planting one on his eye. He laughed and pulled her in tight to his side.

"You belong to Wisconsin now."

"That's not a weird thing to say at all."

"We're weird. Don't act like you aren't into it."

"Not sure that I want to know what you two are rambling about," Carie said as she approached.

"Just sharing friendly sweet nothings," Lisa smiled.

"Kat asked me to sober you two up a bit so that Dottie doesn't ban you from the society."

"I won't be in the circle, but I'll drive you literally wherever you want to go when I'm sober if you could help me out too, Ms. Carie."

"I had no intention of leaving you out, Dan."

Carie grabbed two bottles of water from the drink table and poured them out into cups for her patients. She pinched her fingers, drawing on the powerful threads from the nearby knot, and wove her spell.

"You'll still have the dry mouth and a bit of a headache, but just have some more water after drinking this, sit for a bit, and you should be good to go when Dottie needs us."

Lisa felt like a towel being wrung out. She shot off Dan's shoulder, coughing madly. An ice pick of pain pinged right behind her left eye. She moaned and pressed her face into her hands.

"I told you it wouldn't be pleasant," Carie said, a bit smugger than Lisa thought was warranted.

"Think I'll just stay drunk, thanks," Dan said. "Gonna go grab some water."

"Grab me one too, please?"

Carie patted Lisa's shoulder. "Take a minute. I'm sure Dottie can wait a few..."

Lisa looked up from her hands as Carie trailed off. "What's wrong?"

"Look there," Carie pointed across the harbor. "Is that just the light from the bonfire?"

Peering over the water, Lisa tried to follow the angle of Carie's finger. For a moment, she stared and was about to say that she didn't see anything, but then there was a flash of something. It was tinted bluish-green rather than the reds and oranges from the fire.

"I don't know what it is, but there's definitely something."

"Shit."

Carie patted Lisa's shoulder again before running back to Jo. She pulled her off the bench and rushed her close to the bonfire.

"Dottie," Lisa called for the hostess as she jogged over to the water's edge.

"I see it too," Dottie shouted. "Ladies! Archie! We need to get this going now!"

The authoritative tone in Dottie's voice brought the festivities to a halt. Kat pulled her parents from the food tent back to the circle, while Dan stumbled back over with several bottles of water balanced in his arms.

"Can they stay in the circle?" Carie asked. "Or would they be safer in the house?"

"I have no idea what that is or if it's coming this way," Dottie said. "I'll defer to your judgment."

Carie clearly didn't want to be the one responsible for the decision. She looked between the house and Jo and back again before stepping close to Jo.

"I need you to stay close to Dottie," Carie whispered fiercely. "Stay in the ward, but if it breaks, I want you to take Dan and Kat's parents into the house. Dottie and the ladies will keep you safe, okay?"

"Where are you going?"

"I need to see what's going on over there."

Jo shook her head. "Why? Why can't you just stay here? It might not be anything."

"But it might be something. And I don't want anything happening to a knot this close."

"Please don't go alone."

"Kat can come with me. Lisa will stay here with you."

Jo nodded, but she clung to the sleeves of Carie's sweater.

"I'll be okay, Josie. I deal with this kind of thing all the time."

"Just be safe," Jo said with a quirk of her lip. "I bought so much food for Christmas."

Carie huffed a laugh. "And I wouldn't want to miss out on your cooking." She pulled away, but not far enough to break contact. "Dottie, do you have a boat I can use to get over there?"

"It's December, dear. The boats are in storage for the winter."

"Shit," Carie swore. "That's fine. We'll take the long way around."

Lisa trotted back up. She'd heard the entire exchange. "When are we going?"

"You're staying here."

"Absolutely not. You need me with you."

Carie shot Lisa a warning look. "I need you here."

"Kat can stay and help with the circle. I'm coming with you and that's that."

"She can help you, dear," Jo added. "Let her go with. You two can keep each other safe."

Grinding her teeth, Carie bobbed her head once. "Let's get in the car then. Dottie, as soon as we're clear, start the ward. Hopefully its nothing, but I doubt it."

"We'll hold down the fort here," Dottie agreed. "A circle around the fire, people! That's the only invitation you all are going to get!"

✳

Jo had to consciously pry her fingers from Carie's sweater as she stepped away with Lisa. Something felt off the second Carie stepped away, but Jo couldn't find a way to vocalize it. A large hand clasped around her heart and was slowly tugging. She could feel the muscles in her chest tense. She barely registered

Dottie clapping her hands and gathering everyone around the bonfire. She picked up bits of panicked conversation from the witched. She could only stare at the intensifying glow from the lighthouse. Some distant part of her mind thought she should warn someone, but her mouth seemed glued shut.

Around her, the witches joined hands. Jo wanted to help, but her attention remained fixed across the water. No one tried to include her, so she remained inside the ring, useless. They had all taken their gloves off to better channel the power from the threads. There had been grumbling, but Dottie insisted.

"Let our combined skills weave together a blanket of protection," Dottie called out in a strong voice. It boomed over the snapping fire. "We offer up each bit of ourselves to shield our families and neighbors from the hidden entities that haunt the woods. This is just like any other year. Ignore the distractions."

Jo tried to focus on Dottie's familiar voice, but her ears roared with the sound of the fire. The heat of it blazed at her back. She could feel sweat beading under her layers. It was all becoming too much to bear. She squeezed her eyes shut, trying to pull herself back to some base line of normalcy. When she opened them, the sky had gone white. She was no longer at the harbor. She was at the bay.

She blinked again, and Dottie was back before her.

Another blink, and she was standing just at the water's edge in the contrasted world. The hand in her chest pulled, and she nearly stumbled forward into the water. A hand grabbed her wrist, jerking her back to reality. She shook her head and turned to see Dan swaying beside her. Jo couldn't tell if he grabbed her to steady himself or to stop her from bolting. Either way, he looked terrified. Jo could feel the tug of magic in the air and in her chest. The circle around them was chanting together, and a shimmering ball of twisting magical protection grew above the fire. It spun and expanded, like a mound of clay on a potter's wheel. The sides grew long enough that they hit the ground enclosing the circle in the dome. The apex continued to supply the magic, and the shield continued to cascade over the land, pouring out in all directions.

Jo tugged Dan closer with a crippling grip on his hand. He stumbled a bit and tipped against Jo's shoulder. She leaned into him, willing him to keep her grounded. The tug in her chest pulled again. She felt like a pie being portioned into slices. Each piece pulled away was agony.

"Something's very wrong," she managed to whisper.

No one heard her.

The magic passed like oil over the harbor, crashing like the tides over the islands on the far side. Jo's vision of the world was starkly contrasted. The sky was so white it burned her eyes. The aqua glow from the lighthouse turned to a sickly mucus green. It called to the power generated from the circle. The magic spun into a vortex around the lighthouse until it touched the green light.

Jo opened her mouth to shout a warming, but the explosion from across the water drowned out anything that she hoped to say. The force of the blast reverberated off the shield, but the magic held.

"It's feeding it!" Kat broke the circle and flipped Dottie to look across the water. The protection spell had been completed, so the shield held despite the break.

"It's not just feeding." Dottie grabbed at her chest and held onto Kat to keep from keeling over. "It's drawing from the threads. It's...it's trying to unwind the knot at the lighthouse."

Jo could feel the pull. Her heart lurched again, every muscle tensed against the insistent pressure. It forced her forward as her vision swam. The landscape swirled into a kaleidoscope of nonsense, but eventually reformed into Kat's familiar face.

"Jo...Jo are you alright?"

"Something's wrong."

"That's quite the understatement."

Jo couldn't articulate it. She tried to jerk away, but Kat kept a tourniquet grip on her arms. The bonfire burned brighter, throwing the shadows among the trees into sharp relief. They danced as they had been in the corners of her mind since the spring.

Interesting that their ritual should affect you so.

Like an old friend calling after months of phone tag, the voice was familiar now. Too familiar. It had been speaking even when she wasn't listening. Drawing her forward to an unknown fate.

Not completely unknown. Haven't you been seeing it? I'm sure that you've been there before. It's tucked out of the way. Quiet. A lovely place for some introspection. Lonely. Isolated. We can have all the time in world to ourselves. Unwind for a while.

"Jo, if something happens to you, both Lisa and Carie are going to take turns killing me," Kat all but shouted. Her voice was tight with panic. "Can you focus on me?"

Jo resisted the pull. She twisted and felt it loosen for a moment only for the pressure to return even stronger. She gasped and stumbled into Kat.

"Jo?!"

"I'm here. I'm okay. It's...it's just a lot..."

"She's only just discovered her weaving, Kat," Dottie moved next to them and placed a cool hand on Jo's cheek. "Whatever is happening over there is taking a toll on us all."

"How can it still be drawing from the circle if we broke it?" Kat asked. She never took her eyes off Jo's pallid face.

"I don't know if it has something to do with the knot being nearby or because there's a concentration of weavers here, but it's never happened before."

It has. They may not have been paying attention. Creation is always painful.

"Yes, it has..." Jo echoed.

The voice was so familiar. A purr. A whisper of smoke.

They're not ready. Neither is your pet witch. But you will be, Josie. I'll make sure of it.

"NO!"

Kat blanched and fell back into Dottie as Jo violently ripped her arms free. Jo whipped around, looking for the source of the voice, but the roar of the fire and the manic dancing of the shadows became too much. The sky flashed white, and the waves lapped at her ankles in the unknown bay, and the world inverted.

The snow crunched below her as she collapsed. Kat's frantic calling of her name faded into darkness as her eyes drifted shut.

Chapter Thirteen

"I'm pretty sure the speed limit is like twenty-five here," Lisa said as she leaned over into Carie's space. The speedometer was pushing passed sixty-five when a sharp curve sent her crashing back into her seat.

"We need to get over there. Anything fucking around by the knot is there for only one reason, and I'm not too keen on letting it be unraveled that close to all those people."

Lisa helpfully kept her mouth shut instead of noting that Carie really only meant Jo. Instead she asked, "What are we heading into?"

"It's either a possession on par with what we saw at Eagle Bluff, or something's trying to punch through."

"Punch through sounds ominous."

"You remember Aldred? Easily dealt with and contained, but they aren't from here."

"Wisconsin?"

"This plane of existence. Something could be trying to use the knot to tear the fabric between dimensions. We can't let that happen. One thing coming through is hard enough to deal with, but the tear could let all kinds of other things through."

Carie slowed the car down as they approached the end of the road. The sky was glowing with a new aurora, and the cage at the top of the lighthouse was the epicenter.

"Aldred managed to cram through some minuscule hole over the course of years. Most entities are fine with their lot where they came from. Forcing their way through a tear isn't appealing, but sometimes they feel it's the only option. I'm worried this is something larger."

"I'm starting to get why you guys try to keep this all to yourselves."

"What, you think the general public wouldn't be in a constant state of panic over the notion that not only are there other dimensions out there, but some of them are definitely filled with beings that could wipe out this universe with a thought? Let them think the witches are a glorified bridge club that can light a cigarette with a flick of a finger. Easier for everyone."

"I'm never going to be able to sleep again."

Carie flashed a grin. "Yes, you will. You're tough. And you can stop it from happening."

She pulled the car to the side of the road. Not bothering to turn it off, she flung open the door and started running for the source of the aurora. Lisa struggled with her seatbelt before following. She immediately wished she had thrown on a few more layers. The bonfire and booze had tricked her into thinking it was warmer out than it actually was. She quietly followed in Carie's footsteps through the beach front property. The small house on the beach appeared to be empty, but Lisa didn't want to tempt fate. She had no desire to meet finally meet one of the Door County police when she was trespassing on private land.

She was contemplating a warming ward when she ran right into Carie, who had stopped at the edge of the water. The lighthouse was on an island. The ice wasn't thick enough to walk on, and Lisa wasn't keen on falling in the water.

"Something tells me they won't have any boats over here either."

"You stay here then," Carie looked down at the water with a shiver. "I'll go over and check it out."

"How the hell am I supposed to help from here?"

"We've practiced at a distance."

"But I can barely see the lighthouse from here."

"Then I guess you're coming over with me."

Lisa opened her mouth to retort, but the sound caught in her throat as movement drew her eye. Dottie's circle had completed their casting, and a wave of protective magic was washing towards them.

"Let's go. Looks like they've got the ritual started. Run fast and try to follow my exact path. If you do fall in, I'll get you. We have that warming ward that Archie showed you. We'll be okay."

They both ran out onto the ice. Lisa winced as it cracked as soon as Carie's boot hit it. On instinct, Lisa pulled on the threads and wove a spell to strengthen the ice. Carie's next step was on solid ice, and she was able to dash across to safety. Lisa was right behind her. She felt a rush of excitement that they had made it, but that was quickly quelled when the lighthouse came into view.

The building had clearly been abandoned for years. The foliage had reclaimed most of it with vines and leaves curling up the rough stone of the lighthouse. At the top of the stone column, inside the metal cage that once housed the light, a swelling circle of miasma was asserting itself. Lisa squinted, trying to make out details, but the being defied definition.

"There's something up there," Lisa said.

Carie looked up and grit her teeth.

"It's an entity," Carie shouted. "But it's been here for a while. Get a defensive ward up. I'm going to draw it down."

Lisa nodded as Carie clapped her hands together. It was loud as a crash of thunder. It certainly grabbed the attention of the being trying to siphon power from the knot. Carie screamed as she drew her hands apart. They shook and quaked as she formed two crackling spears of white lightening. She hurled one up at the creature. The beast leered over the top of the building, shrieking as the spear crashed into it. It flared itself out, giving the impression of a vast wingspan, as the magic from the witches' circle crashed into the lighthouse back. The energy was pulled up the walls, swirling around the building like water down a drain. The creature screamed again drawing the magic into itself. Its howl was powerful and strong, until it became pained. The magic was overwhelming the beast.

"It's too much!"

Carie came charging towards Lisa, pulling her spear apart and reweaving it as a ward protecting her from above.

"GET DOWN!"

The beast swelled with the magic it was inhaling, and in the instant before it exploded, Lisa could see the cracks forming in the lighthouse. She remembered the map over Dottie's fireplace. She remembered the knots. She could feel it unraveling and the threads going loose around her. She closed her eyes just as the stone foundations shattered and the beast exploded.

Lisa's ward held--which she took great pride in-- but the backlash knocked her to her knees. Carie crossed the threshold just in time to shove Lisa to the ground. Heavy debris hit the ward. Each impact was like a punch to Lisa's chest. She could feel Carie entangling their wards, strengthening them and easing the strain.

"You okay?" Carie rolled off Lisa and pushed herself to her knees.

Lisa took a quick inventory of her body, wiggling her fingers and toes, before she sat up.

"I think so," she answered. "What the hell was that?"

"That's what happens when something that isn't very smart starts munching on a knot."

"I... I think I can still feel it. It wasn't destroyed?"

Carie nodded. "You'd know if it was. It's still intact. Dottie's warding ritual made sure of that."

"But the lighthouse..."

The structure had sunk into the ground, and a deep crack had shot up the side. The cage that sat atop the lighthouse looked as if the creature had ripped its way out. It was twisted and cracked. Despite the damage, Lisa could still feel the knot at the end of the threads she tested. She pulled harder and could feel the witches on the other side of the bay still distantly connected.

"I might need some help, but since it wasn't destroyed, I should be able to fix this. Are you up to weave? That was a lot back there."

"Yeah. Will it take long? I want to get back and make sure everyone is okay."

"Shouldn't take longer than a few minutes to patch the crack and fix the cage. I'll need to shore up the wards too, but I've been meaning to show you how to do that anyway."

Before they started, Lisa sent off a quick text to her aunt, making sure that everyone on their end was alright. She stuffed her phone into the deep pocket of her outer most layer and followed along as Carie walked her through the repair and then the protective ward.

The building did not appreciate being jostled a second time but eased under the magic as if it could sense their intention to help. Lisa had no experience in architecture, but Carie did her best to guide her.

"Don't think about it too literally. This isn't about logic. You want to support the building. Doesn't matter how. Just lift it and let it make its repairs."

Carie made weaving seem natural. Magic was just an extension of the self. There was no strain, no exertion. And unlike the other witches, she seemed to be able to do almost anything with her magic. Lisa could feel her among the threads, plucking them like an experienced harpist. Lisa wondered how she felt to Carie. Like a child failing at embroidery. A novice struggling with a loom. She could feel her magic weaken as her mind wandered. Lisa shook the doubts from her mind and trusted the stone to knit itself back together as Carie instructed.

The light faded, and Carie let out a breath.

"Alright, now the hard part."

Lisa rolled her shoulders and nodded.

"This is just the same as any normal ward you would summon, you're just going to set it around something else. Draw more than you typically would. We want this strong and lasting. I'm going to do the same, and then we'll start the ritual."

"I haven't done a ritual yet."

"It's not difficult," Carie said. "We can feel each other on the threads, right? Just follow my lead. The lighthouse is just the marker. If it's contained too, great, but we definitely want the protection focused around the knot. Ready?"

"As I'll ever be."

"Let's get started."

The ritual wasn't too different from the repair. The ward that Carie had placed before was still there, but it was shattered. She felt Carie as the glue between the cracks, adhering the shards back together. Carie pressed back, giving Lisa confidence. She pulled more from the threads. She didn't hold the magic close but let it flow freely through her. She channeled it into the fixed ward, forcing the barrier stronger and thicker. She pictured a meteorite bouncing off it and into the bay. She imagined a missile detonating harmlessly against it. Nothing of this earth or any other world would get through.

Carie was still there, winding between Lisa's ethereal cinder blocks. She let Lisa steer the ritual, giving her the space to build and to create. Lisa felt Carie's encouragement through the threads. It bolstered her resolve, and she placed the last protections. With a flourish, she sealed the last crack and fixed the ward.

"That's much sturdier than when I do it on my own," Carie said.

"I can feel it. I don't mean to brag, but I don't think anything will be able to get through that for a while."

"Nicely done," Carie smiled. "You can tell Dottie that you led your first ritual."

"I don't think this was the first," Lisa said.

Carie cocked an eyebrow.

"That night," Lisa started. "When we brought you back to Auntie Jo's house, she asked me to help heal you. She didn't know yet. About her magic. I haven't really thought about it, but I suppose she must have unknowingly helped."

The corner of Carie's mouth twitched upward as her eyes went a bit wobbly. "Second one, then."

"Can we do this with the others?" Lisa asked after a moment.

"Absolutely," Carie answered. "Before the holiday, we'll swing around the peninsula and shore up the rest of them. This is strong enough to hopefully hold until the new year."

"Really?"

"Definitely. You'll know if it's breached. It'll feel like a door slamming in a different room in your house. Like a vibration."

"I'll keep that in mind," Lisa said, shivering as the wind began to pick up over the water. "I'll drive back."

"I've got it."

"We're in no rush, and I'm not trying to wreck our only car that has a habitable back seat."

Chapter Fourteen

T he bonfire was burning low when Lisa pulled back onto Dottie's property. Half of the cars were gone, and a few of the witches were meandering on the front yard. Lisa could feel Carie's hackles rise as they parked.

"They must have called it after they saw the explosion," Lisa offered by way of an explanation. "Most of them are pretty old. That spell must have taken a lot out of them."

"Maybe," Carie said. She didn't wait for Lisa to turn off the car. She was jogging towards the house before Lisa could even get it in park.

Lisa didn't bother locking the car. She pulled off her top layer and flung it in the back seat. It stunk of lake scum and broken wards. She wanted nothing more than to grab a boozy hot chocolate and sink into a hot bath. Though the smell of nicotine lured her away from her path to the house. Evelyn and Archie were passing a slim cigarette back and forth, tittering quietly over the night's events.

"Everyone okay?" Lisa asked as she approached.

Archie blew a smoke ring to Evelyn's delight. He smirked.

"I've been trying to get that right all night," he said. "But yes, my girl. Your aunt had a bit of a fainting spell, but Dottie seems to think that she was just overwhelmed by the sheer force of magic that we were weaving."

Evelyn took the cigarette from Archie's slim, knobby fingers. "It's really never been like that before. We've never been able to draw that much from the threads, even that close to one of the knots."

"Could have been that thing that was on the lighthouse."

"Carie said it was one of those entities that--"

"Oh," Archie interrupted with an elegant wave of this hand. "We don't deal in particulars, dear. I'm just up here to enjoy the quiet and lend a hand where I'm able. My weaving isn't anything special. I use it keep my tea forever warm and my bed cozy. I like the camaraderie, and your aunt's pastries are divine. Dottie asks me to help with a spell, I'll help, but I do not want to hear about whatever is actually going bump in the night. I'm up in my years, but I do still need my beauty rest."

"Better we don't know, really," Evelyn added. "We're all terrible at running our mouths, and we wouldn't want to say anything to the wrong person. Folks up here know that there's the odd happening, but if they were looking out for them, they might get hurt. We don't want that on our consciences."

"Well said."

Archie took the cigarette back and finished it with one last inhale. He ashed, and then flicked it out of existence.

"Dear Dottie gets very put out when we smoke. Especially on her property."

"You should go inside and check on your aunt," Evelyn said. "We were just about to head out."

"Ralph should be here soon to pick me up. We're leaving early for the drive to Ann Arbor to see his nephew."

Lisa nodded and accepted a quick kiss on the cheek from both of them before she hurried towards the well-lit foyer of Dottie's home. The door was open, and a few of the ladies were lingering by the stairs. Dan was perched on a stool in the kitchen. He was draped over the countertop with his head braced on his folded arms. Kat was beside him, absentmindedly rubbing a hand over his back while chatting with her shell-shocked parents. Lisa caught her eye as she entered the room, and Kat pointed to the ceiling. Lisa nodded gratefully and doubled back to the stairs. She took them two at a time and once she got to the second floor, she followed the quiet voices down the hall.

A door swung open, and Dottie stepped out. Her normally regal demeanor was diminished. Her hair was askew, and her shoulders were slumped. She rubbed a hand over her exhausted face before she noticed Lisa approaching.

"Oh, thank goodness," she gasped. She pulled Lisa into a tight hug. "Carie just rushed inside with barely a word and only eyes for your aunt."

It took all of Lisa not to completely sink into Dottie's hug. The other woman was clearly ready for a lie down, and Lisa didn't want to burden her.

"Is Jo okay?"

"Seems to be. She was a bit rattled after she fainted, but Kat managed to keep her head from hitting the ground."

"Carie's in there now?"

"Whispering sweet nothings into her ear, no doubt."

"We shouldn't hold our breaths for that."

Dottie pulled away and rubbed Lisa's arms. "Old hurts are the hardest to heal. This isn't just all about them. They'll get there. Give them time."

"You should go sit down. Being the anchor of a spell like that must be taxing."

Dottie flashed a smile and smoothed back her hair. She pulled herself together and stood at her full height.

"I still have guests in the house, dear, but as soon as I send them on their way, I'll make myself a cup of tea and have a sit. I have a feeling you all will probably be spending the night. We'll get you sorted with towels and all that in the morning. For now, check in on your aunt, and then find a room. The beds are all done up."

Lisa felt her chest warm with gratitude as Dottie gave her arm once last squeeze before heading downstairs to bid her guests good night. She leaned against the wall as she watched Dottie disappear. She needed just a minute to gather herself. Part of her wanted to just slide down the wall and curl up on the floor. She'd never pulled that much from the threads before, and now that she'd stopped moving, she had never felt so drained.

The door opened again, and Carie poked her head out.

"You look about ready to keel over," she observed. "Your aunt's asking after you."

Barely nodding, Lisa shuffled into the room.

A generous king bed anchored the room between two large windows. The overhead fan spun lazily, more for the white noise than anything else. Jo was under the comforter and propped up on every pillow that Carie could find. She still looked a bit dazed, but her expression pulled into a relieved smile when Lisa walked in.

"I'm glad you're alright."

Lisa forced herself to the bed and collapsed next to her aunt. She felt fingers running through her hair. Squirming close as she could, Lisa plastered herself against Jo and gave in to the welcome warmth of sleep.

***

Falling unconscious had protected Jo from strange voices and the bay. She fought to stay under, but the smoky tendrils of the voice refused to leave her in peace. It sounded like Aldred, humming in her ear, drawing her back to consciousness. Carie said they were harmless. Jo wasn't so sure.

Her interactions with the entity were colored with malice and hunger. Jo had no idea why. She was a novice at weaving. She didn't have the ability that Carie and Lisa had. Why she had attracted Aldred's attention was a mystery. Were they warning her, or did they see her as an easy target?

Another possibility had hit her like a punch in the stomach. She could be sick. This could all be caused by a brain tumor. The voice could just be the restriction of blood flow in her brain. Healthcare wasn't something discussed when she was still living at home, so there could be a history she wasn't aware of.

That was becoming a common theme in her life.

Hovering in twilight, Jo wondered why she wasn't worth a history. If she'd known she was magic, she could have done so much more to help. She could guide Lisa, contribute with the witches, and been more than a burden for Carie.

She hoped Lisa would keep to her own path. Her niece was positioned for happiness, fulfillment, and friendship. Jo would do anything to help her achieve them all.

When she finally woke, Jo felt Carie's familiar presence and the weight of her niece leaning against her in the bed.

"I think you might be running her a bit ragged," Jo sighed. She felt her niece go boneless beside her. Not a moment later, her breathing evened out and Lisa was asleep.

"I know," Carie said apologetically. "Her weaving is powerful, Josie. Her wards are even stronger than mine."

"She's not used to all this."

"We all deserve a little bit of a rest for the holidays. We'll take a drive tomorrow to the lighthouses and fortify the wards."

"You might need a boat for that too. Aren't there a few up north that are on isolated islands?"

"Let me worry about that. I'll keep an eye on Lisa too. If she's overexerting herself, we'll come home for a rest and then finish before Christmas Eve."

Jo's eyes fluttered shut. She concentrated on the feel of Lisa's hair under her fingers.

"You need to be careful too," Jo whispered.

"I'm fine," Carie assured her. "Always am."

"That's not true."

Jo groped for Carie's hand, threading their fingers together when she found it. She could feel herself dropping back to sleep, and her tongue wasn't as guarded as it should have been.

"I often dream of you in the summer," Jo murmured. "You're sitting on the dunes near the water. It's peaceful. You're quiet. Introspective. You're safe. You're at peace. And you're with me."

She felt a gentle pressure against her fingers, and then the fleeting brush of soft lips against her forehead. She slipped away before she could say anything more.

Her dreams that night mirrored that little summer fantasy exactly. Carie reclined on a gingham picnic blanket. Her skin was pink from too much sun. Her eyes were closed, and she didn't see the water swiftly retreating from the beach. The sky bled down into the water until the horizon was a thick line of dripping blue. The water churned out further, leaving fish flopping on the ever-expanding beach. It was gathering in a massive wave on the horizon.

Jo tried to move forward, but tight arms held her back. She could feel the hand back in her chest, surrounding her heart, testing the tensile strength of every vein and artery.

Let her relax, Josie. She already does so much for everyone.

"But--"

She has enough to concern herself without fussing over you.

Of course, she knew that was true, but if she didn't warn her, Carie would be swept away by the wave. If Jo could get there, they could run from it together.

I know that you care for her. Deeply. People need her. You know this. Let her lay in the sun for a bit, eh?

Jo stopped fighting against the arms. She slumped, letting the hold on her heart keep her on her feet. Hot breath whispered in her ear, soothing and loving.

There we are. Stop pulling yourself if so many directions. I've got you.

Jo hovered there for a bit, between sleeping and waking. She could feel Carie close, resting in the bed, but Jo kept herself from rolling into her warmth. She could keep herself comfortable. She couldn't depend on others to help her. It would hurt more when they left.

It wasn't just about Carie anymore either. Lisa needed a strong support system. She needed a marble pillar, not a wet cardboard box. Lisa would be amazing. Jo wanted to give her everything she had lost.

Jo's mind wandered from Carie and Lisa. She conjured an image of the grad student that she had crashed into after hours at the library years ago when Jo was in college. It had been so long that Jo could barely remember what she looked like. The memory was painted in broad strokes. Short, dark hair. Piercing eyes. A wickedly funny smile. Jo felt her heart jolt in her chest again, just as it had when they sat at the same study table. Coupling had never been appealing before they started sharing looks over their calculus text books. It was correct. It was right.

If she hadn't thought so she never would have told her parents.

Jo hadn't looked back to the dinner she told her parents she met someone in ages. They were having a benign conversation until she mentioned it. Her mother tittered with excitement. A man would help her wayward daughter get back on track. A man meant a proposal, engagement parties, and a wedding to plan. Jo's mother spoke this language perfectly, so when Jo said a woman's name, her mother stared at her as if she had spontaneously started speaking Latin. Her father raged, shouting about how she would end the relationship and attend the next church mixer. She was in her twenties after all. She should have some prospects. Jo hadn't seen the trap for what it was. She gently declined, only to be met with fury. They told her to leave and think about what she had done. Once she was willing to contort herself to their box, she would be welcomed home.

Fifteen years later, and Jo still wondered if she spontaneously showed up with a man all would be forgiven.

Celeste hadn't been an option either. Jo didn't bother reaching out. Since Lisa arrived, Jo couldn't help but wonder what would have happened had she called her sister. Celeste already had a family. Her perfect husband and a little girl that Jo had barely known.

The last few months, Jo thanked anything that would listen that Lisa was brave enough to reach out to her. She could help Lisa thrive. She wouldn't leave her out in the cold, even if it meant that Lisa would flourish and eventually leave Jo alone again.

When she woke, Jo felt the crust of dried, salty tears in her eyelashes as she blinked open her eyes. Lisa had burrowed closer and was gently snoring into the wet spot of drool that had accumulated on the pillow. She could still feel a weight against her chest, but when she shifted, she found it was Lisa's arm wrapped around her. Rubbing the crust from her eyes, she took a deep breath to center herself. She eased off the bed, leaving Lisa to sleep. She made sure the comforter was tucked around her niece and pulled the curtains a bit tighter before she went out to the hall to find a bathroom.

The walk down the corridor was still a bit dreamy. Jo kept her fingers tracing against the wall, a physical reminder of where she was. The beach still loomed in the back of her mind. She focused on the texture of the wall. She was inside. It was winter. Carie was downstairs.

Taking the steps slowly, Jo could hear the welcome and familiar voices below.

The large foyer windows revealed a gentle snow fall. She admired the view for a moment, almost getting lost in the gentle crash of the waves, but she shook herself. She pinched her leg and forced herself to move into the kitchen. Dottie was at the stove, minding thick slices of frying bacon. She was chatting with Kat, who stood beside her with a foot braced against the cabinets and a mug of coffee in her hands. They both heard the floorboards squeak when Jo entered the room.

"How are you awake?" Kat asked, aghast.

Jo pushed the images of the water from her head, the voice telling her to let go. "I've never needed much sleep, and that bed up there is probably the best one I've ever slept on."

"My grandchildren are notoriously picky," Dottie chirped, "so only the finest for them."

"I'll be dwelling for a while on the fact that your grandchildren's vacation beds are nicer than the bed I sleep on every night."

"Whatever gets the job done," Kat said. She pressed a warm mug into Jo's hands. "You're shaking. Warm up a bit, huh?"

Jo sipped from the cup and shivered as the heat crawled through her body. She jumped a bit as a blanket draped itself over her shoulders.

"Heard Kat," Carie said. Her hands lingered a moment on Jo, making sure the blanket was tucked around her before moving over to the coffee pot to refresh her own cup. "You looked cold."

"Thank you."

Carie smirked and nodded before peeking over at the stove.

"Did Dan get home alright last night?" Jo asked between sips.

"We dragged him upstairs once we were sure he wasn't going to puke all over Dottie's fancy furniture. He'll be asleep for another six hours," Kat said. "I let his parents know he'd be crashing with me, so they wouldn't worry."

"And your parents?"

Kat let out a strangled laugh. "After I assured them that there is no safer place than Dottie's house, I had them take the car back home. This is a little too much weirdness for them, and I don't need them worrying every time I come up for a visit."

"We might need to rethink you and Dan coming out on patrols, then," Carie said. "If you both had come last night, I don't know that Lisa and I would have been able to protect you."

Kat rolled her eyes and lit a fire at the tip of her finger. She plunged it into her coffee to warm it up. "We've talked about this already. We know it's dangerous, but this is our home too. We're still helping, even if it's just to drive you around and help you back to the car when you inevitably get injured again. Someone's gotta make sure you get back to Jo in one piece."

Carie's face flared red as Jo became very interested in the swirl of steam from her coffee. Dottie laughed as she moved the cooked bacon from her cast iron pan. She immediately replaced it with four more slices.

"Sit down, all of you. The frittata will be out shortly, and this bacon is up for grabs. Kat, be a dear and pull down some plates and check the biscuits. They should be just about done too."

Jo took her coffee and plopped into one of the stools around the island. She grabbed a piece of bacon and ate it as quickly as polite company allowed. Carie sat beside her, and Jo felt herself leaning into her instinctively. Carie tensed at first, but soon relaxed and draped an arm over the back of Jo's chair. She shifted closer, all but whispering in Jo's ear.

"Are you sure you're okay? You look a bit shaken."

Jo nodded. She was pleased to see Carie filling her peripheral vision, instead of the shadows that had haunted her these many months. She knocked her head against Carie's. Her skin sang with the contact.

"I'm fine. I don't want you and Lisa to push too hard, but the idea of a quiet winter's rest over the holidays sounds lovely."

"Then we'll do everything we can to make that happen, Josie."

Bumping her head again, Jo pulled back with shining eyes. She wondered if she would ever be brave enough to kiss Carie again. If they had woken up in their home this morning, would she have done it? Sharing coffee and leaning into each other at the breakfast table would have been the perfect domestic scene to top off with a show of their affections. But if Jo couldn't do it in private company, how could she ever do it among people?

Jo tipped her head just so. Kat was busy with the dishes, Dottie with the bacon. She felt lips at her temple, pressing a promise to her skin. She snapped her full attention to Carie, who looked at her with deep affection. Jo wished it was love. The moment was there and gone. Kat dropped the plates along with a basket of steaming hot biscuits and started rambling about how Dottie had finally started sharing some of her recipes. Carie had pulled away but left her arm behind Jo's chair. It was a comforting pressure, and Jo leaned into it. She would steal glances at Carie as they discussed anything but magic over a delicious leek and onion frittata. She wanted this domesticity. She wanted to look forward to this every day of her life.

She wanted to ask for it, but Jo wondered if she was ready to take that leap again. She had been so sure last time she asked. She sighed, trying to relax into the moment, but then the fist closed around her heart again. The voice tittered in her ear. She tensed, sloshing her coffee, but coughed to hide it. No one noticed but Carie.

Chapter Fifteen

Lisa suggested they make a day trip of their drive to the wards. Jo settled into the back seat. She recruited Dan to handle delivering bakery orders for the day and spent the day observing Carie guide her niece through warding the knots.

After the last lighthouse was warded, Lisa and Carie both looked exhausted. Jo drove home as they both slept in the back seat. They settled on ordering a pizza for dinner, and then spent the evening watching the classic Muppet movies. They all crashed on the couch, confident that the wards would hold.

Jo woke early to finish off the orders for the holiday. She opened for a bit just to have something to pass the time while the others slept. Carie eventually wandered over and kept vigil over the coffee. Lisa was still asleep on the couch when they came back in the early afternoon. Carie scooped her up as if she weighed nothing and carried her back upstairs. Jo settled into the couch while she waited for her to come back. She flipped on a random cooking competition and fought to keep her eyes open. Eventually, Carie came back down and sat on the opposite end of the couch.

That just wouldn't do.

Feeling brave, Jo shuffled over, drawing her blanket around Carie. She tucked herself into Carie's side, hiding her face in Carie's neck. She had so much she wanted to say. But before they addressed any of it, Jo wanted to settle in for a winter's rest with the most important person in the world. In that quiet moment, she didn't care what was out there. Let the voices whisper and the wind blow. Carie was warm and soft beside her, and that was all that mattered. Carie seemed to feel the same. She snaked an arm around Jo and pulled her in tight before criticizing one of the competitors' decisions to try to cook a risotto in a half an hour.

Cordially declining invites from Dan's and Kat's families for Christmas Eve dinner, Jo insisted on making a gingerbread house from scratch. She set Carie loose on the pantry to scrap together every piece of candy she could find. Lisa was charged with finding a template online they could use as a guide. The dough was resting while they debated between a more complicated Victorian home or a more basic structure. Ambition won out over practicality, and Jo started another batch of dough. With a ten-hour fireplace video streaming on the television, and a playlist claiming to contain thirty years of alternative music, they set to work. Carie had vetoed Christmas music on account that it was the same five songs sang in increasingly terrible versions. Lisa for the most part respected the veto but made sure to slip in a few choice selections from Mariah Carey's classic nineties Christmas album.

After several royal icing coated hours, they were laughed out and exhausted, but the proud builders of a slowly collapsing gingerbread mansion. Jo had made them a batch of gingerbread cookies from the scraps for a nibble before they went to bed.

Carie had retired upstairs after a warm hug from Lisa and a gentle kiss on the forehead for Jo. Lisa settled into her nest of blankets on the couch while Jo went to wash her face and pick the dried icing from her hair. She turned off the water and heard the telltale sounds from the living room of someone trying to cry silently. She tossed an oversized sweater over her ratty camisole and hurried to her niece's side.

Lisa didn't notice Jo until she was sitting beside her.

"Shit," she swore. "I'm sorry. I'm fine."

"You're clearly not."

Lisa waved her hand dismissively, but then slapped it over her mouth in a vain attempt to hide a sob. She squeezed her eyes shut. "It's stupid. I shouldn't be crying,"

Jo rubbed her back. "Take it from me. It's absolutely fine that you're crying. It's hard. I know. My first Christmas up here was hard too."

Lisa shook her head. "It's not that at all. I stressed so much about calling them or texting them for Thanksgiving, but I didn't even think about it today."

Jo stilled her hand. She wasn't sure what to say.

Lisa sniffled and rubbed her sleeve under her nose. "They didn't bother to text either, but I didn't have a single thought about mom or dad. It didn't matter because I was up here having a great time."

Unsure of what to say, Jo resumed her soothing back rubs. She had been desperate for that kind of distraction her first year alone.

"I'm a terrible daughter," Lisa sobbed.

"That's absolutely not true. You're taking a break from each other. And a much needed one at that."

"How can I not think of my parents at all on the holiday?"

Jo bit her lip before responding. "Because they weren't worth thinking about?"

Lisa shot her a snotty look.

"That came out harsher than I intended," Jo said. "I just meant that--"

"They weren't," Lisa said. "I don't know if it was different when you were still around, but Christmas Eve we'd eat a bland dinner, and then sit around while grandma ranted about how the Democrats were destroying the fabric of society. Tonight was amazing. This is exactly how I've always wanted to spend the holiday, and I had to be kicked out to do it."

Her eyes welled with tears again, so Jo gently guided Lisa's head to her shoulder.

"It took me a very long time to be okay with not worrying about them anymore," Jo said. "It's a hard thing to break from your parents. But it doesn't necessarily mean it's forever. Who knows? Maybe next year you'll be doing this with them. Maybe you'll talk it all out, and it'll work out the way that it should. But if it doesn't, you are welcome here."

Jo didn't want her to say thank you again. The first few weeks Lisa stayed with her, it felt like every other phrase out of her mouth was a thank you. Jo was just happy to provide a port in the storm. She dropped her head on Lisa's and tried to fight off a wave of unexpected melancholy. She was a stop, not a destination.

And everyone moves on eventually.

"Let's get to bed, huh," Jo suggested, tamping down on her own tears. "We have a very busy day of sitting around and eating pasta ahead of us."

"I love you, Auntie Jo."

"I love you, too, hon."

Jo laid awake for hours that night, and when she finally fell asleep, she was fitful. She was back at the bay, watching a small boat row further and further into the lake while she stood on the shore. She woke before sunrise, shivering in the field behind the house. Her legs were scratched from the dead, dry plants sticking out of the fresh layer of snow. She hurried back to the house, hoping the flurries would mask her path if her house mates decided to look out the window. Quietly as she could, she snuck into the bathroom. She cleaned the worst of the cuts, trying to come up with a story to explain them away. It was winter, and she could just wear leggings and her wool socks until she healed. It wasn't like she would be getting naked for anyone in the near future. She slipped back into her bedroom and lay awake until she heard stirring on the stairs and in the kitchen.

As she watched the ceiling fan lazily spin, Jo debated mentioning her dreams and the voice to Carie. The witch wasn't stupid. She could clearly tell that something was up, but despite their renewed friendship, Carie would never pry. She would trust Jo to ask for help if she needed it. After the Yule bonfire, Dottie had surmised that her fainting spell had been a result of weaving without knowing just what she was doing. It was the simplest explanation, but it didn't account for the voice or the shadows. They all had enough on their mind, and Jo still wasn't sure that her worries were magical.

Jo half expected the voice to crack into her thoughts, but it was her own voice that cautioned against saying anything. If the voice was Aldred as Jo suspected, shouldn't that be easy to handle on her own? Carie had said they weren't a problem.

She told herself that she was being ridiculous. She could deal with this. She would call up a therapist after the holidays and see about dealing with her issues. She didn't need to burden Carie or anyone else.

Originally, Jo had said no gifts. It was more important that they were spending the day together, but Lisa had insisted. She bought Jo a new apron and potholders to replace her threadbare ones. For Carie, she had finally found a way to clean the ichor and bloodstains from the back seat of her car. In the end, it wasn't magic, but an old remedy that Dottie suggested. With the way Carie's face lit up, it was the perfect gift. Jo and Carie had gone in on a gift together for Lisa and signed her up for a baking class down at the community college in Sturgeon Bay. Kat had helped her pick out the course and had offered to let Lisa crash on her couch should classes ever run long. Lisa could barely contain her excitement and squeezed them both tightly. Carie's gift was smaller. Jo had found a small frame and printed the picture of the three of them from Thanksgiving.

"It's small enough that you can carry us with you wherever you go," Jo explained as Carie stared at the frame.

"We already have one over the fireplace."

Jo flashed a sad, knowing smile. Carie wouldn't stay here forever, and Jo wanted it to be clear that she knew that.

"This is to take with you."

Carie's eyes pinched in confusion for a moment before she nodded.

"Then it will go with me no matter where I am," she said. She then handed Jo a package.

Jo pulled the wrapping off and stared. In neat handwriting on the cover, it said 'My Recipes'. Inside, she found page after page of the recipes that she'd been making with Lisa since the fall. Further into the book, she recognized her pastries from the bakery. Each page was written in the same neat script from the cover. At the very back of it were blank pages for new additions.

Jo looked up at Carie with wide eyes.

"You said you've been wanting to get organized," Carie said, "so I thought that I'd give you a hand."

Because it was the holiday, and she deserved a little treat, Jo clutched the book to her chest, pressed up to her tip toes, and placed a peck to the side of Carie's mouth. The witch blushed immediately as Jo demurred, looking to the floor.

"This is very sweet. Thank you."

They spent the rest of the day babysitting the giant pot of marinara sauce that Jo prepared from scratch. To match the sauce, they made spaghetti as well. They ended up eating entirely too much pasta.

❦

Like Carie said, Lisa could feel the sturdy power of the wards holding. Despite her confidence, Carie insisted on driving around a few days after Christmas to check on them. Lisa called in Kat and Dan, though Carie was a bit hesitant to include them after the bonfire. There was a brief argument that resolved when Dan showed up in his truck to ferry them on their rounds. Jo waved goodbye after pressing a box of her pastries into their car. She promised dinner when they got back.

Jo spent the day cleaning. The week between Christmas and the new year she kept limited hours at the bakery. She moved the appliances that she could manage alone and deeply cleaned the floors. Inventory needed to be taken, but she decided that would be a three-person job. She locked up and dashed back to the house, pausing halfway across the yard. The sky was overcast, but the snow cover reflected white everywhere. Suddenly, she could smell the brine of the beach and feel the phantom lapping of water at her ankles.

"What do you want?" she asked with a hint of desperation in her voice. "What do you want from me?"

"That's the big question, isn't it?"

Jo startled, stepping back and yelping in surprise as she slipped on a rock beneath the dark water at her feet. She crashed back, splashing into the bay. Above her, a familiar twist of smoke formed into a vaguely humanoid shape.

"It's been you?" Jo asked.

Aldred shrugged.

"I wanted something to keep me occupied this year," they answered. "New, emerging powers like yourself seemed diverting enough. And let's be honest. You seemed so very lonely. Oh, you mean this nonsense?" They waved to the scenery. "I know this place, yes, but it appears to be calling to you."

"How are you here, then?"

"I'm not bound by the laws of mortal minds. I was just stopping by for a quick check in with dear Carie. How surprising to find something so much more interesting going on."

Jo shivered in the water, losing herself in the realistic brush of algae and the poke of the sharp rocks. "My magic is baking. Cakes and cookies. Nothing special."

"Oh, Josie, I think your magic touches so much more than that."

"Please don't call me that."

Aldred quirked their head to the side. "What? Josie? A special name from a special lady?"

Jo looked down into the water.

Aldred laughed above her. "I am a creature from a world beyond your understanding. I do not care for the miniscule lives of mortals. You've called into the ether nearly every night since the snow began to melt last year. How could I not respond?"

Cold fingers hooked under Jo's chin and forced her to meet Aldred's gaze. The smoke had formed a sharp figured face with burning deep purple eyes.

"There's something odd going on. You've been languishing up here in exile for years, but never before have you thrummed with such delicious magic. I've some scores to settle back home, and I've been looking for such strength. I would have sensed it. Would have come to say hello earlier, too."

Jo tried to turn away, but Aldred kept her fixed in place.

"That niece of yours seems to be blossoming up here. Helping you come into your own as well. Her wards are strong. Even stronger than Carie's. I'd love to have a conversation with her. I haven't been able to reach her, but winter has only just begun. She's built up quite the support system for herself. No quiet yearning spilling over the threads from her."

"Stay away from her," Josie spat.

They knew where to prod, and Jo felt each thrust in her chest. Lisa wasn't planning on staying forever, was she? She'd leave in the spring, just like Carie would, and Jo would be alone again, slowly being driven mad by the strengthening voices in her head.

"Oh, sweet lady, I can make sure you're never alone again. After all, connection is so very important. You'll learn that lesson very soon."

Aldred leaned down. Their firm grip grew sharp as claws pierced Jo's cheeks. Jo went very still.

"I'll be back for you, Josie. You're going to wake up in the snow outside your house, concerned that you have some kind of medical malady that's been causing these hallucinations. I'll keep to the periphery for now, but don't worry. I won't leave you. I'll stay. I promise."

Aldred pushed forward and kissed Jo's forehead. The contact leached the heat from Jo's body. She shook violently, then shot up to a sitting position in her snowy yard. She sucked in great gasping breaths, trying to keep from full blown panic. She hurried inside the house, immediately flipping open her laptop and searching for a neurologist. She found one down in Milwaukee, but the earliest they'd be able to see her was April. She booked an appointment and tried not to worry about if her insurance would cover it.

Since arriving, Lisa had become well versed in the language of Jo. She could tell as soon as they walked back into the house that something was bothering her aunt. Jo had warmed up a potluck's worth of leftovers for the group and was sitting at the kitchen table staring into the middle distance with her leg bouncing absently.

"I really think that I could have driven that boat," Dan said as he pulled off his boots. "How different can it be from a car?"

Kat rolled her eyes and brushed the snow from her hair.

"I have no idea how different it is, because I know just as much about boats as you do. Which is nothing."

"I could have all the knowledge on that deep boat lore, you don't know."

"Even the idea that someone was going to ask you out on that boat with Lisa and Carie made you turn green. You don't know how to swim. Water and you? Not compatible."

Carie stepped passed them all without pulling off her shoes or her coat. She seemed acutely attuned to Jo's distress and tried to be subtle as she bent to grab her attention. Lisa sighed and pushed between her two friends.

"I thought that went well," Lisa said, breaking into the conversation. She kept one eye on her aunt. Jo's leg stopped bouncing as soon as Carie touched her shoulder.

"Again, aside from the boat debacle, I thought it was great,' Dan said. "Seems pointless for me to be the driver if I can't work one of the vehicles."

"We'll mention it to Dottie when she's back in town," Kat suggested. "I'll bet if we spun it the right way, we could probably get her to pay for lessons."

"And a license," Lisa added.

"Do you need a license for a boat?"

"Again," Kat sighed. "None of us have any idea about anything relating to boats."

"I'll look it up when I get home," Dan said. He turned his attention to the food spread out on the counter. "Is that all open season, Jo?"

Looking around Carie, Jo nodded with a trying-too-hard smile.

"Go to town."

The meal was quick, and Lisa watched as her aunt slowly untangled herself from whatever had her wound up. As Dan chattered on about how it was impossible to get everyone together for the campaign this time of year, Lisa noted how tired Jo looked. They had been consciously taking it easy since the Yule bonfire. Lisa hadn't slept so hard in years. Even Carie was looking a little less pale, but the dark, bruised skin under Jo's eyes had only grown more pronounced. Lisa's own exhaustion had pulled her deep into sleep each night that she hadn't been able to keep tabs on Jo's nocturnal habits. Something was clearly wrong.

"So, what do you think?"

Both Lisa and Carie startled from their vigil as Dan looked at them expectantly.

"Think about what?" Lisa asked.

Kat rolled her eyes.

"Dan was asking if you were free to meet up on New Year's Eve for a drink at the Blue Ox."

Dan nodded. "Michelle has to work, and Jack is spending it with the family, so I thought instead of sitting in my basement we could go out and be social."

"Yeah, I can get into that," Lisa said.

"Carie and Jo are obviously invited too."

Carie looked to Jo, who shrugged.

"I haven't been to a bar for New Year's since college, so as long as it doesn't get too nuts, I'm game," Jo said.

"The Ox isn't exactly known for their raucous parties. They keep it pretty chill," Kat said.

"Great," Dan said. "We'll meet there at nine?"

With their plans set, the others left. Lisa stopped her aunt from starting the dishes.

"What's wrong?" She demanded. "And please don't say nothing, because there's clearly something bothering you."

Jo braced herself against the counter. "This is a hard time of year, Lisa. I've been a bit in my own head about things lately, but I'll be okay."

Lisa felt her eyes go hot with angry tears. "Please don't lie to me. We're both really worried about you."

"You shouldn't wo--"

"Of course, we're going to worry," Lisa exploded. She shocked herself at her own outburst, slapping her hands over her mouth as Jo flinched.

"I'm sorry," Lisa said after a tense moment.

Jo didn't turn to face her, but softly said it was all right.

"I just meant...You don't have to bear this all by yourself anymore," Lisa said. "I know you felt like you have to because you were all alone, but I'm here now. Carie's here too. Shit, Kat and Dan are too. So is Dottie. We're here, and we care, and we just want you to be okay."

"I know, hon," Jo breathed. She finally turned from the sink. "I know...it's just hard to remember that sometimes. You get used to being all you have if that makes any sense. It's hard to unlearn all that."

Lisa nodded, feeling the anger bleeding out of her.

"I didn't mean to yell," she said.

"There's nothing wrong with being passionate."

"Can you please be as understanding with yourself as you are with other people," Lisa pleaded.

With a strained laugh, Jo offered a nod. "I promise that I'll try."

"And just know that we're here when you're ready to talk," Lisa said. "Okay?"

Jo smiled sadly, knowing she couldn't burden them with her problems. "Okay."

Chapter Sixteen

As promised, the Blue Ox was very relaxed. Since it was New Year's Eve, it was more crowded than a normal weeknight, but nowhere near as packed as it could be. Dan had gotten there early, grabbing two tables for their group. Lisa caught sight of him waving when she walked in with her aunt and Carie. She immediately felt warm. Not only from the heat in the bar, but from the gaggle of people waiting to greet her. Kat was already a few daiquiris in and sloppily kissed both Lisa's cheeks in greeting. She explained it away as a new thing she was trying and immediately turned to Max to do the same thing. Dan pulled her into a tight hug, saying he was so happy she could make it.

Lisa found herself wondering what her younger self would think. When she was in high school, finding a niche like this seemed impossible. Other people slotted into similar spaces, but Lisa could never find her nook. Talking to new people seemed insurmountable, and the world outside of school, according to her parents, was hostile and just not worth the effort. She had to focus on her studies after all.

Since Christmas, Lisa's mind didn't wander to her parents often, but she did genuinely wonder what they were getting into that night. In years past, her mother would complain about not being invited anywhere, and her dad would suggest a dinner reservation for the two of them. That would devolve into a fight because reservations at any restaurant worth a damn would be impossible to get the day before the holiday. They would retire to opposite sides of the house, doors slamming behind them, and Lisa would be left in the middle wondering why the hell they were still together. She would retreat to her own room, more than happy to avoid the questions about why she didn't have anyone to spend the night with. Didn't she have friends? If she was staying in, why waste the night on video games? There were college applications that she could be filling out.

Her phone remained silent in her pocket, but Lisa pulled it out anyway. She opened the messaging app and started typing out a long message.

...I know you're both still mad, but I wanted to reach out and say that I hope you're having a good night. I know you spoke with Auntie Jo, so you know that I'm up here with her. It's been a really nice experience, and I'm discovering a lot about myself. I don't think that college was ever really for me. At least, not college the way you guys were hoping for. I'm looking at taking some culinary classes up here. I've been working with Jo in the bakery, and it's something that I can see myself pursuing. It's not business, but I think it can make me happy...

...I don't want the last time we spoke to be it. We're different people, and we don't have much in common, but you're still my mother, and even after everything I do still care about you. Dad too. I'm hoping that in the time apart, you can come to accept that my path is going to be different from the one you laid out for me. That isn't anything against what you wanted, but I don't think I can do it. I don't know exactly what I want yet, but I'm hoping that I figure it out soon...

...Hopefully we can chat in the new year. I don't know if you'd be interested in coming up here, or if things between you and Aunt Jo are irreparably broken, but either way. Hope to talk to you soon...

Lisa read over her words a few times and before push sending the message. She immediately turned off her phone and stuffed it in her back pocket. Whatever response she got, she would deal with it later.

After he had gotten hammered at the bonfire, Dan had promised to ferry Kat around for the evening, so he decided he would have a drink at midnight so he could toast with everyone. In the meantime, he was encouraging everyone else with shots and drinking games as if prohibition had just been lifted. Carie had offered to be their designated driver, so Lisa started working her way through the local beer selections. Jo ordered an old fashioned and had been nursing the same glass since they got there. She was engaged in the conversation, but something was still weighing on her shoulders.

"That still hasn't been figured out, huh?" Kat asked, nodding at Carie and Jo. She set down two lemon drop shots.

Lisa groaned, but as soon as Kat was counting down from three, she shot it back with a loud gasp.

"Nope," Lisa said, popping the 'p' loudly. "When I tell you that it's the hardest thing I've ever done to not just shove them both in a room and lock the door..."

"The pining is getting a bit sickening."

"It's not just that," Lisa said. "There's something up with my aunt. Beyond the pining."

"A place beyond the pining," Kat muttered.

Lisa snorted in her drink.

"She did just find out that she has magic too, right," Kat asked. "That's a big thing to suddenly have dropped in your lap. You know. It just happened to you too."

"It feels like more than that. She hasn't been sleeping. I'm sure she doesn't think we remember, but we found her sleepwalking right around Thanksgiving. Happened again a few weeks ago."

"Which is weird, but is that bad, necessarily?"

"When it leaves her standing outside in the cold? And she doesn't realize how she got out there?"

Kat shuddered. "Yeesh. That's not great."

"I haven't had a chance to talk about it with Carie, but she's definitely worried too. I don't know if she has an idea of what's going on, but she hasn't mentioned anything to me."

"Carie seems like the type to want to take care of it herself. If we're honest, I'm shocked she's letting me and Dan tag along while you guys play witchy avengers all over the place."

"You should run that name by her," Lisa hiccupped. "She'd loooove it."

"I'll make her a shirt. See how she feels about all that."

They ducked their heads together and snorted laughing. Lisa rubbed her eyes with a wide grin. She craned her neck, looking for a sign of her aunt or Carie.

"Did they step out?"

Dan dropped two more shots on the table.

"Your aunt did," he said. "She mentioned that she needed some air. Carie, I think she went to the bathroom?"

Lisa sighed theatrically. "Maybe if we all wish hard enough at midnight, they'll finally figure it out."

Kat threw back her shot. "Hope springs eternal."

"Holy shit!"

The girls startled at Dan's exclamation. When they faced him, he pointed out the window. They looked and huge smiles spread across their faces.

***

Jo breathed in the rapidly dwindling December air. The bar had gotten a bit too stuffy, and the juke box just a little too loud. She leaned against the railing around the bar's front porch, listening to the water break against the beach across the street. The ice accumulated on the sand jingled like wind chimes as the waves lapped the shore. It was hypnotizing, and she felt herself being drawn towards the noise. A voice, welcome, familiar, and warm, broke her from its spell.

"Bit cold out here without a jacket," Carie said.

"I just needed some air. Was getting stuffy in there."

Carie kept a bit of distance between them as she joined Jo on the railing. Jo ached to drift closer, but she stopped herself from indulging. She clung to the banister, rooting herself in place.

"You can go back," Jo said with a half-smile. "I'll be in soon."

Biting her lip, Carie pulled her gaze from Jo's face to the harbor.

"It's too loud in there," Carie said. "Peaceful out here. With you."

Jo's cheeks flushed. They stood in silence for a moment. The outdoor speakers faded from one song to another. A gentle flurry of snow had covered the sidewalks, reflecting the sparse light.

"I'm sorry." Carie said.

Jo looked up at her with a frown.

"For what I said," Carie continued. "Before I left. I...it feels like I needed to say it again."

"Oh," Jo shrugged, feigning nonchalance. "I shouldn't have pushed. It wasn't fair of me to expect you to drop everything and endure the tourist season. It can be a lot."

"You don't have to do that."

"What?"

"You're allowed to push. You're allowed to want more."

Jo couldn't help the heat prickling in her eyes. She huffed a quiet laugh and looked away. "I don't know about that. It's better to keep it to myself. Harder to be disappointed that way."

Carie sounded like she'd been punched in the chest as a traitorous tear slipped down Jo's cheek. Jo went to wipe it violently away but found Carie had beaten her to it. She brushed it gently away with her thumb and kept caressing Jo's cheek.

"I'm so sorry that I've made you feel that way, Josie. I want you to ask things of me," Carie said. "I'm...not great with this emotional stuff. I've never been happier than when you opened your house to me."

Jo wanted to grab Carie's wrist. She wasn't sure if she just wanted more contact or if she wanted to push her away. She stayed frozen, only moving to squeeze her eyes shut, sending more tears over her cheeks. She pressed her lips together, desperate to keep herself from sobbing.

Carie whined deep in her throat. She brought her other hand up to frame Jo's face.

"Hey hey hey," she whispered. "Please look at me."

Jo slowly opened her eyes. "I was fine with it all, you know. When we reconciled, I said that I wanted to be your friend. If that's all you want, I promise I'll be okay with it. I just might need some time..."

"I don't want you to be fine with it. I want you to ask the world of me. And if you don't, I may just give it to you anyway. You gave me that picture for Christmas, and you were so sure that I would be leaving. I'm not. At least, I'm not planning to." Carie leaned in even closer, her eyes boring into Jo's. "I'm so sorry I reacted like that when you asked me to stay."

Jo nodded as much as she could, framed in Carie's hands.

"I should have told you I loved you then."

The world paused. Jo searched Carie's face for a trace of a lie. "What?"

"I love you, Josie," Carie said, her own eyes welling up. "And I'm so sorry that I made you think that I didn't."

Jo released her death grip on the banister and grabbed Carie's wrists. "You love me?"

Carie nodded. "For a long time."

Finally, like the first bud of spring reaching towards the sun, Jo's smile unfurled, bright and wide. She laughed, light and disbelieving.

"May I kiss you?"

"Please," Jo said, only a bit desperately.

Carie leaned in and gently pressed their lips together. Jo wound her arms beneath Carie's coat and around her waist. They parted but pressed their foreheads together. Carie pulled Jo tight to her chest, wrapping her in the warmth of her coat.

"You should have a jacket on," Carie said as she nuzzled into Jo's hair. "You'd think as long as you've been living up here, you'd know that."

Jo huffed a laugh before turning her face into the side of Carie's neck. "I'm just used to it. And I like the cold."

"I like you warm."

They swayed for a moment before Jo pulled away.

"You said you want me to ask for things."

"For everything."

"I'd like you to take me home," Jo said with just a hint of suggestion in her voice. "I've had a bit too much to drink, and I probably shouldn't be driving."

"Good thing that I already said I would," Carie said. "I'll make sure Lisa has a ride home."

"My coat is inside."

"I'll grab it. Sit tight. I'll be right back."

Carie kissed her again before heading back into the bar. Jo immediately felt cold at the loss of her touch, but she tucked her hands into her armpits and tried to stave off the shivers.

You'll be just as cold when she eventually leaves.

"She's not going to," Jo said to the falling snow.

Aldred laughed, loud and painful in Jo's head.

We'll see. The high season starts in five months. That's plenty of time for someone to change their mind.

Jo refused to close her eyes. She strained to keep herself from blinking. She wouldn't cede that territory. The voice faded, having said its piece, and soon Carie walked back onto the porch. Her cheeks were a furious red. Jo looked from her to the windows, where she could see Lisa and her friends flashing thumbs up and waving enthusiastically.

"Had a bit of an audience," Carie said apologetically.

Jo felt her own cheeks flush, but she let herself giggle quietly. She wiggled her fingers to the group inside. "We'll have all the privacy in the world at home."

Carie's expression went soppy. "I love when you say home like its ours."

"It is, love. Has been for a long time."

Jo let Carie help with her coat and then pressed herself tight to Carie's side as they made their way to the car. The wind picked up off the water, and the flurry turned into a heavier snow fall. The drive was slow and dark, only illuminated by the high beams reflecting off the snowflakes. The world had narrowed to the car, the road, and each other. They stayed silent for the drive, listening to the soft singing over the radio. They held hands the entire drive home, only letting go when they were standing at the front door and Jo had to find her keys. The door was just closed as Carie unwound the scarf from Jo's neck. When Carie turned to hang it up, Jo tripped trying to get out of her boots. She scrambled for Carie as she fell. Carie grabbed her arms and hauled her up, over correcting and crashing into the console table, sending keys, spare change, and a picture frame flying. Jo tucked her face into Carie's chest and started giggling uncontrollably. Carie held her out at arm's length, worry on her face before the concern melted away to laughter.

"Think we can manage without destroying the house?"

Carie shrugged. "Doubtful."

Pulling herself up, Jo unbuttoned Carie's coat and slipped it off her shoulders. She placed it on a hanger and into the hall closet. She did the same with her own coat before taking Carie by the hand. Tugging gently, Jo led her back to the bedroom. She flipped the light on as they entered and stopped Carie at the foot of the bed. Slowly, Jo began to tug off Carie's clothes until she stood bare. Carie raised her hands to do the same to Jo, but Jo took her hands again in hers. She kissed Carie's knuckles before drawing them to her chest.

"I want to take care of you. Will you let me?"

Bereft of words, Carie could only nod. Jo smiled and released her.

"Lay back, love," Jo said. She grabbed the hem of her sweater and pulled it over her head as Carie sat on the bed. Jo pushed her back before crawling over her. Carie's gaze flicked to Jo's hair before she snaked a hand up to pull the hair tie holding it back. Her hair cascaded down her shoulder, and Carie tangled her fingers in it.

"Sorry," she said. "Couldn't help it."

Jo crooked an eyebrow before leaning down to capture Carie's lips.

"I forgive you," she said when she came up for air. "But maybe don't do it again."

Carie grinned and ran her other hand up and down Jo's back, stopping at the clasp of her bra. Jo leveled her with an unimpressed grin, but Carie pinched and twisted her hand. The clasp came loose, and the straps slipped down her arms.

"Not a very good listener."

"Never was."

Carie flipped them so that Jo was beneath her.

"You've taken care of me for years," Carie whispered, tickling the soft shell of Jo's ear. "Please, please, please let me..."

She trailed off and tugged on Jo's leggings. Getting the message, Jo removed them, baring herself completely. She tried not to squirm. Her stomach was soft, and her breasts sagged. With Carie, it didn't matter. Carie looked at her in that moment like she was perfect, stopping when she saw the still healing scratches on her legs. Her gaze snapped back to Jo's; the question obvious in her eyes.

"I fell when I took out the garbage the other day," Jo lied. "It's not a big deal."

Carie clearly disagreed. She slid down Jo's body to reverently lift her left leg by the ankle. Carie pressed gentle kisses to the marks, repeating the tender motion with the other leg. Jo propped herself on her elbows and watched with shaky eyes.

"Anything that hurts you is a big deal to me," Carie said. She nudged Jo's knees apart so she could settle between them. She traced her fingers along the plush skin of Jo's thighs.

Jo's skin sang with Carie's gentle touch. She clutched at the headboard, dug her toes into the sheets, and sank into the bed under Carie's enthusiastic ministrations.

⁓ℓℓ⁓

January had arrived, and saw Carie plastered to Jo's back with an arm wrapped around her waist. The rhythmic puff of Carie's breath at her neck had lulled Jo to sleep.

When she opened her eyes, she was at the bay, but the colors were duller. Her old bedroom set from her parents' house was strewn across the beach. The water lapped at the legs of the frame and the comforter hanging over the side. The water pulled at the blanket, tugging it further away with each cycle of the waves. Jo could hear raised voices in the woods on the bluffs around her. She could pick out the sounds of her mother and father--she had plenty of practice listening to their arguments through walls-- and even fainter, further away, she could pick out Carie's quiet rejections from months ago.

The water was peaceful and inviting behind her. Quiet and inviting. Jo watched as her blanket finally pulled free of the bed and floated out into the bay. She took a step towards the water but felt something gently tug her back. She blinked awake, back in the safe darkness of her bedroom with Carie's arm a tight anchor around her.

Carie mumbled behind her, confusion and worry evident in her tone. "Where are you going?"

Jo turned a bit, seeing Carie's concerned face looming over her.

"Do you need to get up?" Carie asked.

Jo shook her head and turned around in Carie's embrace. She resettled, tucking herself into the nook of Carie's neck. She felt arms curl tighter around her, keeping her safe until morning.

Chapter Seventeen

"You still live with your parents, right?"

Kat and Lisa stood in line at the Piggly Wiggly. They had been charged with picking up snacks while Dan drove Carie to get gas. Kat had been waffling about what candy bar to buy before they paid, when Lisa sprung the question.

"Kinda. It's a similar situation to your aunt's place, but more of a proper two flat. They used to rent my apartment out for the summers, but then I asked if they'd mind me staying there. Worked out for everyone. We have our own space, but we're close if they need me."

"I did get to move back upstairs."

Kat dropped the sweet she was holding and snapped her attention to Lisa. "So, what we saw on New Year's..."

Lisa clicked her tongue and nodded coyly.

"That's wonderful," Kat said with a clap on her hands. "I'm so happy for them!"

"It's made things a lot less tense around the house, that's for sure," Lisa said. She bit her lip and started placing the groceries on the check out belt. "I'm still worried about my aunt."

"What's wrong?"

Lisa shook her head. "Honestly, I don't know. She's happier than I've ever seen her, but she's jumpy. And I don't know that she's sleeping."

"Carie must have noticed if she isn't."

"She's worried too. I mentioned something to Jo before New Year's. We haven't spoken much about it since, but I can tell they're both so worried about ruining things."

"They just got together!"

"I guess after what happened with our family it's really hard for Jo to trust that a good thing will stay. If your parents functionally disowned you for just being who you were, trust doesn't come easily."

"She still isn't worried about Carie leaving, is she?" Kat asked.

"I don't know if they've talked about their plans for the summer. I would have thought that would be the first thing they sorted out, but what do I know?"

They paid for their groceries and took their bags to wait on the curb for Dan's truck to reappear in the parking lot.

"I guess I can kind of understand why Jo wouldn't want to say anything," Kat said. "They've decided to make a go of it, and it's this new, fresh, wonderful thing. Exactly what they've both been hoping for since they've met, yeah? She wants Carie to move in, to stay. But, when she asked before, she got a no and they fought. I mean, it makes sense when you think about it."

"But if she's working herself up to a point where her health is being affected, then she needs to address the situation."

"Might be worth trying to talk to her again?"

"Definitely," Lisa said. She caught sight of Dan's truck and nodded towards it. "I should see what Carie thinks. And what she's thinking for the summer."

"If she's not planning on staying--"

Lisa shrugged. "I mean, what if she doesn't, but she comes back a few times to visit? Would that be the worst thing?"

Rolling her eyes, Kat sighed theatrically. "They just need to talk."

Dan pulled up, and the girls clambered into the back seat. Carie looked at them in the rearview mirror as if she knew exactly what they were talking about. Lisa spent the rest of the drive debating with herself about whether she had any business sticking her nose in her aunt's relationship. She didn't want to be overbearing. Didn't want to push anyone away. She let her forehead fall against the window, closing her eyes and trying to quiet her reeling thoughts.

The car was quiet for a moment, until Lisa yelped. She felt a sharp ping in the back of her mind. She shot up and found Carie staring back at her.

"I know it must be bad if I felt it," Kat said. Her expression was pained, and she had a hand pressed over her right eye. "What the hell was that?"

Lisa scrunched her eyes closed, feeling for her wards. It was just as Carie described. She could feel an opening where she had placed a seal.

"Cana Island," she said. "Dan--"

With a nod, Dan stomped his foot down on the gas pedal, lurching everyone back into their seats as he sped to the eastern coast of the peninsula and the lighthouse.

The road ended at a rocky causeway buffeted by waves. The tide was coming in, and the path would soon be completely underwater. A small, tree lined island sat across the causeway. The lighthouse wasn't visible, but Lisa could feel the knot thrumming beyond the foliage.

Dan pulled over, nodding to Carie as he unlocked the doors. Carie clapped his shoulder as they got out of the car. He cracked his window so he could hear them calling for him and cranked the heat up a bit.

"Glad I thought to toss the boots in before we left," Lisa said as they approached the causeway.

During the summer months, a tractor would ferry people across the uneven terrain. Most opted for that option, but some brave souls would traverse the rocks for the full experience. Lisa had suggested asking Dan to drive them over the first time they made these rounds, but Carie had quickly shot it down. She didn't want Dan anywhere near the knots or for anything to happen to his truck.

"It's not just one thing," Carie said. She fought to be heard over the crashing waves. "Do you feel them?"

Lisa could. Something was knocking at the wards, but not just from one spot.

"I'll throw a ward around the island," Lisa said, already pulling from the knot in the lighthouse.

"Kat, stay with Lisa. I'll call for you if I need you."

Kat shot Carie a look. "Are you sure that's smart?"

"No, but I want them contained so that if I can't get them all, you two can come in and help."

Lisa narrowed her attention, drawing everything she could manage from the threads. Something seemed diminished. The power she drew forth wasn't as much as she was expecting, but she was able to secure the island as Carie requested. A low keening noise echoed over the water. It was immediately met with three separate responses.

"So that's four?"

"Sounds like it," Carie said. "Keep an ear out for me."

Before she could step through the ward, another low moan shook the island.

"What the hell is that?"

Lisa opened her eyes and followed the line of Kat's finger. She was pointing towards a copse of trees just by the island's ticket office. The creature slowly plodded onto the path, standing tall on taloned, three-toed paws. Its legs were spindle-thin and long. The creature stood at least eight feet tall. Its neck stretched high, ending in a thin head with a long snout and tall, jagged ears. It was completely bald with translucent flesh that pulled and stretched over taut, firm muscle. It lifted its head again, bellowing as it lumbered deeper into the heart of the small island. Two similar creatures pushed out of the trees, stretching their necks and calling to the sky.

"That's a new one for me," Carie said. She cursed under her breath and spat on the ground.

Connected as she was to the threads, Lisa felt Carie tug on them as she wove a personal warding spell. A shimmering silver light encased her body for a moment before dispersing into the air. Goosebumps raised on Lisa's skin as she felt the tingle of Carie crossing her barrier. As she did, Lisa caught the barest notion of something else on the island. Something vaguely familiar. She opened her mouth to shout her observation to Carie, but the creatures had clocked her. They stopped in their tracks, regarding Carie with a benign interest.

Methodically, Carie approached the nearest one. She held out a hand as if she were looking to pet the creature. Its wide eyes tracked her movement, and when she was close enough, it ducked its head so she might touch it. Her fingers slid up its leathery nose, pausing just between the eyes and gliding back down.

"You don't belong here, bud," Carie cooed at the beast. "Let me send you home."

The creature bellowed again, low and warm, as Carie completed the exorcism. Her hand stayed firmly on the creature, while her other went through the motions of tugging on the threads. Her brow furrowed in concentration. Lisa thinned out her own spell and loosened her hold on the threads, hoping to free the magic for Carie. She knew that she'd hear about it later, but after Carie received that extra surge of power, the creature closed its eyes and faded from existence.

"I've got this,' Carie shouted back. "Keep the containment up. I just need to send the others back."

"I felt something else there, Carie," Lisa answered back. "Right when you crossed over, something tugged on the threads."

With a wave, Carie indicated she had heard and moved towards the next creature.

"Do you feel anything, Kat?"

"Sorry," Kat said with a shake of her head. "I'm not as in tune with the knots as you and Carie are."

"Really?"

"Yeah, like, I can kind of feel something, but I think it's all in relation to how much power I can control."

She snapped her fingers and the small flame ignited at the tips. She wiggled her fingers, and it danced along them before settling over her pointer. "I can do this, and I can weave an exorcism. Those take a little more magic, but for the most part this is all I can do."

"Weird."

"What you guys can do is weird," Kat said, blowing out the flame. "You saw how many witches it took to cast that ritual at the bonfire. Dottie was able to amplify it a bit since she can actually feel the threads. And then you fly in being able to just pop up a ward whenever you want. Even Carie has to take a couple seconds to think about it."

"I guess having no preconceived notions of weaving helps," Lisa said.

"You're also having a full conversation while holding up a huge ward."

"More than helps, I guess."

"There's no way your great great grandmother or something isn't a weaver."

"A bloodline thing?"

Kat shrugged. "I mean, your aunt has magic too, yeah? Maybe someone a little farther down the family tree did too."

"Doubt I'll ever have a chance to ask," Lisa said. Her text to her mother had been read but left unanswered. She'd been tempted to block and then delete the number, but she couldn't bring herself to do it. It was foolishly optimistic to think that her parents would come around eventually, but every day that went by without an answer seemed like response enough.

Kat studied Lisa's face for a long minute before turning back to face the island. "Their loss."

Lisa felt her heart swell with affection for her friend. "Yeah."

Carie returned soon after, looking almost disappointed that a fight hadn't broken out. They replenished the breached ward around the lighthouse and were picking their way back across the causeway when Kat asked, "What the hell were those things?"

"Nothing I've seen in the time that I've been coming up here."

"That's more than a little concerning," Lisa said.

"It's possible that they're entities that forced themselves through the cracks between spaces," Carie said. "Most sentient creatures won't do that. It takes ages to pass through. They could have been created here, but that kind of weaving takes an enormous amount of strength. Even Mildred would have been able to feel it."

"This all just feels like we're spinning our wheels," Lisa said. "The hits on the wards are escalating, and we don't know any more than when we started. I feel like we're just waiting for the eventual breach that we won't be able to stop."

Dan must have seen them crossing back because the truck was as close to the causeway as he could get. He had gotten out of the car and was watching them cross. The closer they got, it was clear that he was looking at something else. His mouth hung open as he stared over their heads.

Lisa turned, picking her steps carefully. Kat gasped beside her and grabbed her arm. A ward popped up around them as Carie pushed them both behind her. Lisa finally looked up. Her hand clapped to her mouth. The waves were loud enough that they had masked the slow emergence of the creature from the water. It was large enough to straddle the lighthouse. Lisa was sure you could see it from Michigan. Its neck extended the length of the island, and it slowly dropped its long face just in front of where Carie's ward began.

"That could be what I felt before," Lisa whispered.

Carie didn't respond. She focused completely on the creature. It studied them with genuine interest, sniffing the air as Carie held out her hand to it.

"You don't belong here," she said.

The creature didn't speak, but Lisa could feel its calm intention through the threads.

No, I do not. But you were able to send my kin home, yes?

Lisa and Carie winced at the sheer enormity of the voice. Kat looked worriedly at the two of them.

"I can do the same for you, but you must not return here," Carie said. "This place doesn't understand creatures like you."

It was not our intention to come here. We fell through the space between worlds.

"That's not possible," Carie said. "Those tears are thin. No one can get through without intention and desire."

That is not the way of things anymore. Something here is forcing the cracks wider, allowing for easier passage.

"Do you know who pulled open the tear?"

Such workings are not permitted on our side. There are many in our realms that do not want to share power. For an untapped source to exist, it is too tempting for some.

"Where did you come through? Tell me that, and I'll send you home."

The creature swayed its head north.

There is a tear that way. We found ourselves under the water, but there were small islands we were able to feed from. We wanted to explore this new land, and we followed the power from this place.

"Thank you," Carie said sincerely. "Please bend down. I'll send you back."

The creature's massive head came to rest on the rocks. The waves lapped against its skin. Carie touched its muzzle. She closed her eyes and concentrated. A moment later, the creature was gone. The water crashed in to fill the space it had occupied, splashing them with freezing spray.

"Did you hear any of that?" Carie asked.

Kat shook her head, but Lisa met her eyes and nodded.

"We need to let Dottie know," Carie said. "Immediately. We're not far from the house and she should be back from her trip."

"How are we going to find where it came from?" Lisa wouldn't help the waiver in her voice. She could feel Kat shaking beside her. Everything they had seen so far had seemed manageable. Beasts, no matter how benevolent, rising from the sea was more than they were mentally equipped to handle.

Carie could sense their distress immediately. She took both their hands and tugged them forward.

"I promise you that we can handle this. We're just going to need help. I will not ask either of you to do anything that I don't think you can handle."

"Carie..."

The witch stooped to meet Lisa's gaze. There was a faint tremor running through her body.

"I promise, Lisa. We can handle this." She didn't move until Lisa offered a nod. "Let's get out of this water. Dan, close your mouth. You'll start catching flies."

The group drove in silence to Dottie's. Lisa couldn't find any words. She kept reaching out for the threads, just to see if anything else was tugging on them. Dottie, rested and tan from her Christmas trip to Florida, was waiting for them on her front porch. She was pleased to see them, but then her mood soured when she saw the looks on their faces. Carie had explained, after suggesting they all have a sit and something to drink if Dottie didn't mind them crashing. As Carie told her what had happened at the lighthouse, Dottie had stalled in taking a sip from her mug. She held it suspended halfway up to her lips.

"The creature made it sound like the tear was up north. It's either near Pilot Island or Plum Island. Possibly between the two."

"I don't know that we've ever had a tear to seal before," Dottie said. Her voice was soft and wobbly.

"As far as I'm aware, you haven't," Carie said. "But I do have experience with sealing them. I'll need a ritual circle, similar to what we had set up on Yule."

"I can put out the word. I know some of us head south for the colder months, but I think we can get a sound circle," Dottie said, finally putting her mug down. "Ladies, you'll help?"

Kat was staring out the large windows in the kitchen as if she was waiting for another creature to erupt from the water. Lisa nudged her with an elbow to bring her back.

"What was that?"

"Of course, we'll help," Lisa agreed, nodding at Kat who offered a bob back before looking back out the window.

"How soon do you need the circle?" Dottie asked.

"We need to get the tear sealed now. We're going to head back to the house to regroup, so make your calls then let us know how we're expecting."

Dottie fixed Carie with a pleading look. "You can fix this, can't you?"

"I don't want to make a promise that I can't keep, Dottie," Carie sighed. "I will do everything in my power to make this right. I... I've come to see this place as home. I care deeply about the people who live here. We were lucky that those creatures were benevolent."

Dottie nodded, taking a deep breath to steady herself as Carie continued.

"Call me when you have everyone. I can try a few things back at the house to see just what we're dealing with."

Lisa watched as Dottie pushed up from the table. She looked her age in that moment, but she regained her regal bearing as she approached Carie. She took the witch's face in her hands.

"I trust you, Carie. Have for over a decade now. We'll defend our home together."

Carie allowed Dottie to pull her into a brief, tight hug.

"Let's get going then," Dottie ordered. "I'll grab my address book."

Chapter Eighteen

J o woke on the floor of the bakery. Something had wrapped its oily fingers around her head and squeezed tightly as possible. She had been closing the bakery for the evening with an eye on the road. That was the last thing she remembered before opening her eyes to the ceiling.

It's calling. The draw is loud and powerful. Perhaps it is time...

She closed her eyes tightly. The whimper that escaped her lips was pathetic. Jo was grateful no one else was around to hear it. She reached for the counter and heaved herself up. The voice had retreated completely, and a familiar truck was turning into the parking lot.

After checking her reflection in the oven door, Jo tried to pat her hair back into something presentable. She quickly pulled it back into a messy bun, hoping that she would just look harried from a busy day. She had seen the concerned looks passed between Lisa and Carie in the last few weeks, but Jo didn't want to worry them until she knew what was happening. Her appointment with the neurologist was coming up in a few months, and she was planning on asking them both if they would mind taking the drive down to Milwaukee with her. She anticipated that it would be a rough trip, and she hoped they would agree to be her moral support.

Giving up on her appearance, she tossed on her coat and locked the bakery behind her. Carie was stepping out of the truck, pointing towards the house as

Kat and Lisa hurried by her. Jo jogged to reach her, pecking her on the cheek when she was close enough.

"Is everything okay?" Jo asked.

Carie cupped the back of Jo's neck and pressed her lips to Jo's forehead. "No. We have a bit of a situation."

"You aren't hurt?"

Carie shook her head. "There's something bad happening near the knots up north. We've got Dottie calling up the witches. Soon as we hear back from her, we'll be heading up to fix it."

"What can I do to help?"

Expression gone warm and fond, Carie tugged Jo in close to her side. "I want you to stay as far from this as possible. I'm tempted to tell you to get in the car and drive south until I tell you it's safe to come back, but I know there's not a chance in hell that you'd actually listen. I want you to stay here. If we call you, we're in big trouble and need to be driven out."

Jo bit her lip against her protestations. What if she collapsed while Carie was in the middle of fixing whatever was wrong? She couldn't ask her to split her attention like that.

"What do you need here and now?" she asked.

"A wide, shallow bowl filled with water would be very helpful."

Jo started cycling through the catalog of bakeware she had. "Would a twelve-inch cake pan work?"

"Perfectly."

After settling the others on the couch, Jo dug out the pan and filled it with water. Carie had moved the kitchen table and was sitting cross-legged on the floor. Whether she had chosen that specific spot for any reason was beyond Jo. She knelt before Carie and set the pan on the ground between them.

"This might get a bit weird," Carie said apologetically. "I need you all just to stay calm. Dan, keep an eye on my phone. If Dottie calls, Lisa, you can tug on the threads. I'll feel you there, and I'll stop."

"What are you doing?" Jo asked.

"It's a far-seeing spell. I can't feel anything coming through the rift, but that doesn't mean that there isn't something there pushing through. I want to know what we'll be facing once we get up there."

Carie looked at Jo as if she expected her to move to the couch. Jo just stared back, daring her to tell her to move. A defeated smile slipped over Carie's face.

"It's going to be fine. I promise."

Jo felt a swelling in her chest. For some reason, she was certain that wasn't true. She backed away, but she stayed in the kitchen. She didn't want to go far.

Carie passed her hands over the pan and the water glowed with an ethereal light. The pan was only a few inches deep, but Jo could swear that it went far deeper than that. Carie bent over the water as her hair lifted around her head as if a sudden static wave passed over her. It fell a second later, and Carie's body went rigid. She was elsewhere, and that was when Jo felt the cold arms around her shoulders.

None of them can see me. Don't you think that's a bit odd? Or are they all just so wrapped up in these silly games that they don't notice what's actually happening right in front of their faces?

Jo shook her head, trying to dislodge the voice, but Aldred bent close and hissed in her ear.

I'm not going anywhere. I've been dancing in the corners of your eyes for months now. Why would I leave? You'd be so lonely without me. Especially since it seems that you're either too much of a liability or a dead weight they just can't be bothered to bring you with them.

The grip tightened.

You'll stay with me, and everything will be just fine.

The embrace loosened, and the pressure at her ear disappeared. She looked over to the couch, hoping someone had noticed her distress. Dan was hunched over Carie's phone while Lisa had Kat leaning against her side. She whispered quiet assurances to her friend, promising that they would deal with this and make everything okay.

It warmed Jo's heart to see the woman Lisa had become in the few months she'd been there. Jo had a hard time imagining the directionless girl that showed up all those months ago comforting anyone.

Jo was so proud of Lisa. She hated herself for wondering when her niece would inevitably leave too.

Because that's what they all would do. Dan made his deliveries to her because he was a kind man helping out a lonely woman exiled in the countryside. Kat was warm and friendly because she had bonded with Lisa. Lisa loved her, Jo knew that with all her heart, but Lisa needed to thrive. She should get her own place, maybe open her own bakery somewhere people would discover her and appreciate her.

And Carie...

Carie would save the day, and then she would move on.

Jo's eyes watered, but she did not brush the tears away. She wondered if someone would notice. Perhaps it was unfair. Something big was happening here, but she wished for a glance.

The shadows in the room grew longer and sharper. Carie's weaving threw odd light all over the room, and the shadows began to dance. Jo tried to ignore them, but she could swear that she saw that familiar smokey face of Aldred appearing before her with a wide and welcoming smile on their face. Jo kept her eyes trained on Carie, taking strength and comfort from her presence, but the shadows became overwhelming. Jo worried that once Carie's light was gone, they would swallow her whole.

It seemed like hours, but Carie was only under for a few minutes. She gasped, popping out of her spell and sending the shadows scurrying. Jo dropped to her side immediately.

"Are you okay?"

Carie shook herself, blinking rapidly. "Yes. I'm fine. Just takes a minute to readjust."

Lisa jumped off the couch and stood beside her aunt. "What did you see?"

"I could see the tear. It's not huge, which could explain why I didn't notice it before. Still, if something that big went missing from the other side, that's not to say that other entities didn't notice it was gone. We need to get it closed as soon as possible."

Dan looked up from Carie's phone. "Ms. Cambridge just texted. She'd asking where to meet us."

"Northport," Carie said. "We'll need to hike out to the beach and weave the ritual there. I'll need to be as close to the tear as possible to close it, so we can grab a boat if we need to."

Dan pushed off the couch and jingled his keys. "I should have enough gas to get us there. I'll get the car warming."

Jo could feel them slipping away from her. Their work was important, but that certainty that something terrible would happen to her as soon as they left weighed heavily on her shoulders.

"Wait, Dan. You don't have to come with us," Carie said. She was still kneeling and had pulled one of Jo's hands into her lap.

"I'm gonna stop you right there, Carie," Dan said. "Every member of the party is important, even the no power guide who's just showing them the way. Let my overly curious delivery driver show your mighty wizard the way."

Carie laughed, a bit stunned and so grateful. "Lead on, good sir."

Dan nodded and hurried to his car.

"We need to get going," Carie ordered. "It'll take a minute to get up there."

Jo kept quiet as they moved around her. She picked up the cake pan, careful not to spill the water still in it. She busied herself with pointless tidying in the kitchen, aware of the presence in the deep corners that no one else seemed to notice. She wanted to say something about it, to call attention to it, but that old fear kept her mouth shut. The old fear that it was nothing. That she was blowing things out of proportion.

A heavy weight slamming into her back pulled Jo back from the edge of that deep pit. It was Lisa, clinging tightly.

"We'll see you in a bit, Auntie Jo."

Jo turned in the embrace and framed Lisa's face with her hands. She didn't want to delay them, so she didn't say how proud she was of Lisa. How she admired her for being able to roll with the punches that the world had flung at her. How she was so honored to have been a port in the storm for her. She hoped she was a good influence on her niece. That her insecurities and flaws hadn't ruined her.

Instead, she smiled as brightly as she could and kissed Lisa's forehead.

"You're going to be magnificent, hon," Jo said. "Go and keep us safe."

Lisa shook Jo's hands from her face and burrowed deep into her aunt's chest.

"Those assholes back in Illinois don't deserve you," Lisa said.

Jo dropped a kiss into her hair and squeezed Lisa tight. She caught sight of Carie, who was watching as Kat waited impatiently for her own hug. She swooped in for it when Lisa finally pulled away.

It all felt so final.

Carie lingered in the doorway after the others rushed out to Dan's truck. "You'll stay here?"

Jo nodded though she wanted nothing more than to go.

"Lock the doors," Carie said. "Maybe lock yourself in the bedroom."

"Why?"

"You've been sleepwalking. Not as much since I've been staying over, but it's happened enough to worry me. Lisa too."

"I've made an appointment with a doctor," Jo said after a long moment. "They can't get me in until April."

"We'll get it sorted then," Carie said as she ran her hands through Jo's hair. She studied Jo's face like she wanted to remember it forever. "But just in case, will you do that for me? I don't want you wandering when I'm not here to follow."

But she wouldn't ask Jo to go with her. She had to stay behind so she wouldn't interrupt their important work.

"Okay," Jo agreed. "I'll stay in the bedroom. I'll lock the door."

Carie took Jo's hand in her own and pressed a kiss to her knuckles.

"I hope we're just making a bigger deal of the tear than we need to, but I'd rather be overly cautious."

"I understand."

"I love you, Josie."

Jo forced a smile and pressed close to Carie, tucking her head under her chin. She believed Carie, but it was so hard when she was being left behind.

"I love you, too."

The door pulled shut, and Jo turned the deadbolt, knowing that it wouldn't make any difference. She stood in the dark living room and watched through the window as Dan's truck pulled onto the road. Those unwelcome hands reappeared on her shoulders, pressing down just enough to show an endless well of strength.

They didn't notice at all.

"They have a lot on their minds," Jo said, her voice quivering.

I know, and I appreciate the distraction. Let them close that tear. They won't notice another knot being plucked apart with all that raw power being thrown around.

"What...," Jo felt something tug in her chest. She pressed a hand there, trying to ease the strain.

I could lament all the time we could have had together, Josie, but all things happen for a reason. I've been wandering this forsaken little nothing of a world for centuries, looking for my chance to get back. I have things I need to do back home. And who would have thought that someone as inconsequential as you could help me. A fresh knot, pulled into existence through ancient magical bloodlines and good old-fashioned connection.

"My parents--"

Maybe they knew what you'd become. Maybe that's why they got rid of you. A girlfriend would have been shameful in their social circles, but a new knot? Something magical? Unnatural? Wrong? That would invite all kinds of scrutiny. You weren't worth their perfect little life, Josie. Let me fix it.

The pressure in her chest tugged again. She gasped in pain and tried to turn but found herself rooted to the floor.

Easy, Josie. I want them a little further afield, and then we can get going. Why don't you sleep for a bit? It'll be less painful that way.

Chapter Nineteen

The day had been exhausting, and night was turning out to be even more so. Lisa struggled to keep her eyes open as the dark country roads flew passed the windows. Kat was softly snoring, tucked into a warm ball against the car door. Carie had been arguing with Dan about the fastest route north, but Dan eventually won out. He put Northport in his GPS app on his phone and insisted that was the best way to go. The brief argument seemed to take it all out of Carie. She was snoring a few minutes later.

"If you're tired too, don't try to stay awake on my account," Dan said. "I can always flip on a podcast. I'm a little behind on the latest Critical Role campaign."

"Hardly seems fair for you to have to stay awake while we all snore around you."

Dan shrugged. "I usually drive for my parents when we go anywhere farther than an hour away. If my mom isn't driving, she's asleep, and dad refuses to let her drive for whatever reason. I usually just end up doing it. I'm also just going to be hanging in the car when we get up there, so I'll grab a nap while you guys save the world from ripping apart or whatever."

"I remain in awe of how you just roll with all this weirdness."

"Eh, you get used to it. Kat's always been so open about it, and Ms. Cambridge would rather people know and are comfortable with what they see. Obviously they want to keep all this big stuff under wraps."

"It has been nice to see it all accepted. Any little different thing in my family back home, and they lose their minds."

"I'm sure there's people like that up here too, but you don't have to deal with assholes unless you chose too. And life's too short to waste any time on them."

Lisa smiled and nuzzled closer to the window. Her eye lids began to droop.

"I'm a little mad that it took me so long to realize that," Lisa said. "I'm sure I've mentioned it before, but we should go to the renaissance faire in Bristol this summer. I've always wanted to go with friends."

"You, Carie, and the witches make sure the world isn't overwhelmed by a bunch of nonsense from dimensions beyond our reckoning, and I'll make sure we get to Bristol this year."

She meant to say thank you, but she was asleep before she could get the words out.

When she woke, Lisa wasn't in the car.

She blinked and rubbed the sleep from her eyes, but the view remained the same. She was in an expanse of white. A liminal space with no sharp features. If she strained, Lisa could just barely hear the gentle lapping of the waves against the shore. The ground seemed to expand and contract, like she was minuscule and standing on a giant's chest. She spun in place, trying to make sense of the vision.

Under the cresting waves, she could make out another quiet noise. She focused solely on that, desperate to make out what it was saying.

The voice was familiar. Her aunt whispered to her.

Keep going. I'll be fine.

Lisa jolted awake just as Dan slid to the side of the road. She looked beside her, almost expecting to see her aunt, but only the empty middle seat looked back. Kat was already out of the truck, swearing about how cold it was. Unable to shake the unease she felt, Lisa pulled her phone out and typed out a quick message to Jo. The phone couldn't send it; there was no service this far north. Cursing, Lisa tossed the phone onto the seat as she followed everyone else out of the car.

Carie eyed Lisa as if she were able to sense her unease.

"Just had a weird dream on the way up," Lisa said. "I'm alright. Just a little rattled."

"Same," Carie said. Her voice was tight with tension. "Let's go handle this so we can get home."

This close to the tear, Lisa could feel the odd energy. It was different from the knots but warm and welcoming.

"Carie, can a tear draw power from the knots?"

"Wouldn't be the weirdest thing," Carie said, staring out at the water. "But if it is, we want to get it closed quickly."

Lisa closed her eyes and tugged again. She could feel where the tear was by its own pressure on the threads. It wasn't far off the coastline, but entirely too close to the ferry's route to Washington Island in the distance.

"Has there ever been a breach that caused any substantial damage out here?"

"Nothing that I couldn't contain, but we were lucky with that last creature. It must have emerged late at night for no one to have noticed it. There's things that you can kinda laugh off as just weirdness, but then there's a giant monster crashing out of the water and destroying a boat full of unsuspecting people."

"Do you ever worry about that?"

"I try not to," she said honestly with a shrug. "It doesn't make a lot of sense to get all worked up about possibilities I can't control. I'm focused on what Dottie hired me to do, and that's keep the knots up here safe. No point in looking beyond that. Now, if something were to come crashing out of the tear, then I'd let myself worry. Fix what you can fix and don't pull focus for something that might not even happen."

"But it could. Happen, I mean," Lisa said.

"Sure, but aliens could land and start nuking every major city in the world. Dinosaurs could suddenly walk the earth again. Anything could happen."

Lisa nodded and looked back down the road they drove in on. "Think Dottie and the ladies are far behind?"

Carie sighed. "Dottie Cambridge is many things. A fast driver is not one of them. It's a little quicker from her side of the peninsula to here, so hopefully she gets here soon. We can get started while we wait."

Carie called Dan over, asking if he could find a boat for them to borrow for a bit. She charged Kat with keeping an eye out for Dottie before pointing down the beach.

"We'll be over that way, setting up. Tell them to try and be quiet. I have no idea if these beaches are private and the last thing we need is an angry local interrupting."

Kat offered a cheeky salute as Carie nodded to Lisa.

They were a ways down the beach before either spoke again.

"I think I heard Jo while I slept in the car."

Carie tripped on her feet. "I... I think I did too."

"Is that one of those things that we should worry about?"

Carie's face suggested that it was for a moment before she managed to pull her authoritative expression back into place. "We need to deal with this first."

Lisa bit back what she wanted to say. It wasn't cruel, but she didn't want to pull Carie's attention away from the task at hand. She felt a deep dread in her chest. She had kept a hand on the threads since they'd arrived, and there was a low-level hum of something that was throwing her. It hadn't been there before. She could chalk it up to being so close to the tear, but for whatever reason, Lisa was positive it wasn't that. It felt like that first spark of magic when she was cooking with Jo.

She followed Carie's advice and focused on what she knew was happening. They were quiet again as they walked, and Lisa stared up at the sky. There was barely any light pollution this far north, and the sky was awash with stars.

"Shit."

Lisa's attention snapped immediately to Carie. "What?"

Carie pointed out to the water. Lisa had taken a breath to ask what she was looking for, but it was obvious. The water was churning off the shore. Below, a vibrant purple light was pulsing, faster and faster as Lisa watched.

"Stay here. Once Dottie gets here, tell her to start the sealing ritual."

"How's that--"

"Same as a ward, but you pull it together from the sides, like a torn seam."

"Got it," Lisa insisted.

"Get it started. You won't be able to cast it until the others get here. It's too powerful for you to do on your own. Something is coming out of the tear, and I need to send it back before it gets all the way through."

Lisa nodded, though she knew as soon as she felt the spell quicken, she would cast it. She had been able to draw wards before she even knew anything about weaving. She wasn't about to risk Carie getting hurt if she could seal the tear on her own.

After weaving a quick warming ward, Carie had stripped down to her underwear and bra before diving into the water. Lisa winced in sympathy. It was January and no matter how warm Carie insisted she ran, a swim had to be horrible. As she vanished under the waves, Lisa took a deep, cleansing breath and reached again for the knots. One, then two, and then a third, from further south. She furrowed her brow in confusion at that. She thought the closest knot to the south was Cana Island, and that should have been further than she was able to reach. As soon as she had that thought, her connection with it cut. She jolted at the sudden loss. A knot had never been wrenched from her like that before. It felt almost physical.

Lisa snarled as she shook her head. She had to stay in the now. She pulled with all her might on the remaining connections. They jolted at her touch, pleased and happy to help her. The magic was warm and welcoming in the frigid air. The threads fed Lisa a power that she hadn't felt before. Her body swelled with the overflow of energy, and just before she was sure she would pop, Lisa forced the magic outward. She didn't form a dome around herself but wove it over the tear. She could see it clearly in her mind. Her hold on the threads worked almost like an echolocation spell. She could see the negative space around the knots, where the tear was, where Carie was swimming, and where an incomprehensible thing was forcing itself through the tear.

The wave of panic almost broke her connection, but Lisa tightened her grip. She vaguely felt her legs give out and the crash of her knees to the cold sand. Someone was calling her name. Familiar and welcome hands touched her back, and Lisa could feel the strain of the spell lessen as others took up some of the burden. Her vision cleared, though she could still feel Carie beneath the waves.

"Compensate for Carie," Lisa managed to grit out. "She's down there trying to exorcise whatever is trying to get out."

"Archie, take the boat out with Dan," Dottie shouted. "She'll need a warming spell when she surfaces."

Lisa focused back on the warm magic of her fellow witches. The entire might of the Witches of Door stood beside her, bolstering her against the immense power she had drawn. With their guidance, she wove the spell around the tear, cutting off the abomination pushing through. She could feel Carie's relief, though it was tinged with the familiar hurt of lungs burning for air. She called out to Carie over the threads, telling her they were finished. The message appeared to go through, and she could feel Carie start to swim upwards. She commanded the tear to seal, cutting whatever tendrils were reaching towards Carie with the promise of pulling her into the unknown. With the spell woven, the tension in Lisa's body released her. She smiled, wondering if it was possible to venture into those other places beyond a tear. She was falling backwards, bracing for an impact that never came.

Lisa felt her entire being shift with the world around her. She opened her eyes to that white space one more, though now the threads were showing. Every color the eye could conceive cut through the unending white space. She startled as a hand touched her shoulder. She looked back to see Carie dressed and dry.

"We need to work on your listening skills," Carie said.

"There wasn't time to wait," Lisa explained. "I think Dottie got there just in time."

"Not the first time she's flown in at the last minute with a save."

"Think she can get us out of here?"

Carie looked around, confusion and panic colliding on her face. "I'm not sure where this is."

She trailed off. Her eyes went wide and her mouth hung open. Lisa turned to follow her gaze. Fifty feet away from them, Jo stood amid a tangle of threads. She was dressed as she was when they left the house in an ancient college sweatshirt and threadbare yoga pants. Her feet were bare and dirty as if she'd been wandering again. Her hair was windswept and damp. She shivered.

"Josie?"

Jo startled out of her rigid dreamy state. Her eyes focused on Carie and something like relief passed over her face.

"Carie," she breathed, "Something's wrong."

Jo twitched like she wanted to approach them, but she didn't move. A heavy shadow rose behind her, sizzling against the threads.

Carie bolted into action, rushing forward to grab Jo's arm, but she couldn't reach. The magic thrummed, keeping her and Lisa away.

The shadow shimmered. An arm stretched from the torrent, winding itself around Jo's waist, pinning her arms to her sides. Another arm pulled itself free of the shadow, forming spindle-long fingers tipped with sharp nails. The hand twisted over Jo's throat, forcing a terrified whimper from her mouth.

A chin hooked over Jo's shoulder and sharp, taunting eyes regarded Carie and Lisa with mirth.

"Hello, again." Aldred smiled. "You didn't tell me what you had hidden away, Carie. Made her all the more tempting."

Jo's expression remained rigid with terror.

"See, she's been toying with the idea of telling you about the odd dreams she's been having since you left her last spring. She was so worried about saying anything when you came back, weren't you, Josie?"

Aldred nuzzled at Jo's temple. "I was pleased beyond measure. I've been skulking around this shit heap for ages, searching for a way back. I have business back home. Those places of power...your knots...they were too much for me. They've been concentrating their power for so long that I would have disintegrated in my weakened state. It takes so much out of a body to crawl through the cracks between the worlds. But I had to come here, horrible though it is. I needed to find a way to get stronger. There's so much to do back home."

"What are you talking about?" Carie demanded.

"There are so very many realms beyond this pathetic dimension, witch. You know this. I need to get back to mine. Your exorcism didn't send me back, so I needed another way. None of you realized what you had sitting right under your noses," Aldred said, squeezing Jo closer. "See, Josie? I was right. They never really saw you at all."

"Stop calling her that," Carie yelled.

"Hitting a nerve?" Aldred mocked. "You still don't realize what she is, do you? Did you ever wonder why your weaving seemed to strengthen over the winters? Why this year you felt so weak until you were back with her?"

Carie could only gape at Aldred.

"Connection, you fool. You make connections with those places of power. Pulling your strength from the threads and the knots. What you didn't realize is you've had a newly forming knot at your side for a decade. Which of course begs the question of what those lighthouses are actually hiding."

Lisa felt like her head was going to explode. She remembered her aunt's hand in hers as she healed Carie after Eagle Bluff. She remembered every meal they made together and the tickle of magic that accompanied every bite.

"You weavers may be accepted now, but you can't think that was always the case. You know what I think? I think the meat bags that lived here long ago killed the weavers that dared to show their gifts. Those secrets were buried beneath brick and stone. Lost and unnoticed. No one caring to look." Aldred glared at Jo. "Sound familiar?"

"Stop it," Lisa shouted.

"Oh, but this is partially your fault, baby witch," Aldred said. "The connection you forged with Josie is what finally awakened the knot. The one with dear Carie had practically been severed, but then you waltzed in and wove that connecting thread so tight that you pulled her latent power up from the ether. Thank you. I plan on making very good use of it."

"No..."

Aldred ignored Carie, barreling on. "So many creatures could feel that power emerging. That's why so many of us were drawn south. Why you were so close to being overwhelmed. Thank goodness you had some help."

Their gaze darted to Lisa again. "You made it much harder to get to her. Those connections you forged with her strengthened her threads, making her even more tantalizing. I've been flitting around in the shadows of her mind since the witch left her. It was easy to whisper in her ear, to convince her that no one would ever stay, to weaken the protection of those connections so I could finally swoop in.

"You left her alone tonight, when all she wanted was to come with you. To help those she loves. But you didn't see her distress. You left her to my kind devices."

"I'm sorry," Josie whispered. "I--"

"Hush, dear," Aldred cooed. "She was so worried she would ruin things after you finally came back to her, witch. You know how terribly lonely she gets. Though you don't really care, do you? If you did, you might actually stay."

"Carie--" Jo tried to speak, but Aldred pressed their clawed thumb into the tender flesh under her chin. It forced Jo's mouth shut as a red bead of blood rolled down the column of Jo's neck. Her eyes squeezed shut.

"But not to worry. She can help me. You know how she likes to be useful. If she's useful, someone might actually stay."

"If you hurt her--"

Aldred laughed. "Oh, Carie, I'm already hurting her," they said, gleefully. "I'm going to pluck her threads apart, devour the power she possesses, and then I'll return home to claim what is rightly mine. I would rather have kept you in the dark, but she's figured out how to call for help along the threads. Took her long enough."

Lisa opened her mouth to speak, but Carie beat her to it.

"Josie, we're coming," Carie said, terrified and breathless. She could feel the edges of the space fraying as Aldred started to pull away. The voices of the witches on the beach were piercing the space. "Hold on, okay?"

"Don't get her hopes up, witch," Aldred said. "Come and find us. I'd love to finally settle up with you after all these years of humiliation."

Jo was pulled back into Aldred's shadow. She squirmed and managed to get an arm free. She stretched her hand out to Carie, her mouth opened to beg for help before Aldred folded them into space and vanished.

Lisa's eyes snapped open. She regarded the stars for the briefest moment before Carie's face appeared above her.

"You saw that?"

"They're close," Lisa said. "I can feel her. She's not far. She's a knot? The lighthouses were built on dead weavers? What the fuck is going on?!"

Carie pulled her close, ignoring the questions and concerns from the gathered witches.

"I'm not going to let anything happen to her. We're going to save her. I promise."

Chapter Twenty

"Among all your blessings, Ms. Waverland, staying warm in the water in January might be the most unbelievable," Archie said with a shiver.

He wove a warming ward to dry off Carie, who had rung out her wet hair and pulled on her clothes before shouting for Dan. Lisa could still feel the residual echoes of her aunt's essence reverberating over the threads. It was pointing her south. They decided a ride over the water would be faster than taking the back roads and hiking in. Though, Carie asked Dottie if the witches wouldn't mind doing just that for back up.

"For Josephine? Of course," Dottie replied. She'd clapped her hands together and herded the witches back to their cars. Kat opted to ride with the witches, since the boat wasn't meant for more than three people. She tugged the three of them in close, commanded them to be safe, and hurried to follow her ride.

Lisa kept her mouth clamped shut as Dan steered the little boat along the icy coastline. She had a thousand questions whirling through her mind, but she didn't want to ask them. Carie was tense and ready at the bow. She stared forward, completely ignoring her companions. Lisa wanted to offer some trite line of comfort, but she couldn't force the words out. This was on them both. They both had noticed the sleepwalking and the odd hours Jo had been keeping. If they did bring it up, Jo had waved their concern away, saying she just needed one good night's sleep to bounce back.

The more Lisa thought about it, the more sense it made. Hadn't Jo been thrown out of the family for sharing the most basic truth about herself? Lisa only had vague memories of Jo from childhood, and she was never spoken about after she left. Any photos of Jo that may have hung in her grandmother's home were gone, replaced with pictures of Lisa's mother alone. A stranger would think that there had never been another girl living in the house. After such a betrayal, Jo didn't want to give anyone else a reason to cast her aside.

And then, there was the situation with Carie. Even though they were together now, clearly Jo still worried she would be left behind.

With a fortifying breath, Lisa shifted further up the little boat and placed a hand on Carie's back. The witch startled, looking over to Lisa for the briefest second before resuming her vigil.

"We're going to get her back," Lisa said with all the conviction she could muster.

Carie nodded once. Lisa could already feel Carie's grip on the threads.

"I can feel her," Carie whispered. "It...it's just like tasting that pastry you made back at Dottie's a few months back. It's her, but I don't understand how I missed this."

"Doesn't matter," Lisa said. "We'll get her back, and we'll figure it out."

They rode in silence for a minute or two more, until the waves grew choppier. The freezing wind howled in across the Death's Door strait, buffeting the boat and blowing their hair in their faces.

"We're close," Carie said. "Can you feel her, Lisa?"

Lisa had discovered her power right alongside Jo. She felt like a part of their weaving would forever be intertwined. She touched the threads and felt all that was her aunt screaming back at her.

"We're right on the coastline of Newport State Park," Carie said. "I'm pretty sure that's Lynd Point. There's a little bay after that outcropping. We should be able to--"

The wind screamed over her, sucking the breath from her lungs. She choked and tipped forward, but Lisa grabbed her jacket and hefted her backwards. Dan let go of the motor to press both his hands over his ears. He huddled as low as he could get, silently screaming as the wind howled. Lisa tugged at the threads--trying to avoid drawing power from her aunt-- and cast a ward around their boat. Their bubbles was still and warm, but the atmosphere around them roared.

"Are you both alright?" Carie asked. She touched Dan's shoulder as if assuring herself that he was still there.

"This is bonkers," he responded.

"And that's why we tell you to stay in the car," Carie said.

Lisa cast her hands out and tried to move her ward back and forth. "If we can get the boat to the shore, I think I can keep us safe from the wind."

"Excellent," Dan said as he regained control of the motor. He angled them towards the shore and set off.

"We'll set Dan up with a fixed ward with a beacon for Dottie to follow," Carie said. "I'd prefer if we could get him set up with something safer..."

"Don't have to talk about me like I'm not here," Dan said with a laugh. "I knew the objective when I came. Jo is in dire need of assistance. She's the priority. I'll be fine for a bit on my own."

"You're a rock star, Dan," Lisa said. She leaned over so she could kiss his cheek.

Lisa kept her ward up as Carie helped Dan drag the boat out of the water. The shore was rocky, and they tried to find a spot where the boat wouldn't float away. They trudged a bit further into the tree line and quickly found a spot they deemed safe enough for Dan to wait out for the witches. Carie weaved a quick ward around him, giving it a bit of warmth to keep him comfortable. Lisa watched the woods around them, straining to hear anything over the howling wind.

Further down the path, the forest was devoid of any color. The trees looked like an unfinished drawing. Beyond them, a blinding whiteness burned Lisa's eyes. She reached for the threads, and for the first time, felt them recoil from her. They hung loose in her grip. Her aunt's magic was still present, but it had dimmed.

"Carie, we need to go."

"What's wrong?"

"She's fading."

Dan waved them off. "I'm fine! Get going!"

Jo could feel her body being picked apart by long, sharp claws. Every muscle was tense and taut. Unwelcome hands manipulated her body, tugging her arms and legs into place, pulling hard enough to ache. She was pinned in that place of just-too-far. She moaned in distress, but a clawed finger pressed on her chin until her mouth clacked shut. The finger became a hand, gripping her jaw and forcing her neck to elongate. The tendons in her shoulders screamed as her head was pulled away. She groaned again, trying to twist away, but another hand clamped over her mouth. She heard muttering, and her tongue froze to the bottom of her mouth.

"They'll be here without you calling them, Josie," Aldred murmured. "But if they're much longer, I'm afraid there won't be anything left to save. Let's get started."

The world went wrong around them as the knot unraveled. Lisa felt the color dripping from her limbs as she raced through the woods. She shivered as it melted, slopping to the ground and fading into the dull gray nothingness. She held out a hand to shield her eyes from the intense white light that shone through the woods. Beneath them, the forest floor had fallen away. When Lisa reached out with her magic, it felt like the tear they just closed. With each step, she worried that her foot could crash though the texture-less ground sending her careening into the void that loomed below. They needed to stop Aldred, or the whole world would be unmade.

Lisa focused on Carie's confident stride beside her. The witch had called upon whatever strength she could gather from the threads. Carie's hands were the only splash of color in the muted world they ran through. The color threw just enough light to highlight Carie's body, making her seem like the only three-dimensional being in a two-dimensional world. That warmed Lisa's heart. It made her run faster. It made her reach again for the threads, grasping desperately for her aunt and promising her they were so close.

The path led them to a rocky bluff that dropped about ten feet down into the choppy water. Beyond the drop, the water rushed into the small bay as if the lake had been tipped to spill into it. Lisa recognized it instantly. She had dreamed of it on the ride up here. Color bled back into the world around Aldred and Jo as they hovered above the center of the bay. The water whirled around them, forcing everything into motion.

Lisa felt Carie tense beside her soon as she saw the tableau before them.

"They're pulling her apart," Lisa screamed as she tugged at Carie's sleeve.

Carie's eyes darted back and forth, taking in the scene before her and trying to come up with something. She closed her eyes, took a deep breath, and looked back to Lisa.

"Grab her threads. Hold tight. Call her. I'll get Aldred to drop her, but you need to catch her."

Lisa nodded, taking solace in Carie's steely nerves. She watched as Carie dropped into the water, letting the current draw her close to whirling torrent. She kept her eyes open, wide and all seeing, as she reached for the threads that made up her aunt. She wasn't a practiced witch. She didn't know where the knots came from, or even how her aunt could possibly house one within her chest, but none of it mattered. What mattered was her aunt's heart. Her kindness. She fumbled through until she found the threads that made up Josephine Phines and pulled them close to her chest.

"You remember when we cooked together for the first time? I had never done that with anyone before, and it was a beautiful experience," Lisa said.

She felt the threads buck and squirm, but she held them fast. She set her jaw and stared through the walls of raw energy flashing before her with tears in her eyes.

"I've never created anything that I got to share with someone. You showed me that cooking is a love language. Carie could taste you in those pastries we made. That's an incredible thing. I need you here so we can spread that joy to everyone we meet. I want to do that with you. I want Sundays where we're cooking together with Carie. I want Dan and Kat and all those old biddies from the Witches of Door to join us."

Her aunt shrieked, and suddenly Lisa's vision was filled with a gray cloud of smog. She startled back as the smoke resolved into an enormous face. Its eyes burned with malice as its mouth ripped open like old stitches in a festered wound.

"SHE'S MINE," Aldred screamed.

Lisa bellowed back, "SHE'S OURS!"

She pulled everything she could from the threads and forced it at the beast before her. She couldn't tell if she shoved it away. She dropped backwards at the impossible expulsion of power. She never hit the ground. Lisa felt herself pass through where rocks should have hit her back, flipping over so that she could see the entire scene before her from beneath. Her mind tried to drop into unconsciousness instead of making sense of the vision before her, but she flailed for the threads, using them to pull herself back. She swam through the void, moving beneath her aunt. She could feel Jo's agony as the tangle of power at her heart was being unraveled. Carie's panic and rage and despair ripped through the threads, hitting Lisa with all that raw emotion. Her head felt like it could explode, but then she breached the ground beneath her aunt's hovering body.

Her fingertip crested that horizon, and everything slowed. The knot was just about to loosen, but Lisa forced her body back into reality and up to cradle her aunt's body close. She pressed her hands-- technicolored and perfect-- over Jo's chest and forced a protecting ward around the loose tangle of the knot. She could feel their tension give, but the ward pressed them close, forcing the strands to stay together.

"Carie," Lisa screamed over the din. "She needs you!"

The witch shoved away from Aldred, pouring every last ounce of energy and speed she had within to get to Jo's side. Lisa immediately forced another ward around them, just stopping Aldred from getting to them.

Aldred's form wavered, their arms shifting long and muscled and monstrous. Their mouth was suddenly full of razor-sharp needle teeth. They roared, impotently, as they pounded against the protective ward. Lisa could feel every blow, and she knew they only had a little time left.

"Talk to her. She's almost undone."

Aldred screamed, "You can't do this! She must unravel. I need that power! I have to get back! You don't understand! I can't stay here! I NEED TO GO BACK!"

Lisa shut her eyes and focused all of her strength on her two fading wards.

ele

"Josie...Josie, love, I need you to listen."

The voice was so far away. So quiet. But she latched onto it before she could completely vanish. It was a beloved voice, just like the last one. That was...Lisa. Her niece.

This was Carie.

"You can't leave me. You can't leave any of us. We need you here. Me and Lisa and everyone in this stupid county. There is so much that I want you to show me. Little things. Things that I could do alone, but they wouldn't mean anything because I wasn't doing them with you.

"I was lucky enough that you let me back into your life. I'm not going to let it end like this. You're not going to die because of some magical bullshit. How could I ever live with myself if the one thing I couldn't protect was you? I want you here. All of you. The way you snore and hog the blankets. The way you tuck your freezing feet under my thigh when we watch tv together. I want to find you slumped over a book of recipes, so I can have the pleasure of carrying you to our bed every night for the rest of our lives."

Jo felt the tension ease. Her tendons and muscles relaxed and fell into repose. She could feel Aldred's magic trying to command her back into that fixed position, but her body refused. Her heart wound back upon itself, secure and strong. Feeling came back to her fingers and toes. She lifted her arms and let her fingers search and scramble until they were cupping a familiar and beloved face.

"That's it, Josie. Come back to me."

She could feel it now. The tension of the threads that wrapped around the very core of her being was an embrace of magic. She took a deep breath, exhaling against the threads. They danced, welcoming her back and willing her to use them.

Her mouth struggled to form words, but Jo managed to grit out, "Will you help me?"

Carie's voice cracked with joy when she replied.

"Of course, I will. Anything you ask of me, all of me, is yours. I can't promise that I'll always be at your side, but you'll be with me no matter where I go. And if I do have to go, I promise that I'll always come back."

Jo felt one of her hands be pulled away. She touched paper, rough and worn. She struggled to open her eyes, but when she finally did she saw the photo she had given to Carie.

"You carry it with you?"

Tears crested Carie's cheeks. "I told you I'd carry you with me."

"I love you very much," Jo said. She pitched forward, brushing her lips against Carie's.

━ꝇꝇ━

Somewhere, in that white blank space, Lisa could feel her aunt's very essence in her hands. Her ward kept it from unraveling, but the warm cadence of Carie's voice wove the threads of it back together. Lisa watched as the threads looped and pulled, strengthening the bonds. Soon, the knot was whole again, and Lisa let her magic slowly absorb into the threads, leaving her own mark on the newly forged connection.

The water stilled beneath them as the wind quieted to a gentle breeze, but Aldred, still monstrous and furious, pounded against Lisa's remaining ward.

"You foolish sacks of flesh don't understand," they bellowed. "I need that power. She doesn't even know what she has! It's a waste! I can use it! I have to use it!"

"She isn't a thing to be used," Lisa said. She could feel her body failing under the strain. Her arms shook as she struggled to hold up her barrier. "She's ours, and you can't have her."

"You pathetic little witch," Aldred screamed. "You have no idea the limits of my strength. I can draw on the powers from beyond your mortal comprehension. As soon as you drop this pathetic barrier--and you will, I can see how its draining you-- I will devour you and pull her apart in the slowest and most painful way I can."

Lisa tried to summon the energy to speak, but she could only manage a gasping sob as she struggled each second to keep the ward in place. She screamed as she felt the power from the threads cut off. She saw victory in the murderous red eyes of Aldred.

But then the surging strength of a new connection filled her senses. Lisa felt Carie and Jo behind her propping her up. She looked beyond Aldred to the rocky bluffs. Dan had found the witches and led them to the bay, where Dottie had led them in a ritual. Lisa could feel them all offering up their power. Archie and Mildred and Evelyn and Kat and all the rest had their arms outstretched, feeding into Lisa's spell.

Aldred dared a look back, snarling as they moved to attack. Lisa decided then that they wouldn't touch anyone she cared about ever again. She gathered all their magic together, finding each individual thread and then weaving them into something more. Her hands crackled with energy as the spell wove around her fingers. The magic shot at Aldred in a violent bolt, crashing into their back. Upon impact, the water in the bay cascaded towards the shoreline, breaking against the bluffs. Aldred shrieked at a pitch loud enough to pierce an ear drum. Lisa held her ears, feeling something liquid and warm dripping onto her palms. She made herself watch as the magic burned Aldred from the sky. The screaming petered off until it was a low whimper, and the barest hint of smog was blown away in the breeze.

Lisa felt for Aldred along the threads but couldn't find them.

"I think I got 'em."

Her feet found the sand, and though she tried to mind the minnows wondering where the water went, Lisa was more focused on staying upright. She failed when Dan and Kat both crashed into her.

"That was fucking awesome," Kat screamed. "Holy shit!"

Dan did his best to cushion the fall, but they all ended up as a tangle of limbs on the damp sand.

Lisa let herself revel in her friends' touch. Everything had a vague sense of unreality, but Kat's hands on her face and Dan's fingers tangled with her own grounded her. She had no way of knowing exactly what happened, but she was pretty sure that she had somehow traveled outside their reality. She would have to bring it up with Carie later. If anyone knew, she would.

"Oh shit, Jo!"

Lisa shot up, scrambling against the tangle of limbs. She got to her feet and finally spotted her aunt and Carie. They were both awake. Jo leaned heavily into Carie's side, looking ready to sleep for a month. Carie's arm was slung around her shoulders, keeping Jo snug to her side. They were surrounded by a gaggle of witches. Dottie had tears in her eyes as she inspected Jo's form. The older woman wrapped her arms around both Carie and Jo, burying her head between theirs. Jo lost herself in the hug, but Carie locked eyes with Lisa over Dottie's shoulder. She flashed Lisa a reassuring smile. They were safe. They were whole. They had a lot to work out, but in this minute, everyone was okay.

⸎

No one had the energy to leave the bay just yet, despite the group looking like an unhinged family reunion making use of the empty beach in the middle of the night in January. Evelyn conjured some blankets to cover the beach. Archie let Dan help him with a fire, but the older gentleman touched each of the blankets in turn, weaving a cozy, radiating warmth into them. Lisa insisted on taking the boat they stole back up to Northport, but Dan and Kat managed to talk her out of it. Jo was happy that Lisa had friends to look out for her. It was important to have people who cared for you. They knew her well, too. As soon as Lisa plopped down on the blanket, she fell asleep propped between the two of them.

Jo had so much she wanted to say, but she was exhausted. She wanted to apologize to Carie for her constant insecurity. She had kept so much of herself secret for fear of driving people away even when she craved that connection. She was angry at herself for thinking so poorly of Carie.

"You know, if you wouldn't mind, I could go with you sometimes."

Carie startled. "I'm surprised you're not sleeping?"

"It still feels a bit weird when I close my eyes," Jo said. "I've been seeing this place in my dreams for months, but now it feels like being...somewhere else."

"I'm here."

"I know. There's plenty enough time for sleeping."

Carie smiled and gently brushed Jo's hair from her face. "Where do you want to go?"

Jo snuggled closer to Carie. "Anywhere. Everywhere. I do love it up here. I love my bakery, and I love that Lisa has carved a life for herself there."

"But..."

"But I think I've gotten too comfortable in my sadness up here. Part of me has accepted that I'll never have the relationship I used to hope for with my family. That's fine, but there was always a little corner clinging to the notion that they'd call. That they'd reach out and I wouldn't be alone anymore."

"Josie..."

Jo silenced Carie with a kiss. "I know I'm not alone. I've had you for years, even though I never let myself believe that it was real. It was easy to let myself believe that you would just up and leave. That's why when we fought last May I took it so hard."

"I'll never leave you like that again."

"And I think it's time that I committed to believing that," Jo said. She took one of Carie's hands and held it over her heart. "I can still feel you in there. You're in the very thread that holds me together."

"We'll figure that all out," Carie said, leaning in to steal a kiss of her own.

"We can build a life together."

"I'd like that. Building something. The two of us."

"It's more than just us, love."

Jo pointed over to the tangled trio a few blankets over. Kat was having a spirited discussion with Dottie about what the last few weeks meant for the Witches of Door while keeping Lisa's sleeping form balanced against her shoulder. Dan was trying to listen, but his head kept drooping.

"I wish that I had known the importance of that before Ethan..." Carie trailed off. She swallowed, steadying herself. "If we had allowed ourselves to accept help...shit, if we had asked mom and dad...maybe he'd still be here."

"He'd be happy for you."

Carie nodded, her brother's cocky smile passing through her memory.

They were silent for a moment, watching the scene play out before them.

"We've gone and built ourselves a little family without even realizing," Jo sighed.

"It's a great foundation for what's to come."

Jo settled on Carie's shoulder, reveling in the warmth.

Carie leaned closer, brushing her lips against Jo's ear as she spoke. "And you can follow me anywhere. I meant what I said. I never want to be without you again."

Jo smiled and stared up at the endless sea of stars.

<h1 style="text-align:center">Epilogue</h1>

"Lisa? I think that's Dan out front."

Jo dried her hands in a kitchen towel as Lisa came pounding down the stairs.

"I can't find my boots!"

"You left them by the door so you wouldn't forget them," Jo said, pointing towards the pile of bags stacked in the foyer. "You have everything else?"

"Yeah," Lisa said, pressing a quick peck to her aunt's check as she rushed by. "I was going to wear my corset, but three hours in the car in that thing just sounds terrible."

"I picked the coziest t-shirt I could find for those witchy avengers shirts. Just wear that!"

⁓ele⁓

Half a year could make all the difference in the world. With the tear closed and Aldred exorcised, quiet settled over the peninsula. Carie had remained on high alert in the weeks after the encounter. The first drive out to the lighthouses had been tense and quiet. Carie insisted on checking the tear was still closed, which drew unwanted attention from an elderly beachcomber. When she emerged from the water with barely a shiver, he had lectured her for nearly a half hour on how insane it was to swim in those temperatures. He waggled his metal detector at her during his tirade while Kat and Lisa struggled to keep their laughter to themselves. Dan had run up with blankets Archie warded with warmth and explained away his crazy aunt. The man eventually left, and the fog of stress that had been hanging over the group finally dissipated.

The tear was closed, and Carie couldn't sense any others. The remaining exorcisms were simple enough that even Kat was allowed to help. The afternoons that the troop used to spend chasing down entities turned into training sessions. Lisa would walk Kat through her process of drawing from the threads, and Kat learned to expand her spell abilities. Carie watched them both with pride.

Dan claimed some of those afternoons for their role playing campaign and graciously allowed Carie to join full time. Jo was invited too, but she was more interested in catering the long adventuring sessions. Most times, she ended up in the kitchen with Dan's parents, walking them through whatever new recipe she had come up with since she saw them last. They would cook together and then invite the adventurers up to sample their wares. Kat would ask her parents up for dinner every now and again as well, if only to assure them that every time she hung out with Lisa wasn't a magical mess.

Lisa came to adore Kat's parents, and they welcomed her just as eagerly. She had taken to staying at Kat's apartment at least one night a week after her classes. Kat would sit up waiting for her, working on her last few electives for a creative writing degree. She had started work on a novel, and soon as Lisa crossed the threshold, Kat would thrust new pages at her, begging for feedback. Lisa would share her latest cooking lessons and would read Kat's writing between chopping and roasting. Lisa came to think of Kat's apartment as an extension of her home back in Egg Harbor. She also figured her aunt and Carie appreciated having the house to themselves for a bit. The walls were very thin, after all.

Carie had finally moved her things permanently into Jo's room. They had spent a Saturday going through all of Jo's old clothes, setting things in keep and donate piles to make room for Carie. The photos on the mantle had been refreshed, sporting photos from Dottie's luncheons and lazy days at the beach. In all of them, Jo and Carie were never further than an arm's reach away.

April had seen them take a tense drive down to Milwaukee, just to verify that Jo was okay. She had wanted to cancel the appointment, but Carie insisted they still go. She reasoned that having Aldred messing about in Jo's head could still have done some damage, and that didn't even mention the sleepwalking and the fainting spells. They made a trip out of it but were all the happier when the doctor called the next week with a clean bill of health for Jo. She prescribed more sleep, less caffeine, and a weekly session with a therapist.

After the clean bill of health from the doctor, Jo asked Carie out to the beach. They sat for hours, snacking on pastries and enjoying each other's company. When the sun began to set, Jo had turned to Carie and asked her to stay for the summer. Carie kissed her sweetly and replied that she would stay forever if Jo would let her. But before they started their life together, Carie felt she had to pay her respects to the past. She asked Jo to travel back west with her. She had some old ghosts to exercise in Washington, among the fields of wildflowers on the side of a mountain. Jo agreed and left the bakery in Lisa's capable hands. She hadn't left Wisconsin since starting her exile nearly fifteen years ago.

When Dottie had arrived that week for her cheat day pastry, she could hardly contain her pleasure for all of them. She also had news that Archie and herself would be performing at the theater annex. Lisa wasn't much for the theater, but finally getting to properly meet Archie's partner Ralph had been worth the whole night. Dottie and Archie had lit up on the stage as well, weaving a whole new kind of magic as their fingers danced across the piano keys. Dottie hosted a reception at her house after. Part way through, Lisa's phone chimed. Her mother had finally texted her back after months of silence. Lisa noted the alert but didn't rush to read it right away. Later, as she laughed with Kat over a stupid joke Dan told, Lisa realized it didn't matter what her mother had said. There would be time enough to parse the message later. She had her people. She would be fine.

The lighthouse remained silent and steady across the bay.

Dottie encouraged more weaving practice during the Witches of Door luncheons. She reasoned that it was unfair to rely completely on Carie to protect them from whatever was lurking out there. Lisa and Carie explained what

Aldred said about the knots, and Dottie set about trying to learn who their fellow witches had been. Even if they didn't find the names of the witches buried there, Dottie promised they would honor the lost.

Spring warmed up to summer, and Lisa was finally able to fulfill a long-held promise to her younger self. She was going to the opening weekend of the Bristol Renaissance Faire with her friends and family.

The door pushed open, revealing Kat in a turquoise doublet, puffy matching shorts and tights, elven shoes that curled up at the toes, and a floppy hat with an enormous peacock feather sticking out of it.

"Did you need help carrying your stuff?"

"I guess some people don't mind being uncomfortable in the car," Jo said.

"Oh, this?" Kat looked down at her outfit before doffing her cap and bowing low. "It's warm, but it is shockingly comfortable. Much better than a whale bone corset. You should have gotten that hobbit one I sent you the link for. I wear that one to Dan's sometimes. It's super comfy."

"You look amazing, Kat," Jo said.

"Thank you! You should see Dan's bard outfit. He's been working on it for years, and he's so excited to show us once we get down to Bristol."

"Are you sure we don't need to have costumes," Carie asked as she walked out of their bedroom. "It really feels like we'll be under dressed if we don't wear a costume."

Jo took one of the bags that Carie was toting. "If it isn't too hot, we can always buy costumes there. We both do better when we have options to choose from."

"There's no way it isn't going to be hot," Lisa said, slipping on a pair of flip flops before digging through her bags again. "Alright, I have my charger, a few changes of clothes, bathroom stuff--"

"We're driving to Bristol, not to the middle of nowhere. There's an outlet mall right over there and a Target if we need anything."

"Now, you remember what you promised," Carie asked as she pulled her boots on.

Jo smiled. "How could I forget? It's a crime that you've been driving up to Wisconsin for over a decade and you haven't been to the Mars Cheese Castle."

"It's one of those things that's just there. I would have gotten to it eventually."

Jo approached her and kissed her deeply. "And I can't tell you how happy I am that I get to facilitate this momentous occasion."

"Don't tease," Carie chastised.

"I'm not," Jo said, swatting at Carie's arm. "You're going to love it."

Jo went through the house, making sure the lights were off and the doors locked. She had a sign up at the bakery letting customers know that she'd be resuming normal hours on Tuesday. She pulled the front door closed and locked it. Dan was helping Kat and Lisa load Lisa's bags into the covered truck bed. Another car behind them held the rest of their group. Jo waved to them as she crossed the parking lot to her car.

"We're still on for dinner next weekend, Ms. Phines," Max shouted from the driver's seat.

"Of course," she shouted back. "You all still need to show me how to finish rolling up my character."

Max beeped his horn in agreement, rolling the window back up so the hot, July air couldn't creep in.

"Did you want to take my car?" Carie asked.

"Did you get the air conditioning fixed?'

"Um..."

"Get in mine," Jo ordered with a laugh.

"Jo, do you know where you're going," Dan asked as he shut his tailgate.

"I've just got it in my phone, but yes, I have an idea of where I'm going. If we get separated on the way, we'll meet up at the main gate."

"Sounds good! See you all in a bit."

Dan hopped back into his truck and led the convoy out of the parking lot. Max's sedan was right on their heels.

"Have you ever been to a renaissance festival before?" Jo asked.

"Can't say that I've ever had the time," Carie replied, leaning in close.

"Well, we'll have to make this a weekend to remember then. We'll need to find you some armor if you want a costume. Maybe something functional. You can wear it come winter."

"If you get to choose my costume, then I get to pick yours."

"I submit myself to your very good taste," Jo smiled.

"Then let's get on the road," Carie said, stealing another kiss. "We don't want to keep the kids waiting."

Acknowledgements

I feel like it would be stupid not to thank you first, dear reader. I'm a big ol' nobody, so thanks for taking a chance on my work. I hope you enjoyed the ride.

All of my love to my darling Bob and Izzy, who gave me the time, space, and encouragement write this story. I wouldn't have been able to do this without them.

I had some very kind people offer to read through this story when it was still called the Witches of Door. An enormous thank you to my oldest and dearest friend, Vicki, who read the very rough first draft even through fantasy is not her genre. A huge thanks to my cousin Sarah, who heard me mention that I was trying to finish a story and offered to give it a read for me. Thanks for the tip about the trauma pad! Thanks to Becky for the quick editing pass. I really appreciated your eyes on this! Without you guys, Jo, Lisa, and Carie never would have come to life.

And just because I can, thanks to my own tabletop crew for giving me the space to tell some rad stories with them. Sheila, Sass, and Christie, you guys rock, and I love you lots.

This story was conceived during a winter trip to Door County in Wisconsin, which is a truly lovely place I've been visiting since I was very little. Buttercup's Coffee in Egg Harbor inspired Jo's countertop oven which really kickstarted work on the book. If you find yourself in Wisconsin, I recommend a visit.

You Were Always Magic was written to an array of music, but I must call out *The Crane Wives* specifically. I've basically had *Coyote Stories* playing on a loop while editing. It's an excellent album that you should listen to immediately. And while we're calling out music, I'll throw some love to Orville Peck's cover of *Unchained Melody*, which is definitely playing when Carie and Jo finally kiss outside the Blue Ox and to *Fair* by *The Amazing Devil*. If you know, you know.

About the Author

Erica L Molinaro has been writing stories in the margins of notebooks since she was a kid. She lives in the western Chicago suburbs with her husband and daughter. She enjoys baking, reading, and running tabletop games for her friends. *You Were Always Magic* is her first novel.